DON'T BELIEVE HER

A GRIPPING PSYCHOLOGICAL THRILLER WITH A SHOCKING TWIST

NICOLA SANDERS

ebook ISBN: 978-1-7636599-1-9
Print ISBN: 978-1-7636599-0-2

v1a

PROLOGUE

She can't breathe. She's coughing. She can't stop. Her throat is on fire. That's what wakes her up. The coughing. So much of it she can't take a breath. The pain.

But then it comes. A sharp inhale. Air. She stands up straight. She's shaking all over. She's standing waist-deep in water. Oh god. Where the hell is she? She touches the walls, but she's so cold she can't feel anything. No, wait. She can. It's rough. Slimy.

'Help!'

She wants to shout but her voice is just a rasp. She can taste blood mixed with dirt. She spits it out. She tries to swallow but it hurts too much.

A drop hits her face. She looks up. Another drop. Rain? It's not pitch black like she first thought. There's an opening above her head, but it's too far to reach. All she can see is moonlight filtering through clouds and the outline of trees.

And then she remembers.

Oh, god. She has to get out of here. She tries to climb up the sides but they're too slimy and she's too cold, so cold. She loses her footing and falls backwards, hitting her head against the wall. Something brushes against her thigh. She spins around. It's floating next to her. She feels it with her hands.

Oh my god. Please no. No!

'Help me! Somebody help me! Get me out!' She can't scream. She can't speak. She has no voice. Her throat is on fire.

Then she hears something. It's coming from above.

'Hello? Is somebody there?'

The sound of metal dragging against brick.

'What are you doing?'

The opening becomes smaller as the sheet of metal is being dragged over it.

'No!!! Stop! No!'

She's hysterical now, splashing, trying to shout, scratching at the brick walls, breaking her nails, scratching her throat. 'Stop! Wait! Please! Don't leave me here! I'll die in here!'

And then, darkness. She's alone now. She knows it. No light, no opening, no way out. She may as well be in a tomb.

She doesn't want to die. That's what she keeps telling herself. *I don't want to die.*

She prays. She cries. She screams. Hours pass. She fades. She is so weak she can barely stand, even when leaning against the wall.

And she is so cold. She's tired of crying, of screaming, of begging. Nobody is coming.

She's going to die.

ONE

'I want you to find my friend.'

On the computer screen, Ashley jerks her head back. 'It's not what we do—'

I half raise a hand. 'No. I know, sorry.' My heart sinks a little. This is not going well. I'd meant to build up to that part. I had it all planned out. I had notes, I was making my case, point by point, and I was halfway into my prepared speech before I heard Ashley telling me I was on mute. Then it took me god knows how long to figure out how to unmute myself, and now I'm completely flustered.

'I didn't mean to blurt it out like that. I'm not good with technology,' I say, as if that wasn't already bleedingly obvious. 'I'm a hairdresser. We haven't figured out how to cut hair via Zoom yet.'

She chuckles. 'That's okay, Ellie. I understand. Let's start again.'

I nod, relieved. 'Thank you.'

Ashley and her friend Kate host a podcast called *Vanishing Acts*. They tell the stories of people who have been missing for a long time, and sometimes they even find them. Although when they do, invariably, those people are dead.

I'd been listening to true crime podcasts with the vague idea that I'd get some tips to help me find Carla, and I came across Vanishing Acts. I binge-listened to the first three seasons, and the whole time I kept thinking, *you're probably never going to find her, but they could.*

And here we are.

'Tell me about Carla,' Ashley says.

I nod, and my heart squeezes a little at the memory. 'I met Carla in our first year of secondary school,' I begin.

It was the first day of term, and I was sitting alone in the playground. I was the girl who'd just lost her mother to cancer, and I guess nobody wanted to be friends with the sad girl.

Except Carla. She walked up to me with her long legs, her self-assured air and a ball under her arm. 'Want to play football?'

Maybe the reason Carla wasn't afraid of the sad girl was that her own father died of a heart attack when she was five. I wasn't that sad anyway, just lonely. I said yes to football even though I didn't particularly like the game, and we became instant friends.

We had more in common than a dead parent. For one thing, we were both tomboys. While our schoolmates were already into make-up and fashion, we were riding our bikes, climbing trees or splashing around in the river. And we were both obsessed with rock music – although, to be fair, everybody else we knew was, too. When we turned fifteen, we decided to start a band. We would call ourselves The Wicked Sistas. We loved that name. We'd see each other in the playground and say things like, 'Hey, Wicked Sista, how are you doing today?' and fall over in fits of laughter. We agreed that Carla would play the guitar – seeing as she already played the guitar – and I'd play the keyboards. We would both sing so there'd be no jealousy, no front person or backup vocals. We would be equal, our voices fitting perfectly in harmony. Eventually. Once we learnt how.

When we weren't at school or out cycling or exploring, we'd be at her house practising our songs. Her house was more practical than my house because it was huge and you could easily keep away from everyone. My father had his mechanic's workshop at the front of our house, so there was always the sound of motors running or panels being beaten. It was loud and noisy, and if I'm honest, I was ashamed of it. It was much, *much* smaller than Carla's, it always smelt of oil or petrol and there always seemed to be a thin layer of grease over every surface.

Now I tell Ashley, 'And then, one day, she ran away. That was twelve years ago. She was sixteen years old. I never saw it coming. I've never understood it, and I never saw her or heard from her again.'

Ashley nods and makes a note. 'Talk me through it. How did you find out she had run away?'

'She called me one night,' I say. It was late, almost ten. I was about to go to bed. She sounded panicky. She said we were going to Liverpool – we'd talked of going to Liverpool one day, when we were, say, twenty, to launch the Wicked Sistas there. We had this fantasy that we'd record a demo, get a record deal and tour the world to packed stadiums. 'We talked about it a lot,' I say. 'Then, one night, she called and said we were going right now. I was to grab a few things and meet her in ten minutes on the road behind her house. I tried to ask questions, but she hung up on me. So I went there just like she asked me to, but I didn't bring anything. I wasn't going anywhere. I wasn't even sure she was serious.

'The back road behind her house is really dark, but I could tell she'd been crying. She was sitting on a tree stump with her guitar slung over one shoulder and a duffel bag at her feet. When she saw me, she stood, hoisted her guitar further up her shoulder and said the train was leaving soon and we had to go now.

'What is going on?' I asked.

'I'll tell you later. Let's go.'

'No way! That's ridiculous. We're not going anywhere. Tell me what's going on?'

'Please, Ellie, I need you. Please, come with me!' She started to tell me how great it would be, and we'd get waitressing jobs and rent a place together and we'd play gigs, like she was selling me the dream, as if it wasn't also my dream. But not like this. I kept telling her no, that it was ridiculous, that she needed to pull herself together and tell me what was going on, but she wasn't listening. She was talking so fast I couldn't make sense of what she was saying, but she looked terrified. 'Please, Ellie! We have to go! Now!'

I thought of my dad. My dad who had tried so hard, sometimes even successfully, to keep it together after my mother died. My dad who did his very best to understand me as I grew into a young woman. My dad who hugged me when I was freaking out hysterically, having got my first period, and then bought me my first box of tampons, handed them to me and coughed something like, 'Read the instructions.'

My dad, alone at home, oblivious.

'I can't,' I said to Carla. 'And you shouldn't either. We're too young. It's dangerous.'

'I don't have a choice,' she said. She picked up her bag and just like that, she took off. I couldn't believe it. I went after her, shouting at her to wait. She turned around and said, 'Don't tell anyone where I'm going, okay? Promise me. Just say you have no idea.' And then she ran down the road towards the train station.

I never saw her again.

'Honestly, I was sure she'd come home two hours later,' I tell Ashley. 'But then her mother showed up at my house the next morning because she'd gone to wake Carla for school and found her bed empty. And that's when I got really worried. The promise I'd made Carla went right out the window. I told her mother everything. She took me straight to the police to tell them my story. Carla's brother, Nick – he's two years older – told me later he didn't believe Carla would run away and never call their mother again. He thought something must have happened to her that night. He'd get into his car and drive all around town in case she'd fallen in a ditch or something. Meanwhile I was calling her incessantly, leaving messages on her mobile, sending a million texts. I only ever got one text back: *I'm fine. I'm living my dream. Don't look for me.* That was it. Then later I heard that the police had spoken to her—'

Ashley raises a hand. 'Sorry, how did you hear that?'

'Her mother told me.' I think about it now. Marjorie, her eyes bloodshot from crying, showing up at our house to tell my father and me. She was always a beautiful woman who looked young for her age, but that day, she looked like she'd aged a hundred years overnight.

'And what did the police say?' Ashley asks.

'That Carla had made it to Liverpool, that she was fine, she was safe, and she didn't want to come home. Since she was sixteen, there was nothing anyone could do. You can't force someone to come home at sixteen.'

Ashley scribbles something. 'And was her mother…?' She looks up. 'What's her name again?'

'Marjorie.'

'Marjorie. Did she speak with or hear from Carla after that?'

I rub my forehead. 'Yes. But this is where things get really strange.'

'How so?'

I take a breath and gather my thoughts. 'You have to understand, I looked for Carla a lot over the years. After I finished secondary school, I moved to London. I was living in Croydon and I still spoke to Marjorie on occasion. For years, she'd had no news from Carla and neither had Nick, or anyone else as far as we knew. Years went by and I kept looking. Marjorie looked up Births, Deaths and Marriages in case Carla was living under a married name, but there was nothing. No mention of marriage, nothing at all. Then, my father died last March—'

'I'm sorry.'

'Thank you. I called Marjorie to tell her. She knew him a little, although he'd moved to a retirement home by then.' For some reason, I feel the need to explain. 'My parents were older when they had me. My father was forty-eight when I was born.'

Ashley nods politely.

'Anyway. At the end of the conversation with Marjorie, I asked about Carla, and she told me she'd had a postcard from her, from Paris, for her birthday. It had come the day before. She was going to call me but I'd beat her to it. She sounded so happy. She read it to me over the phone. "Happy birthday, Mother, thinking of you, much love," signed Carla.'

Ashley frowns. 'And that happened last March? So… three months ago?'

'That's right.'

'So Carla's not missing at all.'

'Except…' I search for the words. 'I saw the postcard

when I came back to Lindleton for my father's funeral. Marjorie showed it to me.'

'And?'

I bite my bottom lip, trying to think of a way of saying it without sounding crazy, but I can't. So I just blurt it out.

'I don't think it's from Carla.'

TWO

I hear a car pull up outside. Is Nick home already? I must have been rambling on for ages. I crane my neck to see, but it's not Nick, it's Meghan, the cleaner, getting out of her Honda Civic.

'Are you sure?' Ashley asks.

I turn back to the screen. 'Yes.'

'How can you tell?'

'Because we wrote songs together, lyrics. I have note-books full of Carla's handwriting, and the writing on the postcard is not the same.'

'What does Marjorie say? Does she think it's from Carla?'

'Absolutely. When I told her I had my doubts, she said I was mad.'

'Was there a return address on the postcard?'

'No.'

'But it was posted from Paris.'

'Absolutely.'

Ashley makes a note. 'Do you have a contact for Marjorie? I'd like to speak to her if I'm going to consider the project.'

'I'll speak to her. I live in her house.'

Ashley looks up. 'You do? I thought you said you lived in Croydon?'

'I used to, until recently. But when I came back for my father's funeral, I spent time with Marjorie, and then I got to see Nick too – that's Carla's brother – and…' I give her a small smile. 'Well, that's the one happy outcome out of this whole story. Nick and I started seeing each other, one thing led to another, and I moved back to Lindleton with my daughter, to be with him.'

'Wow. You really are intertwined with this family.'

I nod. 'I am. I didn't plan it that way, but, yes, I am.'

'So you and your daughter…'

'Karlie. She's six.'

'You and Karlie live with Nick's mother, Marjorie?'

'Only temporarily. Marjorie had a bad fall down the stairs a couple of weeks ago. Nick was renting a cottage nearby, so we gave it up and moved in with her to take care of her while she recovers.'

Ashley taps her pen on her chin. 'Could I speak with Marjorie?'

I hesitate. 'Yes. I'll talk to her and get her to call you.'

I don't tell her that when I suggested doing this podcast to Marjorie, she looked at me like I'd asked her to parade naked in the village square.

'Look, Ellie,' Ashley says, putting her pen down. 'People's handwriting changes over time. Especially between sixteen and… How old would Carla be now?'

'Twenty-eight. And yes, I know what you're saying, but I don't think that's the case here.'

'How can you be so sure?'

'Because she's dead.'

I can hear footsteps coming up the stairs. I wonder if

Nick is home already. Or maybe it's Meghan coming up here to clean.

'What did you say?' Ashley asks. I look back at her. Her face is slack with shock.

'Maybe she's dead. I know it's a terrible thing to say—'

She raises a hand. 'No, no. You said, "Because she's dead."'

'I didn't mean it literally. I don't know that for a fact. But she's…gone, so either she's dead or she's in a cult.'

'A cult?'

'That's the only other explanation I can think of. Some cults cut you off from family and friends. Maybe that's what happened. Maybe she changed her name legally, and now she's called Flowers-in-the-Sky or Gold-Dust-Moon-Shower or something.'

I'd meant to lighten the mood after blurting out that Carla was probably dead, but judging from Ashley's face, I'd failed spectacularly.

'Sorry. I didn't mean to be flippant. Will you help me look for her?'

She taps her pen on her notepad. 'I don't know…'

'Please, Ashley. You and Kate are so good at this. I've listened to every episode of your podcast. If anyone can find her, it's you.'

'I'm just not sure there's a story there, Ellie.'

'But the postcard…'

She gathers her notes together. 'You should be happy about the postcard. It shows that Carla is alive and well. I really think you're reading too much into it.'

'I'm not.'

She stops fiddling with her notes. 'If we could talk to Nick and Marjorie…'

'Yes. Absolutely. I'll talk to Nick and ask him to call you.'

A floorboard creaks outside the door.

Ashley glances at her watch. 'Sorry, I have to go.'

'Or you could call him now,' I blurt. 'He works in town at FitTonePlus, he owns the franchise—'

'Let me know if anything new happens,' she says. 'I really have to go, Ellie.'

'It won't,' I say. I can feel the corners of my mouth pulling down. I feel stupid, a grown woman on the verge of tears because she didn't get what she wanted. I press the heels of my hands against my eyes. 'Nothing new will happen. Nothing new ever happens.'

'Keep me posted. Bye, Ellie. Thank you for the chat.'

The screen goes dark.

I slump in my chair and let my head roll back. I wish Nick were home. I long for him to hold me, to tell me everything will be fine and she'll turn up one day.

I glance at the time on the screen. Ten past three. I should go and pick up Karlie from school.

I turn off the computer and come out onto the landing, closing the door behind me. I'm about to walk down the stairs when it happens: the shock of whiplash, the floor rushing up to meet me, my arms flailing, someone screaming.

Then, nothing.

THREE

3 weeks later.

I arrive at the school gates at the same time as Alex. Alex is my friend Lauren's husband and one of the few dads who does the school run.

'Hi, Ellie.' He points to the pink travel bag decorated with flying unicorns in my hand. 'Is that Karlie's overnight bag? Lauren said I'm not to leave here without Karlie's bag.'

'How could you tell?' I say, handing it to him.

He taps the side of his head. 'Never stops.'

I laugh.

Lauren isn't just my best friend here, but she's also my boss at the salon where I work, which is where she is right now. Our daughters are only a few months apart in age, and they are best friends, too. What can I say? Ever since I moved back to Lindleton, everything in my life has fallen into place so beautifully, so perfectly, it's hard not to think it was all meant to be.

It's Friday today, and tomorrow is Bethany's seventh birthday. When Lauren told me that Bethany wanted to invite Karlie for a sleepover the night before, I have to admit

I was a little hesitant. Is six too young for a sleepover? But Karlie wanted it so badly. 'Please, Mummy!! Pleeeeaaaase!!!' she'd cried, her little eyebrows knitted together, her short legs bouncing like she was on springs.

'Pleeeeaaaase!!!' Bethany had pleaded the next morning outside the school gates, her hands together like she was begging for her life.

'You can have a date night with Nick,' Lauren had said, winking. Was the prospect of a date night with Nick what sealed the deal? Of course not.

Just kidding. It totally did.

The doors to the school building open, releasing a million squealing children. Karlie and Bethany run out together, holding hands. Karlie collides with me, or my legs anyway, and wraps her arms around me.

'Hello, Mummy, did you bring my pink dress with the sparkles on it?'

'Yes,' I say, ruffling her hair.

'And my silver shoes? And my yellow pyjamas?'

'And your silver shoes and your yellow pyjamas and your toothbrush, too. Remember to brush your teeth, okay?'

'Don't worry,' Alex says. 'Lauren is the resident drill sergeant when it comes to teeth-brushing. Come on, girls, let's go.'

I crouch down to Karlie. The back of my eyes sting. It's the first time I've been away from her for a night, and it's all I can do not to snatch her away and shove her in the car before taking off in a cloud of smoke, tyres squealing.

'I'm going to see you tomorrow, okay?' I say. Parents have been invited but attendance isn't compulsory. I don't know, but if it was me, I would absolutely make attendance compulsory. The prospect of managing a house full of six- and seven-year-olds for an afternoon would make me want to curl up in bed and lock the door. But then, that's Lauren for you. If you looked up 'multitasking' or 'unflappable' or 'superwoman' in the dictionary, you'd find Lauren.

I hug my child tightly, kiss her soft cheek, and then I hug her again while she wriggles to get away.

'Jesus, Ellie,' Alex says, shaking his head at me. 'You want to come for a sleepover, too? I'm sure we'll find room for you.'

I laugh. 'No way. I have a date with a hottie, but thanks anyway.'

I kiss the top of Karlie's head one more time. 'I'll see you tomorrow around ten thirty,' I tell Alex. 'I'll be on hand to help. Tell Lauren to text if she wants me to bring anything.'

'Yeah, bring Scotch. I have a feeling we'll need it,' he says, and I laugh, then head home.

I push the front door to our house – it's stuck, again. I keep telling Nick to do something about it. God knows how Marjorie manages to get in and out of this place. And the light above the porch has never worked, even though I put in a new light bulb when I first moved in. But maybe that's just as well because the door desperately needs a paint job.

'Margie? I'm home!' I call out, picking up the post from the floor. Two official-looking letters addressed to Nick. Bills, probably. I shove them in my pocket.

'Hello, Ellie, darling. I'm in here.'

I love my future mother-in-law. And not just because she's Nick's mother, or even because she's wonderful to me, but because she is everything I aspire to be. She's kind and generous, she's smart, she's always helping people, always giving her time to charity events, whether it's a gala or a school raffle. She's a wonderful mother to Nick and very much a mother to me, too. She's beautiful, in a classical way, with blonde hair cut in a wavy bob down to her jawline. And no matter what day of the week it is or what time of the day or whether she's unwell or running errands, she's always impeccably dressed in that tailored, casual look women of her generation do so well.

Oh, and she absolutely adores my daughter.

I put down my bag of groceries in the kitchen, then join Marjorie in her living room. I find her sitting on the couch, perusing the latest British Vogue magazine.

'What do you think of this dress?' She taps the page. 'It would look lovely on you.'

I peer over her shoulder. The model in the picture has a waist not much bigger than my thumb, and the skirt is so short, it could almost classify as a belt. But it does show off the model's perfectly shaped legs.

'I hate it,' I say. Marjorie laughs.

I sit down next to her on the couch and kiss her cheek. 'How are you feeling today?' I point at her bandaged hand. 'How's the wrist?'

'It's much better, look.' She lifts it to show me, wriggling her fingers.

'And the ankle?'

'So much better. Dr Patel says I'll be able to get rid of that cane soon.' She looks at the ceiling. 'Thank god! You have no idea how silly I feel walking around with that thing. And I do miss my Pilates.'

'I know you do, but not long now.'

She turns to me. 'Thank you, Ellie darling. You've been a godsend all these weeks.'

I smile. 'Firstly, it hasn't been that long, and secondly…' I squeeze her good hand. 'I'm glad to be able to look after you.'

She looks at me tenderly. Then she gently puts her fingers on my forehead and squints at it. 'How's the head?'

'It's fine,' I say. After my fall I had a bump the size of an egg, but it's almost gone now.

She clicks her tongue. 'What a pair we are.'

'What a *lucky* pair we are,' I say.

And it's so true. I thank my lucky stars every day that neither of us were seriously hurt. I shudder whenever I think of the day Marjorie fell down the stairs.

Nick and I had come to visit. I was in the kitchen making tea when I heard her scream. I rushed out to the hall and found her splayed on the stairs, her legs at funny angles, one hand on the bannister.

'Nick! Call an ambulance!' I shouted. Nick appeared on the landing above. 'What happened?'

'Your mum fell! Get an ambulance.'

Marjorie tried to pull herself up. 'I just tripped...'

'Just stay there a minute,' I said. I checked her over while Nick called the ambulance. She was fine, in the end. A sprained ankle and a sprained wrist, but it could have been so much worse.

Then, two weeks later, it happened to me, too. And in that split second I remember thinking, *it's her. She's in this house and she's really pissed off with us.*

Except it wasn't a ghost in the end. Just a board on the top step that had come loose.

'Has Nick fixed the stairs yet?' Marjorie asks.

I nod. 'Solid as a rock.'

'Good.' She puts her hand on mine. 'Now, Ellie, dear, I know I ask so much of you—'

'Nonsense. How can I help?'

'I booked myself in for a facial on Tuesday afternoon next week, at three. I'm sorry to be such a bore, but—'

'I'll drive you,' I jump in. 'I finish at the salon at two.'

'That's what I thought. Thank you, darling. I booked you in for one as well. My treat.'

I click my tongue. 'You didn't have to do that.'

'I know, but I wanted to.' She checks her watch. 'Do you think it's too early for a sherry?'

'It's five o'clock somewhere,' I say, pushing myself upright. 'Sherry coming up. And I'll change your bandage too.'

'No, don't. It's your date night.'

'I've got time.'

'Thank you, darling. That would be kind of you.'

I return with my supplies and her sherry. While she sips it, I carefully massage cream into her hand and wrist.

'What are you wearing for your date?' she asks.

I smile. 'I bought a new dress especially.'

'Oh? You did?'

'I can't wait for you to see it. It's gorgeous. It's red, with thin shoulder straps and a flowing skirt. Sexy, but you know, elegant too.'

'You could have borrowed something from me! I know you're being careful with money.'

'Oh, don't worry. It was cheap. Unbelievably cheap in fact. I bought it online. And I'll wear the necklace you gave me with the ruby pendant. It will go perfectly with it.'

We both turn to the window at the sound of a car on the gravel.

'I'd better go up and change. I've got chicken and leek cannelloni for you in the fridge. I'll put it in the oven to warm up now. Oh, and I got you a bottle of Marlborough Sauvignon Blanc. I know it's your favourite.'

'You're an angel,' she says.

'Then you don't know her very well.'

We both turn at the sound of Nick's voice and find him standing there, grinning. I grin back, my stomach filling with butterflies.

If you'd told me when I was fifteen that one day I'd

marry Nick Goodwin, I would have laughed in your face. Don't get me wrong. Every girl at school swooned over Nick Goodwin, myself very much included. But I wasn't the kind of girl someone like Nick would marry. Even back then I was aware of the differences in our circumstances. I was the daughter of a car mechanic. Nick and Carla lived in a beautiful house with a couple of acres of lawn to run around in.

'Look at you two, having a grand old time,' he says, bending down to kiss his mother on the cheek. Then he takes my hand to pull me up.

'When you said date night,' he says softly, pulling me close, 'I thought you meant with me.'

I laugh. He smiles, taking my chin between his thumb and forefinger and looks at my mouth. My heart grows warm. Everything about Nick Goodwin is sexy. His lips, the way his smile curls up on one side, his blue eyes, his perfect jaw, his thick dark hair that I'm dying to weave my fingers into…

I pull away, feeling my cheeks flush. 'I should go upstairs,' I say. 'I still have to get changed.'

'Nicky, come and speak to your mother,' Marjorie says, tapping the spot next to her. 'Have you two come up with a date for the wedding yet? I want to bring it up with Reverend Jeffrey next time I go to church. I think September would be nice, don't you? I love September weddings.'

'I'm happy with September,' Nick says, sitting down and stretching his arm on the back of the sofa. 'What do you think, babe?'

Again, I feel myself blushing. I can't help it. 'I'll check my calendar, see if I'm free,' I say, grinning.

He chuckles and points a finger in my direction. 'You better be free.'

'Then I'm free. September it is.'

'Then it's settled,' Marjorie says, patting Nick's knee. 'How was work, darling?'

'Good, busy. Lots of new clients this week.'

'That's good. You look nice, by the way.'

Nick always looks nice. Today, he's wearing a pair of dark pressed jeans and a pale blue shirt open at the collar.

'I got changed at the gym,' he says.

'Speaking of which…' I gather up the cream and bandages and put them back in the box. 'I'm going to warm up your dinner, Marjorie, and then I'll get dressed.'

'Thank you, darling,' Marjorie says.

Nick winks at me. 'I'll see you upstairs.'

Half an hour later, I'm standing at the bathroom mirror when Nick knocks on the door.

'Just a minute!' I say, staring at my own reflection. I don't know why I even bothered putting it on, I mean, the moment I took it out of the packaging, I could tell.

'If Her Highness would consider relinquishing the bathroom so this faithful subject could comb his hair…'

'Coming!'

Well, there's nothing for it. I shake my fingers through my hair, turn halfway and check my backside in the mirror. I look kind of sexy. If you're into the vacuum-packed look.

I take a breath, pull my stomach in and open the door.

FOUR

'I figured out why the dress was so cheap,' I say, running my hands on either side of my chest. Jesus. I look like I'm about to pop out of this thing like toothpaste. 'It's definitely not a size twelve. More like a ten. A small ten. Or an eight. A zero? Do they have zeros in dress sizes?'

When I look up again, Nick's lips twitch into a smile. I laugh, then put one hand up high on the door jamb and the other on my waist. Kind of Marilyn Monroe in....in anything, really. I'm going for a sexy pose. I hope it's a sexy pose but for all I know, I look like I'm hailing a cab.

'Okay,' he says, laughing. 'I give up. What on earth are you wearing?'

I let go of the door jamb and lean forward, pressing my forehead against his chest. 'I'm an idiot.'

He holds me at arm's length so he can see better. 'Jesus, Ellie. What were you thinking?'

'It looked so good online. The skirt was supposed to be a full skirt, not this super tight tube thing. I can barely walk. I got it from one of those marketplaces... You know the ones. Everything looks fabulous and everything is so cheap?'

'How much did you pay?'

'Four pounds fifty. What do you think, do I look like a mermaid?'

He leans back and tilts his head at me. 'You could pass for a lobster.'

I push him playfully and he lands backwards on the bed. I walk over to him – tiny steps – and hike my dress up to sit astride him.

'Oh, hello,' he says, kissing the base of my neck. 'Hello, lobster…'

I was running my fingers through his hair, and I give a sharp pull. He cries out in exaggerated pain, but he laughs. I love his laugh. He kisses the back of my neck and a shudder runs through me.

He tugs at my dress. 'Can you actually breathe in that?'

'Just,' I whisper, kissing the corner of his mouth.

'You're turning purple,' he breathes.

'I know. We better be quick.'

He flips me over so suddenly that I gasp.

'How does this thing even come off?' he says, sitting up. 'Do I have to get a pair of scissors and cut you out of it?'

On top of the chest of drawers, his phone rings.

'It's not supposed to come off,' I say breathlessly. 'We're going out, remember?'

'You are so *not* going out in that,' he murmurs, trying to pull down the spaghetti straps on my dress. Nick's phone is still ringing. I will him to ignore it, and then it stops. *Thank you, God.*

He kisses the base of my throat. I close my eyes. 'Mmmm…'

The phone rings again.

'Don't…'

He stops kissing me and looks sideways towards the chest of drawers.

'Leave it,' I whisper.

'It's ruining my concentration.' He gets off me and goes to pick it up.

I push myself up on my elbows. 'Who is it?'

'I don't know. A client probably.'

A client? As in, a *personal training* client? At this time on a Friday? What, are they having a bad glutes day? Are their little *derrieres* not tight enough for their Friday night date?

'Leave it,' I say again, but it's too late. He's already answered the call.

I push myself up and go to the wardrobe. I pull my yellow and blue dress off its hanger, then grab my phone.

I message Lauren. *How is everything going?*

I can't hear myself think over the shrieking laughter but other than that, all good, she texts back.

I smile.

Give her a kiss goodnight from me. I'll see you tomorrow at ten thirty. I'll bring balloons.

Bring gin, she texts back.

I laugh as I slip into the bathroom to get changed. Nick is still on the phone.

'I see… Mmmmm… Right.' And then, 'Amazing.'

When I come out of the bathroom, he's sitting on the edge of the bed, gazing into the middle distance, the phone in his lap.

'Everything all right?' I ask.

He looks up at me, then pats the bed next to him. 'Come and sit down.'

My stomach does a little flip. I do as he asks, but then he gets up abruptly, throws the clothes off the chair in the corner and brings it over so that he's sitting in front of me, our knees touching.

He takes both my hands in his. 'There's something I have to tell you.'

My stomach is in knots. I'm already thinking, *the wedding is off. Something's happened. He's getting back with his ex, Edwina. She's amazing.*

'What is it?'

'We found her.'

I blink. 'Who found who?'

He squeezes my hands tightly and takes a sharp breath. 'It's Carla. We found her.'

FIVE

Nick caresses the inside of my wrist with his thumb as a wave of grief crashes over me.

'How did you find her?' I ask, my voice weak.

'Well, do you remember how upset you were after the podcast?'

'Of course I remember.'

I'd told him all about it, before the Zoom call with Ashley. He didn't think it was a good idea, but he didn't try to stop me. And then later, after I recovered from hitting my head, I told him they weren't interested. He stroked my hair and said it was probably just as well.

'You were so upset——' he repeats now.

'I think I was more upset about getting a concussion——'

'——that it got me thinking. Enough is enough. You're worried that something happened to Carla, Mum's confused after getting that postcard, so I got it into my head that I'd find her myself, and then we can all move on.'

I blink a few times. 'But you always said you thought there was nothing wrong. That she was just being selfish.'

'Yep, selfish little brat. And embarrassed, probably. But

after that day, I couldn't get it out of my mind. Honestly, Ellie, it's time to put a stop to the whole charade. She's been a shadow over all our lives for too long. I'm over it. I want you to be happy, and I want Mum to be happy.'

'Okay. Wow. So what did you do?'

'I hired a private detective.'

'You're joking.'

'Nope.'

'When?'

'A few days after the podcast people turned you down.'

'But why didn't you tell me?'

He gives a half shrug. 'I meant for it to be a surprise.'

'Okay, well, that worked. I'm surprised. So what happened?'

'He found Carla.'

We found her. She's dead. 'Oh, Nick…' I wrap my arms around him. 'Oh god. I can't believe it.'

'I should go and tell Mum,' he breathes into my neck.

I pull away. 'Yes, of course. Let's tell her together. This is going to be such a shock. Poor Marge. Where did they find the body? Did he say?'

'The body?' He takes hold of my wrists and pushes me away. 'What the hell, Ellie?'

I frown, confused. 'Hang on… Are you saying…that she's alive?'

'Of course she's alive! Why on earth would you think otherwise?'

I put my hand on my chest. 'Oh my god! Because I thought…'

'Jesus, Ellie.'

'I'm sorry. I'm so sorry. I just assumed…'

'Well, stop assuming. Jesus. Carla's fine.' He pulls me up and takes my face in his hands. He frowns at me. 'Are you happy?'

I hesitate. 'Yes, of course.'

'Are you sure? Because I'll be honest with you, babe, you don't look happy.'

I pull his wrists down and lean into him. I nod into his shirt. 'I'm happy. I'm shocked, but I'm happy.'

He wraps his arms around me. 'Good. Because I did it for you, you know. And Mum.' He releases me. 'Come on. I've got a phone number for her. She wants to talk to Mum.' Then he mumbles, 'Mum's going to have a fit.'

Marjorie didn't have a fit, but she had a good cry with Nick and me sitting on either side of her, holding her hands. Like me, she had no idea Nick had hired a private detective. He explained why, and she cried. Finally, she rose, and armed with the piece of paper Nick had given her, she went to her bedroom to call Carla.

'How did the detective find her, do you know?' I ask Nick while we wait for Marjorie to return.

'I don't know much yet. I know he spoke to people at the French embassy in case she was living there—'

'Oh, of course. The postcard.' Also known as my great conspiracy theory.

'And he put a Facebook post up with his contact details. That's how she got in touch.'

For a moment, I'm not sure I heard him right. 'A Facebook post?'

'Yes.'

'What did it say?'

He shrugs. 'Looking for Carla Goodwin formerly of Lindleton blah blah blah.'

'Wow. That's amazing. I mean, I've posted on Facebook a lot, looking for Carla Goodwin formerly of Lindleton.'

'He probably has his networks.'

I nod. 'Yes. You're probably right.'

Just then, Marjorie returns and we both stand.

Her face is glowing. She rests her cane against the edge of the couch and grins at us, her eyes crinkling with pure joy. She quickly wipes a tear off her left cheek.

'So?' I blurt, unable to contain myself any longer. 'What did she say?'

'She's coming tomorrow,' Marjorie says. 'For lunch.'

SIX

Carla is coming tomorrow for lunch is about the last sentence I'd ever expected to hear. In fact, I still can't believe it's happening. I keep thinking I will wake up any minute now, and realise I was dreaming. Except I'm not waking up, and apparently I'm not dreaming.

Nick and I don't go to the pub, of course. We eat dinner with Marjorie and we talk about Carla. We wonder out loud where she might have been all this time and what she might look like now. Nick thinks she's been living in a commune and she's a hippy now. I venture that she's part of a motor-cycle gang and on the run from the authorities. Marjorie just laughs at whatever we say. It's the happiest I've seen her since I can remember.

I speak to Karlie before she goes to bed. She is breathless with all the fun she's having. At one point I hear Bethany squeal in the background, calling out to Karlie.

'Coming!!!' Karlie shouts before blurting into the phone, '*I'mgoingnowbyemummyloveyoumummy.*' Then I hear a clank, which tells me she's dropped the phone.

'You know how I said I would come and help tomorrow,'

I say to Lauren when she gets on the phone again. 'Well, unfortunately, I have to bail on you. I'm sorry about that, but we have…a visitor for lunch.'

'Oh, that's fine. There's a million adults coming anyway. And that's just the clowns.'

I laugh. 'I would have loved to come and help.'

'I know. Don't worry. Your Karlie's an angel anyway. So who's coming for lunch?'

I pause. 'You'll never believe it.' I tell her the news. She can't believe it either. She makes me swear to tell her all about it tomorrow.

After I hang up, Nick says, 'Aren't you glad you didn't do your podcast?'

I shudder. I imagine myself being interviewed on a podcast, theorising that she's probably dead by now, only for Carla to pop up for lunch three days later. *God.* 'Yes, I am,' I say. I look down at my phone in my hand. 'I'll text Ashley and tell her.'

By the time I wake up the next morning, I am dizzy with the excitement of seeing Carla again. Or maybe I'm dizzy because I barely slept.

I stand in front of the wardrobe, picking out clothes and then putting them back.

'What are you doing?' Nick asks behind me.

I turn around. 'Nothing, why?'

'You've been standing there for half an hour.'

I laugh. 'Hardly. What do you think I should wear?' Nick is wearing beige trousers and a polo shirt. 'Nothing formal, I think. What do you think? It's so warm today. Would denim shorts be too casual? Of course it would. Forget I asked. What would make her the most at ease? How about—'

31

'Hey.' He puts his hands on my shoulders, turns me to him and engulfs me in a hug.

I breathe him in. He smells of soap. He always smells nice, which is another thing I love about him.

'It's just Carla,' he says.

'Right. That's actually incredibly special, but thanks.'

'She's going to be thrilled to see you again no matter what you wear.' He caresses my hair.

'Is she?' I ask. Because according to Marjorie, Carla is fine. She sounded wonderful, and she will fill us all in when she gets here. Also, she can't wait to see us.

Which is why I couldn't sleep last night. I kept asking myself, *then why did she never get in touch? Why did she never reply to my texts or my calls? Why did she never seek me out on social media, like I sought her out?*

He pulls away and lifts my chin. 'How about your yellow skirt and the white blouse with the short sleeves?'

'Perfect,' I say. Then I fall into him and hug him one more time. 'I love you.'

'I love you too.'

'Ellie, sweetheart?' Marjorie calls from downstairs.

'Yes, Margie?' I call back.

'Will you help me with my hair?'

'Of course! I'll be right there.'

I make moves to release myself from Nick's embrace, but he holds on tighter.

'I have to go and help your mum,' I say.

'What about me?' He whispers into my neck. 'I need help too…'

'Stop it!' I laugh, pushing him away. 'We don't have much time. Carla will be here in a few hours and I still have to make lunch.'

I style Marjorie's hair just the way she likes it: with a soft wave throughout. Then I carefully undo the bandage on her wrist and the one on her ankle.

'How does it feel?'

She winces. 'Still tender. Especially the ankle.'

'Dr Patel said that's perfectly normal. It takes time.'

I redo the bandages, then help her dress. I make her a cup of coffee, then I go to the shops to buy supplies for lunch. When I return, I set the table with the prettiest table-cloth I can find and decorate it with a garland of daisies from the garden and wildflowers in small glass cups. I make a quiche for lunch, then help Marjorie prepare Carla's favourite dessert: chocolate mousse.

I'm about to toss the salad when Nick shouts from the hall. 'She's here!'

My heart leaps into my throat. Marjorie and I look at each other and for some reason, we laugh.

I take Marjorie's arm. 'Come on, let's go.' We hobble out of the kitchen, Marjorie leaning on her cane, and join Nick.

The cab has come to a stop and the back door opens. A long, tanned leg emerges, and a perfectly manicured hand rests lightly on the door. I hold my breath. The rest of her comes out, and my jaw drops. She looks incredible. Nothing like the wild, tomboy version of Carla I knew, and yet the same. Her curly hair, which used to look like a rat's nest most days, is slick and shiny, hanging down past her shoulders, with not a single strand out of place. Her outfit – a gold tank top and a green summery skirt – looks simple yet elegant, and probably cost a million pounds. I can't see her eyes because of her sunglasses (gold, mirrored), but her eyebrows could have been drawn by Michelangelo himself. Even her mouth, her plump red lips, looks exquisite.

'Oh my god,' I whisper under my breath. Nick grins at me.

Carla goes first to Marjorie, her arms open wide, a large leather handbag – is that Yves Saint Laurent? – dangling from her elbow.

'Mama.'

They hug for a long time. Marjorie laughs and cries, holding her face and kissing it all over.

'Mama. It's fine,' Carla says, laughing. 'Stop. Please. It's okay.'

When Marjorie finally releases her, Carla turns to Nick.

'How grown up you look!' she exclaims. He hugs her like a bear, his tall frame engulfing her with love.

'You're in so much trouble,' he says, half-jokingly.

'I know,' she says, laughing. 'I fully expect it.'

And I have to say, something gnaws inside me. I get that Nick was joking, but I don't think she should be laughing about it. She's put her family through hell. Some of us thought she was dead. Clearly, she's fine, radiating health and wealth. So what was it all about? And shouldn't she feel some degree of remorse?

But I catch myself and shake the thoughts out of my head. No doubt there will be a logical explanation when the time comes.

'My turn!' I chime in when Nick lets her go. I beam at her, my grin so wide it hurts my cheeks. I open my arms wide to hug her. 'Hey, you…'

She holds me at arm's length, her head tilted to the side, a smile plastered on her face.

'Wow! Ellie! You're here!'

'I know!' I laugh. I move to hug her, but she's not letting me. She's shaking her head at me, her arms still outstretched, locked at the elbows, and the smile still affixed to her face.

'That is so amazing! When Mum told me that you *live* in my house! I couldn't believe it! Wow!'

'I know! Long story. Actually, not that long.'

'You live in my house and you're engaged to my brother! That's so amazing!'

I swivel my head towards Nick. 'Yep. It's been amazing, that's true!'

'Unbelievable!' she exclaims. 'Truly. Unbelievable. I had no idea you even knew Ellie existed, Nicky.'

'Oh, I knew,' Nick says, winking at me. He extends his hand to Carla, which she takes, thereby releasing me.

'Come on, sis,' he says. 'Let's go inside.'

I'd be lying if I said that was the reunion I was expecting. In my mind's eye, I'd pictured us running towards each other in slow motion, Mariah Carey's *All I Want for Christmas Is You* playing in the background. We loved that song. I thought we'd fall over each other laughing and crying and screaming with joy, tears running down our faces. I thought the others would have to tear us apart to get a bit of Carla for themselves.

Not quite.

Nick extends his other arm to his mother and pulls her close, and the three of them huddle together, arms entangled around shoulders, with me following behind. And honestly, I wouldn't have been surprised if they'd closed the door before I got inside, forgetting that I was there too.

SEVEN

It's fine. Totally fine. Obviously I was a little disappointed at the way Carla greeted me, but she's clearly overwhelmed. And reuniting with her brother and mother is so much more important.

We enter the dining room and I swoop in for a quick hug. 'I can't tell you how happy I am to see you, Caramello.'

'Ohhh. That's so sweet!' she says, hugging me back.

'What did you call her?' Nick laughs.

'Caramello! It's my nickname for Carla.' I turn to her. 'You remember? And your nickname for me was…' I tilt my head, already chuckling. I only mean to make a game of it, to pull us into our childhood memories, but she stares at me, that smile again, no teeth, just red lips, thin and straight as a slash.

'Erm…' She looks up. 'It was…' She taps her chin. 'Let me think…. Elli… No wait, it's on the tip of my tongue, truly. My nickname for Ellie… Oh, I'm sorry. It was such a long time ago!' She laughs.

I'm still smiling, but I'm a little hurt.

'Ellie has the memory of an elephant,' Nick says, which I assume is a compliment. He bumps my shoulder with his fist. 'So, what was it anyway? Silly-Ellie?' He laughs and Carla does, too.

I force a smile. 'Jellybean, remember? We did have a fixation on sweets!' I laugh.

Carla clicks her fingers. 'Jellybean! Of course! It was on the tip of my tongue.'

'Sit down next to me,' Marjorie says, taking Carla's hand and guiding her to her chair.

I get the appetisers from the kitchen – broad bean and feta crostinis – and take my seat at the oval dining table. Nick shuffles his chair along to be closer to Carla. There's only four of us, so there's quite a gap on my left, between me and Marjorie, and quite a gap on my right, between me and Nick, and I feel like the odd one out.

I steal glances at Carla while she chats to her mother and brother, and I feel like a total idiot. She looks so sophisticated, so grown up and at ease with herself. I haven't seen her in twelve years, and the only thing I could come up with was to bring up silly, childish nicknames. It occurs to me, with a hollow feeling in my stomach, that seeing each other again means a lot more to me than to her. Maybe I'm still stuck in the past, whereas she has embraced her future. And judging by our respective appearances, I'd say I've hit the nail on the head. She probably has an amazing job that takes her around the world and speaks four languages, whereas I'm just the same person I always was, with a bit more fat on my backside and an amazing little girl.

Cut it out, Silly-Ellie. Move on.

Marjorie and Nick pepper Carla with questions. *How are you? Where have you been? We missed you so much! What do you do these days?*

'You're all so sweet!' She laughs, as if she hadn't expected them to miss her at all. She shakes her fingers through her gorgeous hair. 'Well, I live abroad,' she says, biting into a crostini.

'Oh?' Nick says. 'Where?'

'Don't tell me you live in Paris!' Marjorie says, her hand on her chest.

'That's right!' Carla says. 'I live in Paris. Did you get my postcard, Mum?'

'Of course I did,' she says, her eyes twinkling with happiness.

'That's amazing,' I blurt quickly. I'd hate for Nick or Marjorie to bring up my little conspiracy theory. *Ellie was convinced it wasn't from you at all, can you believe it?* 'And you look great, by the way, very Parisian,' I add, smiling broadly.

'Thank you,' Carla says.

'So what do you do in Paris?' I ask.

'Oh, you know, this and that,' she says with a smile.

'How long have you been living there?' Nick asks.

'Oh, years and years, Nicky. I just love the place. You must come to visit one day, you and Mum. You'll love it. Especially you, Mum.' And I can't help but think, *What about me? Can I come too?*

But I move on. *Cut it out, Silly-Ellie.*

The conversation flows on about Paris and other exotic locations, without much contribution from me. I leave them to it to fetch the quiche and salad. When I return, I notice her wedding band, gold with little sparkling stones.

'You're married?' I blurt.

'Yes.'

I smile, but my heart does a little squeeze. I couldn't imagine getting married and not wanting Carla to be there. The fact that she didn't tell me – let alone invite me – just cements how disconnected we are.

'How wonderful!' I say, sitting back down. 'What's his name? Is he French?'

'John,' she says. 'We got married in London, then we moved to Paris for his job.'

'You got married in London?' Marjorie says.

'Yes,' Carla says lightly. 'A small ceremony. Just a few friends.'

'I see,' Marjorie says, sounding a little hurt.

'And does he have a last name?' I ask.

'Mmm. Smith.'

'John Smith?' I say.

'Yes.'

'Well. I think that's wonderful.' Marjorie says. 'I'm so happy for you. And do you have children?'

'Not yet,' she says lightly. 'Maybe one day. I do love children, as you know.'

I'm a little confused. I try to remember Carla ever mentioning children, let alone that she loves them, and all I can think is the time some kids stole her football from the back of her bicycle, and she said if she ever saw those little shits again, she'd use *them* as footballs.

'What about you two?' Carla says, vaguely indicating Nick and me with the tip of her knife. 'How did you get together?'

Nick smiles at me. 'Ellie came back for her father's funeral, we caught up, spent some time together, and here we are.'

I wait for Carla to say something about my father. Something like, '*Oh, your dad died? I'm sorry.*' But instead, she says, 'How fortunate. Especially considering you always had a crush on Nick. So I guess sparks flew?'

'They certainly did,' I say.

'That's so sweet. Any children on the horizon?'

'We'd love to, one day,' Nick says, smiling at me. My

heart grows like a big warm balloon in my chest. We've never discussed this, so the fact that he mentions it so easily makes me want to drag him upstairs and tear his clothes off.

'And Ellie has a daughter,' Nick continues. 'Her name is Karlie. She's adorable. You'll love her.'

I smile. 'She's six. She's at her friend's birthday party—' I stop mid-sentence. Carla is staring at me, frowning.

'Something wrong?' I ask.

Her face flushes. 'You named your child after me?'

'Are you all right, Carla?' Marjorie asks.

'Yes, of course.' She gives a quick shake of her head and resumes eating. 'It's a bit odd, that's all. I mean, it's very sweet, but it's a little… creepy, maybe? I mean of all the names you could have chosen…'

I feel the back of my eyes sting. Marjorie and Nick look from me to her and back again. I wipe my mouth with my napkin. My hand is shaking. 'Yes, well, I didn't.'

'Ellie,' Marjorie says softly.

'Also it's with a "K", not a "C", so not the same at all,' I say, even though she is spot on. I did name my child after my best friend, but right now I'd rather eat glass than admit it.

'And she lives with you?' Carla asks.

'Well, yes, of course she lives with me. She's six, where else would she live?'

'Ellie,' Marjorie says softly.

Carla extends her hand to take mine, but we are too far away for that, so she lays it on the table. 'I'm sorry, Ellie. I think I've upset you. I didn't mean to. I'm just making conversation.'

'You're not upsetting me,' I say in the tone of someone who is clearly quite upset. 'Karlie has a father, of course. But he's not involved in her life.'

She gives me a quick smile. The conversation continues,

somewhat stilted, and for the next few minutes I sit there, feeling like an A-grade, certifiable, complete and utter idiot. All these years, I've thought about her most days. Some days I missed her so much, it hurt. I grew to be afraid for her because I genuinely believed she was hurt somewhere – or worse, dead. To think that I was about to embark on a true crime podcast to find her makes me want to stick a paper bag over my head. Better yet, curl up in bed and pull the covers over me and stay there until I can think of it without burning with embarrassment.

'I'm surprised you never sold this place, Mum,' Carla says, looking idly around the room. 'Must be worth a pretty penny by now.'

Marjorie is frowning at a piece of tomato on the end of her fork. 'I don't know, I suppose…'

'You'd need to do it up here and there,' Carla continues, looking up at the ceiling. There's a crack that runs from the chandelier to the cornice. 'You could do it,' she says to Nick.

Nick follows her gaze, nodding to himself, like he's only just noticed all the things that need doing. 'Yes. You're right. Good idea, sis. There are a few things I could fix.'

I scoff. 'But I said that.'

They all turn to me. I realise then how petulant I must have sounded. 'I mean, it's true,' I say, looking at my food. I've said to Nick many times that it would be good for Marjorie if he did some basic repairs around the house. Like the front door, for instance.

'Then, we could sell it and move Mum to a care home—' Carla says.

'A home?' Marjorie shrieks.

'I mean a nice one, Mum. One of those assisted living units – is that what they're called? There are wonderful facilities these days. You'd be very independent.' She puts her fork down. 'Come on, Mother. You know this house is too big for you. And don't argue with me. Have you seen the state of the garden? And the lawn?'

Nick's jaw tightens. Marjorie used to have a gardener who cut the lawn on one of those ride-on mowers, but when we moved in, Nick insisted he would do it himself. 'It's a waste of money, Mum, really,' he'd said. And that's the last we'd heard of it.

'It's the right time to sell,' Carla continues. 'There are developers out there who would buy a place like this in a heartbeat. Tear it all down and turn it into a housing estate. That's where the money is. That's what everyone else has done around here. What do you say, Nicky?'

Nicky does not look happy. He's doing that thing with his jaw, grinding it sideways, which is never a good sign. Carla seems oblivious, waiting for a response. Poor Marjorie, however, looks shocked, her fork halfway to her mouth.

'Do you have money problems, Darling?' she asks finally.

Carla shrugs. 'We all have money problems, Mum.'

I just can't believe what I'm hearing. Is that why Carla is back after all this time? Because she needs *money*? She certainly doesn't look poor, with her expensive jewellery and luxury accessories. That's if they're real.

I can't bear to listen any more. I push my chair back and stand up. 'I'm going to get dessert.'

'Thank you, Ellie,' Marjorie says.

I gather the plates around the table.

'I made chocolate mousse. Your favourite,' Marjorie tells Carla.

'Thanks, Mama. I've missed your chocolate mousse so much.'

You can't have missed it that much, I almost blurt. As I reach to pick up her plate, she leans back in her chair, tucking a strand of hair behind her ear.

My hand freezes halfway. I stare at the side of her neck, my pulse racing.

'Are you okay, babe?' Nick asks.

I don't reply. I can't stop staring.

It's not Carla.

EIGHT

I drop the plates in the sink and lean back against the counter. I'm completely confused. That woman in there is not Carla. So who is she? And why is she here? And more importantly, what the hell am I supposed to do now? I can hardly go in there and ask her, 'Are you really Carla? Because I don't think you are.'

I glance towards the door. I need to talk to Nick.

I stand in the archway leading to the dining room and watch the scene for a moment. Nick is laughing at something Carla has said while Marjorie beams at her, holding her hand over the table.

'Nick?' I say, trying to keep the urgency out of my voice. He is so focused on Carla that he doesn't hear me.

'Nick, honey?' I say, a little louder this time.

He raises his hand. 'Just a minute, babe.'

'Nick, please, I need your help.'

'Right now?'

'Right now. Please. It won't take long.'

He follows me through the passage and into the kitchen. 'What is it?'

I take him by the shoulders and stare into his blue eyes. 'I'm so sorry.'

'What about?'

I take a breath. 'It's not Carla.'

He frowns. 'I don't understand.'

'That woman in there—' I point to the dining room, '—is not your sister. She just looks like her.'

He opens his mouth to say something, probably, '*What have you been smoking?*' But I stop him, my fingers on his lips.

'Hear me out. She didn't remember our nicknames for each other—'

He pushes my hand away. 'Are you serious? She forgot your kiddy nicknames? What are you, three?'

'I didn't know her when I was three.'

'Cut it out, Ellie. What's going on?'

'Tell me the truth. Does she seem like Carla to you? Do you recognise her?'

He snorts a laugh. 'Of course I do!'

'If you ran into her in the street, would you know it was her?'

'Ellie, enough. I haven't seen my sister in over ten years. She was fifteen—'

'Sixteen—'

'—when she ran off. She's like thirty—'

'Twenty-eight.'

'—now. People change. What's your point?'

'She doesn't have a birthmark.'

'What birthmark?'

'The one on her neck, here.' I tuck my hair behind my ear. 'Carla has a small brown birthmark, shaped like a cloud, with a dark mole in the centre. And it's not there. I know because when I went to pick up her plate just now, she pushed her hair away. It's not there, Nick.'

'You're sure you've got the correct side?'

'Yes. The left side of her neck. I mean, feel free to check, but I guarantee that you won't see it.'

He rubs his chin and narrows his eyes at me. I have to say, this is not the reaction I expected. I thought he'd be storming back into the dining room, demanding the usurper explain herself. Instead, he looks at me like I'm the one who's up to something shady.

I put my hands on his chest. 'Nick, I'm serious. We have to tell your mother. Right now.'

'Tell her what?'

'That it's not Carla! That she's a pretender!'

He raises his hands. 'Whoa. Hang on a sec. I don't even remember Carla ever having a birthmark. Are you sure you're not mistaken?'

'I'm not mistaken.'

'Because I think you're misremem—'

I raise a finger to his face. 'Wait here. Don't move.'

I walk out quickly, through the passage, past the archway to the dining room and into the living room. I grab a photo album from the shelf, making sure from the dates on the spine that it's one of the older ones. When I return to the kitchen, Marjorie is there, leaning on her cane. I stop in my tracks and quickly put my hands behind my back just as she turns around.

'What are you both doing?' she asks impatiently.

For a moment, I consider telling her, but I can't. Talking to Nick just now has made me doubt myself. Maybe I was mistaken. Maybe Carla's birthmark is on the other side.

'I—'

'Nothing, Mum,' Nick says, glancing at me. 'I'm helping Ellie with dessert.'

'What's taking so long? Have you got the small bowls out? The white ones? Where's the mousse?' She walks to the fridge and opens the door.

'No!' I say quickly. 'We've run out of cream. For serving. Nick and I will go and get some. Right, Nick?' Still holding the album behind me, I grab my car keys from the sideboard.

'What cream?' Marjorie says.

'Cream, you know…'

'Squirty cream,' Nick says.

'Exactly,' I say.

'You know what Ellie's like,' Nick says, rolling his eyes. 'She just wants everything perfect.' Which is completely untrue. Nick is much more of a perfectionist than I am. 'We won't be long, Mum. I'll help you back to your chair.'

She flaps a hand. 'I'm fine. I'm not an invalid, for goodness' sake. Please hurry up, you two.'

I wait until she's out of the room before dragging Nick out through the front door and to my car.

'What the hell are you doing?'

'I need to show you something. Get in.' I open the passenger door and push him inside. I put the album on his lap.

'Ellie!'

I run around to the driver's side.

'Was it true about the cream?' he asks when I start the car.

I look at him. 'Of course not. I don't want—' I drop my voice even though there's no one around '—her to see us talking. I had to get us out of the house and I had to make it look believable.' I drive around the house, which means I have to drive on grass, and I am vaguely aware of Nick looking at me like I've lost my mind. Have I lost my mind?

When I'm sure we can't be seen from the dining room windows or from the front door, I stop the car.

'Nothing you're doing right now looks rational or believable, Ellie. Just saying.'

I pick up the album and scan through pages of

photographs, and I have to say, finding one of Carla is proving surprisingly challenging. The album is basically one long celebration of Nick's accomplishments. Nick as a baby, Nick holding a spoon, Nick playing football, Nick with chocolate all over his face, Nick receiving an award for something, Nick at the beach, Nick riding a bicycle, Nick with a funny hat…

'Ah. There.' I point to a photograph of Carla, aged about ten, making a sandcastle. 'I told you, left side. Right there.'

He narrows his eyes at it. 'You mean, that thing?'

'Exactly. That thing.'

'It's a freckle. She probably grew out of it.'

'People don't grow out of freckles,' I say. *Do they?* 'But the point is, it's not on that woman's neck, whoever she is.'

'Maybe she covered it up with make-up.'

I stare at him. I hadn't thought of that. No. I would have been able to tell.

'Nick, listen to me because this is very serious. She doesn't have a birthmark or freckle or whatever you call it, but it's not just that. Don't you think it's strange the way she talked about the house, just now?'

He shrugs. 'Not really, no.'

'Seriously?' I start counting on my fingers. 'She thinks it would be worth a pretty penny by now. She wants to know how big the land is. She wants you to fix it up. She wants to move your mother into an old people's home.'

He laughs. 'Don't exaggerate.'

I shake my head at him, frowning. 'How can you say that? It's all she's been talking about since she arrived. How much the house is worth and whether you should sell it to a developer. Don't you think it's a strange thing to do after you've been AWOL for twelve years?'

'She's nervous, that's all. She's just trying to make conversation.'

I scoff at him. 'Trying to make conversation? You mean we haven't got anything else to discuss? Like where she's been all these years? Now *that's* a topic of conversation I'd like to hear. But no, she won't, because she can't. And you know why? Because. It's. Not. *Her*.'

He shakes his head at me. 'Are you drunk? You're not making any sense. Why would some rando show up here and pretend to be Carla?'

Am I speaking in tongues? I shift in my seat. 'Because she thinks there's money to be made,' I say. 'What did the Facebook post say? The one your private detective put up.'

'I told you.'

'Tell me again.'

He scratches the back of his head. 'Something about the family wishing to locate Carla Goodwin.'

'Exactly. Don't you think that sounds like it's about an inheritance? Was there a photo of Carla?'

'Of course. Two of them. A school photo from just before she left and another from her fourteenth birthday party.'

I nod, chewing on my bottom lip. 'She's a con artist, Nick. I think she saw the post and the photo, she looked up the family, maybe saw photos of the house. She figured she could pass for Carla. Twelve years is a long time. Carla was only a teenager when she disappeared. She'd be a grown woman now.'

'She *is* a grown woman. And she's in the dining room.'

I ignore him. 'She called the detective and got the information. She's thinking she can trick you all and make a lot of money. You heard what she said to Marge just now. Everyone needs money. I mean, she's so…brazen.'

He drags his hands down his face. 'I think you're going mad, I really do. First the podcast, now this…'

'How can you say that? That woman in there—' I point at the house and jump in my seat, letting out a gasp.

Carla – Fake Carla – is standing at the window, staring right at me.

NINE

I inhale a sharp breath. 'What is she doing there?'

'Who? Where?'

'There.' I point at the window, but by the time Nick has turned to look, she's gone.

'What am I looking at?' he asks.

'Carla. She was staring right at us.'

'From inside Mum's bedroom? Come on, Ellie.'

I put my hand on my chest, waiting for my heart to slow down. 'I'm telling you, she was spying on us. Oh my god. Do you think she's snooping around looking for something to steal?'

'Oh, for Christ's sake,' Nick mutters, letting his head loll back against the headrest.

I start the car again. 'We have to tell Marge.' My hand is shaking. I can't believe she was in Marjorie's room just now. I'm so angry. I want to march in there and give this woman – whoever she is – a piece of my mind.

'Babe, stop. Listen to me. We are not telling Mum anything. Because whatever you think is happening? It's not happening. It *is* Carla. And you know what I think? I think you've been saying that she's missing for so long, that now that she's here, your brain can't compute. You literally can't believe your own eyes.'

'It's not her.'

I park the car back where it was before. I am so angry I can barely look at Nick. Whoever this woman is, she's counting on everyone behaving like Nick: Grateful that Carla is back. Everything is forgiven. Do you need money, darling?

Well, I'm not falling for it. *Somebody* has to protect this family.

We enter the dining room and find Marjorie alone at the table.

'Did you get the cream?' she asks, looking at our empty hands.

Nick grabs the back of a chair.

'Where's Carla?' I ask.

'Don't do it, Ellie.'

'She went to the bathroom,' Marjorie replies. 'What's going on?'

I turn to Nick. 'She must have got lost.'

'Of course she didn't get lost,' Marjorie scoffs. 'She used to live here, remember?'

A floorboard creaks above us. 'I don't think she went to the bathroom.' I rush upstairs, taking quick steps and find her inside our bedroom.

'What on earth do you think you're doing?' I ask, hands on my waist.

'Oh, hi Ellie. Just taking a stroll down memory lane,' she says idly, running her fingers lightly on top of the dressing table. 'So many memories…' she murmurs. 'So this is your bedroom now. Yours and Nicky's.'

I can't believe what I'm seeing. 'Make yourself at home, why don't you?'

She turns to me. 'Are you all right, Ellie?'

'What is going on?' Marjorie asks. I didn't even hear her come up. Nick walks past her to come and stand next to me.

I turn back to Fake Carla. 'You have no right to be in here.'

'Excuse me?' Marjorie says, looking bewildered.

'I'm sorry. I didn't mean to upset Ellie,' Carla says, looking around. 'I'd forgotten how nice this room was. Large, airy. En suite bathroom, too.' She picks up a framed photo of Nick and me from the dressing table and studies it. 'Wasn't this your room, Mum?'

I was going to take the photo out of her hand, but what she's just said stops me. She's a pretender. She's not Carla. So how does she know this was Marjorie's room?

'It used to be, but when Nick and Ellie moved in, Ellie thought it would suit them better,' Marjorie says.

'Not exactly,' I say, scoffing. Marjorie gives me a puzzled look. 'Nick and I didn't want you to go up and down the stairs all the time, remember?'

'Of course, darling,' Marjorie says.

'So you moved Mum next to the kitchen?' Fake Carla says, admiring the tall windows.

'I…' I turn to Nick, looking for help, but he's frowning at me, too. 'That room is near the downstairs bathroom. And it has an adjoining room that we turned into a living room. We thought she would be more comfortable there.'

'I see…' Fake Carla says.

I'm about to argue, but then I remember why we're here.

I raise my hand. 'That's enough. I know what you're doing. Did you take a good look while you were—' I make air quotes with my fingers, 'strolling down memory lane? Plenty of expensive jewellery to swipe on your way out. Although not much here. Pity you picked the wrong room.'

'Jesus Christ, Ellie!' Nick cries.

'Ellie!' Marjorie says.

'I'm sorry, Marjorie. But this woman…' I hesitate. I'm about to break her heart, but I have no choice. 'Isn't Carla.'

Marjorie gasps and puts her hand at her throat. 'What did you say?'

Nick drags his hands down his face. 'It's okay, Mum. Just Ellie losing her mind.'

'No, I'm not.' My heart is thumping. I feel cornered against all three of them, but I have no choice. I have to stop this woman before she enacts her scam, whatever that might be. I take a breath. 'Carla had a birthmark on her neck. This woman, whoever she is, does not have that birthmark.'

We all stare at Carla's neck. You can't tell about the birthmark because her hair – which really is stunning, it has to be said – is draped over her shoulders. But I know. I saw her exposed neck. I know.

I look right into Marjorie's eyes. 'I'm sorry, Marge, but she's not your daughter. She's a fraud, and she thinks she can get money out of the family by pretending to be Carla. But she didn't know about Carla's birthmark.'

Marjorie's face has gone white. Her lips are set into a thin line. She turns to the pretender. 'Carla—'

I open my mouth to speak. *Don't call her that. That's not her name.* But Marjorie has raised her hand at me, her eyes still trained on Fake Carla. 'Can you push your hair out of the way so I can see the left side of your neck, please?'

Honestly, if that had been me, I'd be stuttering my apologies and running out the door. But not her. She looks as bored as if she'd been asked to count blades of grass. She gracefully sweeps her hair to one side, leaving the left side of her neck exposed.

No birthmark.

'I told you,' I say to Nick softly.

'You mean…this one?' She points to the *exact* spot on her

neck. 'I had it surgically removed years ago. There's still a fine scar.'

She actually cranes her neck to show me. I blink a few times, then take a couple of steps forward.

'There,' she says, running a fingernail along it.

I squint. I can just make out a very thin white line, barely there. Marjorie and Nick have also stepped forward to examine the spot.

'Yep, I can see a scar,' Nick says.

'I… I'm not sure,' I lie. I feel my face turn hot.

'You had it surgically removed,' Marjorie sighs in relief. She closes her eyes, puts a hand on her chest and takes a deep breath. Then she goes over to Carla, puts one arm around her shoulders and pulls her close. 'I'm sorry, sweetheart.' She kisses the side of her head. 'When Ellie said…'

'It's all right, Mama.'

'I think Ellie has been listening to too many crime podcasts,' Nick says.

Carla turns to me. 'I understand. I really do. Is there anything else you want to ask me?'

She looks at me kindly, and I feel like a complete bitch. Not to mention a complete idiot. 'I…' I have nothing to say. I close my mouth and bow my head slightly.

'Then, let's go back downstairs,' Marjorie says. She takes Carla's arm and leads her out of the room. 'I know you have to leave soon, sweetheart, and I'd like to make the most of your visit while I can.'

Nick stares at me, raising his arms and letting them fall. 'What were you thinking?'

'I'm…I'm sorry. I really thought—'

He raises a hand, as if to say *don't bother* and walks out, shaking his head.

I sit on the edge of my bed. She had it surgically removed. How did I not think of that?

Nice one, Silly-Ellie.

I drop my face into my hands. I can see exactly what happened. I was disappointed because I'm still stuck in the past and Carla is living her best life. I zeroed in on the missing birthmark because just like that, it would solve all my problems. Of course she was strange and not particularly friendly. It wasn't her!

My stomach is in knots. I have to make things right, and I absolutely have to apologise.

I go back downstairs and find the dining room empty. I glance through the window and see them outside, sitting on the terrace. Carla is talking animatedly while Marjorie is holding her daughter's hand and caressing it. Nick is leaning forward, his elbows on his knees, listening to their conversation.

Somehow, I don't think I'd be welcome right now. I start clearing up and load the dishwasher. I clean the surfaces like my life depended on it – anything to *not* think about what I'd just done. I glance outside again. Maybe I should go and join them. It feels awkward to be in here by myself.

I fill a pitcher with iced water and slices of lemon and take it out on a tray with glasses.

'Thank you, darling,' Marjorie says. Neither Nick nor Carla acknowledge me. Then Marjorie gets out of her chair. 'Can I have a quick word, sweetheart?'

'Of course.'

We walk back a few steps towards the house. We stop at a low wall bordering a flower bed. It's far enough that we won't be heard if we speak in low tones, and it's in the shade. We take a seat.

'What was all that about, Ellie?'

I drop my face into my hands. 'Honestly, I don't know. I really thought…'

'It's like the postcard all over again.'

'I know.'

She pats my knee. 'You could have just asked her about the birthmark, saved us all this drama.'

'I didn't think. I'm so sorry.'

'Well. It can't be helped. But listen, sweetheart. Carla will be leaving soon. I would love it if you apologised to her. I don't want you to leave things like this between you two. Would you do that for me?'

'Of course. I wanted to apologise anyway.'

'Thank you, darling.'

I stand up. Marjorie calls Nick over, 'To give you some privacy,' she whispers to me. She tells him that I'm going to have a chat and apologise to Carla.

'What a good idea,' he says. He sits next to his mother, his hands together in a steeple against his chin. He doesn't even look at me, and I can feel the anger brewing inside him.

TEN

Carla has moved to one of the old recliners – or 'chaise longues' as Marjorie calls them. Nobody ever uses them, so they're a bit tattered by time and weather, but Carla doesn't seem to care. Lying there, with her beautiful, long, tanned legs and her enormous sunglasses, she could be a movie star sunning herself at Saint-Tropez.

I come to stand in front of her. She doesn't move, doesn't acknowledge me. I wonder if she's asleep.

I brush off leaves from the adjacent chair and perch on the edge. I stare at her high-heeled gold sandals, the way her skirt hugs her perfect hips like it was made to measure. I try to make the Carla I know fit into this body, like Russian dolls, but I can't.

I take a breath. 'I'm sorry about before.'

She doesn't reply. Just as I thought, she's fast asleep. Maybe I could pretend to apologise. Just move my mouth and make it look good so Nick forgives me.

Carla sighs. 'Don't worry about it.'

Ah. Not asleep, then.

It's getting hot out here and I can already feel pinpricks

of sweat on my hairline. I pick at the cotton of my top, trying to get some air flowing. I have no idea how Carla manages to remain so cool, but there isn't a bead of sweat in sight anywhere on her.

I look away, towards the trees. 'Nick says I've been looking for you for so long, that now you're here I can't believe my eyes. Maybe he's right. I mean, I have been looking for you for years. And then that man, the detective, he found you so easily…'

'Why were you looking for me?' she asks.

God, this is so strange. She is so cold. But then, I accused her of being a fraud, so I guess I deserve it. 'When I got pregnant with Karlie…it was the happiest time of my life but also the worst, for various reasons. I wanted to reach out to you. I was missing my best friend.' Does that sound passive aggressive? 'But I couldn't find you anywhere. Not on social media, not in the phonebook, not anywhere at all. It was like you'd—' I raise my shoulders. '—vanished into thin air. I even asked your mum to check Births, Deaths and Marriages in case you were married and had a different name…'

I bite my fingernail, an old habit I thought I'd conquered years ago. I wait. I don't know, but if that was me, I'd be surprised, impressed even. I'd say something like, '*Wow, you really went out of your way to find me, that's nice.*' But not Carla. Frankly, it's hard to know why she even asked.

I sigh. 'Anyway. When I came back for my father's funeral, your mother showed me the postcard you'd sent her from Paris for her birthday, and…' I feel like such an idiot right now, I can't even say it.

'What about the postcard?' Carla asks. She hasn't moved, her eyes hidden behind those gold-mirrored sunglasses. She is so cool while I'm sweating from every pore.

Oh well, I may as well put it out there. She'll probably hear about it at some point. 'I thought there was something off about the postcard. I was sure you hadn't written it.' I laugh.

No reply. I mean, I wasn't expecting a reply, but at least some kind of response. Like a pulse. Proof of life. Anything.

Nothing. It's like talking to a log.

'So I went hunting through my things for that notebook we used to write lyrics in, remember?'

Nothing. Log.

'And I found it,' I say, now wishing I'd burnt that thing. 'I went back to your mum's house and asked to see the post-card again. It wasn't your handwriting.' I laugh. 'Obviously, it was, but I don't know. I was on a mission. I told your mum that I didn't think you'd written it. She thought I was crazy, as you can imagine. But I was insistent. And let me tell you, your brother was pissed off with me for putting ideas like that into your mum's head, but I wouldn't listen. I became obsessed with the idea someone out there was pretending that you were…' I let the sentence trail off.

'Anyway. You came home just in time. I was trying to get a true crime podcast made about you.'

She turns her head to look at me from behind her sunglasses.

'You're kidding.'

'Have you heard of Vanishing Acts?'

'No.'

'Well, it's produced by these two women, and every season they focus on finding someone who has disappeared. They're rarely successful, but sometimes they are. Anyway, I told them about you, but they weren't that interested.'

She lies back again and readjusts her glasses. 'You're so strange, Ellie.'

'I know. I'm an idiot.' I rub my hands over my face. I suddenly feel teary and I press the heels of my hands against my eyes. I had imagined this scene so many times: finding

Carla and telling her how hard I'd looked, how I never gave up. But not like this, obviously.

I put my hands behind me and lean back, close my eyes and let the sun warm my face. 'And all this time, you were fine.' I try to keep the resentment out of my voice. I really do, but it's hard.

'You should move on, Ellie. Take your daughter and go make a life for yourself somewhere else. Stop living in the past.'

I pick at my skirt. 'Except that I'm in love with your brother. In fact, you could say it's thanks to your postcard that Nick and I got together.'

'Yeah, well, sorry about that.'

'We're happy,' I say. 'I don't know why that bothers you so much, but we're happy, and he's in love with me too.'

'Of course he is,' she says, clearly not meaning it.

'You don't know what you're talking about,' I say. I think of one of our early dates. We were at the pub. *I love you*, he'd said. It filled me with pure, incredible joy, hearing him say it. *Tell me again. I love you. How much? This much.* That's when he tore off a piece of thread that was dangling off my jumper and tied it around my ring finger. *I love you. Marry me.* I felt my heart, my soul, leave my body. For a few seconds, I was flying.

'Mum says you're getting married in September,' she says.

'Yes. That's the plan.'

'How long have you been engaged?'

'Four months. Almost.'

'Really?' She looks at me over her sunglasses.

'Yes, why?'

She pushes them back in place and lies back. 'I would have thought he could have popped down to Argos and got you an engagement ring by now.'

I look down at my finger. It's not the same thread because they fall apart, but every time Nick will replace it with another one. *I love you. Marry me.* It's actually the most romantic ritual I've ever experienced, and I love it.

'You don't understand,' I say, twirling the thread on my fingers, feeling my cheeks redden.

'Clearly. And to think you always had a crush on him. How lucky is that?' she says.

I tilt my head at her. She said the same thing earlier at lunch, and I still don't know what it means. I did always have a crush on her brother. I would come to her house to hang out with her, and if he was there, I would engineer ways of bumping into him. Carla thought I was an idiot. She hated her brother, but only in the way siblings that age say they hate each other. Still, my crush on Nick was always a point of contention between us. I don't know why she keeps bringing it up. Is she implying I wormed myself into his life?

'I didn't kill my dad so I could bump into your brother in a Lindleton cafe,' I say, chuckling. The joke lands as you'd expect. With a silent, shocked thud.

'Well, anyway, I just wanted to say how sorry I am about before. I don't know what I was thinking.'

'It's all right. Don't worry about it.'

I get up, brush off some leaves that have stuck to my skirt. 'Did you ever do the Wicked Sistas in the end?'

I don't know why I ask. I Googled it until my eyes bled so I know she didn't. I guess what I'm asking is, *Did you start a band in the end? Without me?* Although to be honest, I really can't picture it.

Nick puts his hand on my shoulder. 'How are you two getting on?'

I lean into him. 'Good, we're good.' I turn to Carla. 'We're good, yes?'

'Of course.'

'I'm glad.' I let out a sigh of relief. Nick squeezes my shoulder.

'Why don't we—'

'So did you?' I blurt to Carla. 'Do the Wicked Sistas, I mean?'

'The what sisters?' Nick says, chuckling.

'The Wicked Sistas,' I say. 'Carla and I were—'

But before I have a chance to finish, Carla says, 'I'm sorry, Ellie. I have no idea what you're talking about.'

ELEVEN

'I'll be right back,' I blurt before returning inside the house. I go straight to the kitchen and grip the edge of the sink.

How could Carla forget about the Wicked Sistas? It was such a big part of our lives. We literally spent years talking about it. We wrote dozens of songs. We had scrapbooks filled with pictures we'd cut out of magazines, pictures of what we'd wear on stage or how we'd do our hair or what shiny instruments we wanted to buy.

And yet she had absolutely no idea what I was talking about. It doesn't make any sense. Unless she's had a lobotomy – and at this point, I'm seriously considering that as a possibility.

I mean, she *is* Carla. We've established that. She knew about Carla's birthmark, so of course, she's Carla.

Unless… My pulse races. I clock my handbag on the kitchen counter. I glance outside to make sure no one is coming, then rummage for my phone. I open Facebook and click on Nick's profile. The latest post on his page is the one he shared from Bill Grayson, the private detective.

Looking for Carla Goodwin. We are attempting to locate Ms Carla Goodwin, 28 years old, formerly of Lindleton. Anyone with information about the whereabouts of Ms Carla Goodwin or her legal representatives is kindly requested to contact Mr Bill Grayson at the number provided below.

I study the accompanying photo, and my stomach drops. Carla has her hair tied back in a ponytail and her face turned to the camera, in a pose typical of school photos at that time.

And you can clearly see the birthmark on her neck.

I look out at her, draped over the chaise longue like she's waiting for a waiter to bring her a cocktail with a little parasol. I can feel my heart race. I knew there was something not right about her. This woman doesn't *feel* like Carla. She's cool and strange and she thinks I'm *a little creepy* and she has no idea about the Wicked Sistas.

She's not Carla.

I read the post again. It certainly sounds like Marjorie had died and Carla had been named in the will. Fake Carla must have stumbled upon it and seen the photo of Carla and thought she looked like her. Which she does. She can certainly pass for an older version of Carla. It's like Nick said, nobody looks at twenty-eight the way they did at sixteen.

And the fact that she was living in Paris? That was easy. Marjorie spoke to her for an hour on the phone last night. She must have said something about the postcard from Paris and Fake Carla weaved it into her background. She's good, I'll give her that. She's very good.

I put the phone down and go back outside. There's no point telling Nick. He won't believe me. He'll say I'm going mad.

Outside, he's telling Carla that it's too hot out here for Marjorie, and suggests they go inside.

I stand just behind Nick and to the side, and study her, all of her. Her earlobes. The size of her. Her ankles. Her knees. Her nose. I can't see her face properly, and now I wonder. Is that why she's wearing sunglasses? So we won't look too closely?

'…and then I'll drive you to the station,' Nick finishes.

'Actually…' I bite my bottom lip. 'I have a better idea.'

Nick turns to me. 'What's that?'

'Why don't you stay a few days, Carla? I mean, do you *have* to go now? Marjorie and Nick are so happy to see you. And me, too. It seems such a short visit. Hardly worth it, really.'

She peers at me over her sunglasses, then swings her legs sideways.

'That's a thought,' she says.

Nick frowns at her. 'Don't you have plans? Isn't that what you said yesterday?'

She shrugs. 'Plans change, Nicky.' She pushes her glasses to the top of her head and looks around. 'You know, I'd forgotten how nice this place was. Everyone else around here sold to housing developments, except Mum.' She turns to Nick. 'She must have had a few offers over the years. She was never tempted?'

Nick says nothing. He looks mildly shocked. 'I don't—' he begins, but Carla interrupts him.

'I think I will stay for a few days. Thank you for suggesting it, JellyEllie.'

It's Jellybean, you snake. Get your story straight.

'Wonderful!' I exclaim. 'It's settled, then. I'll get your old room ready. It will be just like old times.'

Nick nods, still staring at Carla, but he looks confused. 'I thought you had to return to Paris this afternoon. You said you had no choice.'

She shrugs. 'Like I said, Nicky. Plans change.'

Nick gives me a big smile. 'That's great. Mum will be thrilled.'

And so am I. Because I know beyond a shadow of a doubt that this woman isn't Carla. And now, I'll have the chance to prove it.

TWELVE

Nick drives Carla into town to buy basic supplies for the next few days. A toothbrush, pyjamas and underwear. I offered to lend her some of mine, and she smiled and said, 'Thank you, Ellie. That's very sweet of you.' Then she added, 'But I like to have my own things. I've always been that way. Haven't I, Nicky?'

There were so many things wrong with that sentence I didn't know where to start. For one thing, Carla and I always shared everything. Clothes, make-up, CDs, whatever. She was never proprietary or materialistic, quite the opposite. She couldn't care less about *things* other than her guitar. Granted, that was a long time ago, but to say, 'I've always been that way,' seems a bit of a risk. What if Nick said he didn't remember that about her? Except he didn't say that. He put his hand on her shoulder and smiled from one side of his mouth. 'You really haven't changed a bit, sis.'

She's so brazen. It's like getting a masterclass in con artistry. She's gambling – rightly, so far – that she could say the most outrageous things and they'd buy it because that's how desperate they are to have her back. She could claim she used to dream of being a pole dancer, and Nick and Marjorie would smile and nod, and their eyes would moisten as they conjured up memories of little Carla twirling around the living room with a broomstick.

But then, a strange thing happened. I was standing there watching Nick open the passenger door of his convertible, which wasn't strange in itself – Nick can be the perfect gentleman – but then as I turned away, I heard the car door slam. I looked again, but it was too late. They were both inside the car. Had I dreamt it?

Nick loves that car. He never ever slams the door of his car.

'Ellie, sweetheart, there you are.'

I turn around. Marjorie hobbles into the room. She's smiling at me, her eyes twinkling.

'All is forgiven,' I say, jerking my thumb towards the window and the departing BMW. 'Carla and I are friends again.'

'I am so delighted with you. Nick tells me that you convinced Carla to stay a little longer.'

This is going to be the hard part. I am not a natural liar, and I hate the idea of lying to Marjorie. Marjorie is like a mother to me. She is the one person I confide in, and she has been there for me in so many ways. Lying feels like a betrayal.

But I have no choice. Not if I am to protect her from that grifter.

'Yes,' I say, mustering as much enthusiasm as I possibly can. 'It seemed silly for her to come all this way just for the day. And she seemed so happy to stay a few more days. In fact, she was very…eager.'

Of course she was. She'd had a good look around the

house. She'd probably already nabbed a couple of things, an ashtray here, a candlestick there, all making their way into her very large handbag. But she also saw a woman desperate to have her daughter back and a gullible brother, all living in a very nice house on two acres of land. *You must have had a few offers…*

Marjorie squeezes my hand. 'You are an angel. Now, come with me, let's make up her room.'

Marjorie clings to the bannister as we slowly walk up the stairs. We stop outside Carla's old bedroom. That room has been locked at least ever since I've lived here. I asked Marjorie about it once, and she took her time to answer, like it had been locked for so long, she couldn't remember why any more.

'I like to keep it the way it was when Carla left. I like to think that when she returned, she would be pleased to find it the same. I know it's silly, but whenever I've thought about cleaning it out and turning it into a guest bedroom, I always feared it would bring bad luck. That it would stop her from coming home.'

Marjorie unlocks the door, and for some reason, I feel a sliver of fear. It's like opening the rooms in Bluebeard's house after they've been shut for years and finding all these dead wives. *Is that how the story went?*

I shake my head. I don't know what's the matter with me, but I need to pull myself together. *Cut it out, Silly-Ellie!* I let Marjorie enter first while I stand in the doorway, taking it in. It's dark with the curtains drawn and so much smaller than I remember. The air is stale and thick with dust. Marjorie hobbles to the windows and opens the curtains, one at a time, leaning on her cane for support. She tries to open the window but struggles. I open it for her, then turn around and survey the scene.

A tsunami of memories washes over me, and for a second, I feel like I've lost my footing.

Marjorie wasn't joking when she said she never changed a thing. The wallpaper – light blue stripes with climbing roses – is peeling off in places. The walls are plastered with posters of bands we used to like. Arctic Monkeys, Florence + The Machine, Fall Out Boy, The Wombats, The Kooks… But the posters have been dulled by time and yellow sticky tape barely holds their curling corners in place, so that it all looks depressing. There's a bookcase with guitar books, some dusty CDs and a couple of Harlequin romances. Then there's her desk with schoolbooks, coloured pencils and an eraser, a scattering of hair ties, and a stack of notebooks covered in doodles. Above the desk there's a corkboard with pictures cut out of magazines and necklaces and earrings hanging off pins. Among the clutter, something catches my eye.

It's a photo of Carla and me, aged around thirteen. We'd just finished a game of tug of war at the fête in town and our T-shirts are covered in mud. We're grinning, one skinny arm over each other's shoulder. Carla's hair is all frizzy tight curls that seem to fly out of her head. My hair clearly started in a ponytail which by then was sticking out sideways. My fringe, which I used to cut myself, is just a few strands of wispy hair. I run my finger over Carla's face. '*She's not you,*' I whisper.

'Did you say something?' Marjorie asks.

'What? No, I was just remembering this day.' I unpin it and hand it to Marjorie. She smiles at it. 'You were both so young,' she says.

I nod.

'That was before all the nonsense. Look how happy you both look.'

'What nonsense?' I ask.

She looks at me, then shakes her head. 'Never mind. You should keep it.'

'I think it's nice here,' I say. I take the photo and pin it back on the corkboard. There. Fake Carla can study it and get her story straight.

Marjorie fingers various things on the dressing table. Carla's hairbrush, a tube of purple lipstick, a jar of Body Shop face moisturiser that must be fully dried up by now.

'Oh dear,' she sighs, looking around. 'I didn't think it would be like this…'

'I'll clean the room,' I say.

'Oh, would you?'

'Of course.'

'Oh, thank you. You really are an angel.'

'It's odd that Carla didn't ask to see her old room earlier,' I say, pulling the duvet off the bed and sending up a cloud of dust. 'I mean, if that was me, I'd want to take a peek. But she didn't mention it at all.'

'Mmmm…' Marjorie says. She opens the jar and frowns at its contents. Even from here, I can tell it's as dry as caked mud.

'Actually,' I continue, removing the pillowcases from the pillows, 'I was wondering, did you happen to mention to Carla that we had your old room?'

She tries to think. 'Yes,' she says finally. 'When she was asking about the house. You and Nick had gone to get the cream. She was asking if I'd made any changes.' She chuckles. 'I told her the only change was the two of you moving in and that you'd moved upstairs and I was downstairs.'

Well. That solves that particular mystery.

'Why do you ask?'

'No reason.' I drop the linen in a bundle on the floor, then open the wardrobe and swallow. All of Carla's old clothes are still here.

'Oh, Ellie, would you mind packing these away?' Marjorie asks. 'Carla will need space for her own things. She can decide later what she wants to keep or throw away. There are suitcases in the utility room. We could store it all in the attic for now. I know it's awkward getting up there, but Nicky can do that for you.'

A part of me wants to say *no*. These are Carla's clothes. They may be musty and dusty and old, but they're still Carla's and I don't want to put them away in the attic to make room for the pretender. It just feels wrong.

'Of course.' I raise my arms full of dusty sheets. 'And I'll take these downstairs and put them in the washing machine, then I'll put the clothes away. You'll see, we'll get this room looking spotless even if it kills us.' Which it well might, seeing all the mould spotting the corners of the ceiling.

'Thank you, darling.' Marjorie takes my elbow, and we walk out of the room. At the door, she presses her hand on my forearm and looks at me tenderly.

'I wanted to say, thank you for being so good about Carla being here. And especially for asking her to stay. I would have, you know, but I wasn't sure that you…' She lets the sentence trail off. 'Anyway. I just want you to know, we love you very, very much. And me most of all, and we are lucky to have you in our lives.' She pats my arm. 'All that business was a long time ago. You were so young. And your poor mother had passed away… Anyway. I never blamed you. I just want you to know that.'

The entire time she spoke just now, I was focusing on her mouth, trying to understand what she was saying, but she may as well have been speaking Icelandic.

'I'm sorry, Margie, but I have no idea what you're talking about.'

'No. Of course not. You're right. I don't want to make a thing out of it, Ellie, darling, I was merely worried it might upset you, that's all. Carla being here, and all that. But I see I was wrong, and I'm glad. We shall say nothing more about it.'

I scoff a laugh. 'I still don't know what you mean. Why on earth would Carla being here upset me?'

She tilts her head at me, a look of confusion on her face. 'Because she hated you.'

THIRTEEN

I pull Carla's clothes out of the wardrobe and drawers and lay them on the bed. I fold them carefully, and the whole time Marjorie's words are swirling around my head.

Because she hated you.

Carla didn't *hate* me. Carla loved me. We adored each other. We were best friends. We were like sisters. Could Marjorie be mistaking me for someone else? But that doesn't make sense either. Carla didn't hate anybody. Well, except for Rob Haley after she caught him kissing another girl behind the toilet block... And maybe Stephanie Parker, who once poured tomato sauce on her head... But not me. Never me.

Could Marjorie's mind be declining? I try to think of instances when she'd said something strange or incongruous, but nothing comes to mind.

Anyway, I have to stop thinking about this or I'll drive myself crazy. I'll have to ask Nick later.

It's depressing packing Carla's clothes. Some of them are mouldy, all of them are stuffy, but each item brings back memories. I take my time, folding T-shirts and jeans and skirts and blouses and it occurs to me that when she left, she really didn't take much. A lot of her favourite things are still here, and I wonder why she never came back for them.

The attic is accessed through a trapdoor in the ceiling. It's quite a large opening, and there's a ladder that extends and retracts, but as Marjorie said, it's awkward to get anything up there. However, since Nick isn't back yet, I decide to do it myself.

I lug the suitcases up one by one, then stop and take a breath, pulling my hair into a loose ponytail. I've only been up here a couple of times. Once when we stored the smaller items of furniture from the cottage, and when I helped Nick move his things out of his childhood bedroom.

The room is cramped, filled with small antiques, a tricycle, Nick's many trophies gathering dust, cricket bats and tennis rackets and god knows what else. I step over a bag full of old dumbbells and pile the suitcases in the corner, next to Carla's guitar case. When I'm done, I take one last look around. There's an old cardboard box, half opened, full of old schoolbooks and notebooks. I pull out one of the notebooks, wondering if they were Carla's, but it's Nick name on the front. I smile to myself, flicking through it, imagining seventeen-year-old Nick hunched over it, writing an essay or figuring out a maths problem. Who would have thought back then that he and I would end up together? Not me, that's who.

As I put the notebook back, something shiny catches my eye. It's caught under one of the books and I pull it out. It's a silver chain with a pendant in the shape of an angel. I hold it up to the light and try to remember where I've seen it before. It must have belonged to Carla. I drop it back in, close the box and go back downstairs to finish getting her room ready.

An hour later and the room has been dusted and aired and vacuumed to within an inch of its life. Surfaces are gleaming, windows have been cleaned and the room is starting to look liveable again. There's fresh linen on the bed and fluffy towels on the armchair. Pity about the peeling wallpaper, but there's only so much I can do.

She hated you.

That's when it comes to me like a bolt of lightning. It's *her*. She's doing this. Of course she is. How did I not think of that before? I think back to the way she and Marjorie were sitting together on the terrace, their heads touching, holding hands. I figured they must have been catching up on what Carla had been up to all these years, but maybe not. Maybe Carla – Fake Carla – was busy spinning lies about me because she knew I was onto her. *I hated her. All that nonsense when we were young. She was always horrible to me. Nobody liked her, of course. What was I supposed to do?*

Oh, my god. Could she be that good? Yes. Resoundingly, yes.

A car drives up to the house. It's Nick and Carla returning from their trip to town. They get out of the BMW, and I raise my hand in a wave. It's important that I show everyone how well I get on with Carla. After all, as far as Fake Carla is concerned, I, too, have been conned. I, too, have drunk from the Kool-Aid she's been doling out. So that's what she would expect from me: a friendly wave from the window, a smile. *I am happy that you're here, and I am sorry about that little snag back there.*

But something is wrong. Nick has walked away, muttering something to her over his shoulder. And judging from his posture, he's not happy. This leaves Carla to pick up her own shopping, which is considerable. There are at least six large bags on the ground. This is not like Nick at all.

I pull my hand down.

I hear footsteps on the stairs. I straighten the bed and give everything one last glance. Carla appears at the door with her shopping bags looped over both arms.

'Oh! My goodness!'

Marjorie appears next to her. 'Ellie! You've been working your fingers to the bone! This is so lovely! Isn't it lovely, Carla?'

Carla wriggles her nose. 'Y-yes…' she almost stutters. 'It's lovely.'

'Is everything all right?' Marjorie asks.

'Well, it's just that…' She bites her bottom lip. 'I do have the most terrible allergies. You remember, Mama? How I would get those allergic reactions all the time? And the mould in here…' She flaps a hand in front of her nose. 'Goodness. The smell…'

I stare at Marjorie. Carla didn't have any allergies. Surely Marjorie is going to say something. But instead, she knots her eyebrows together. 'Oh, dear…'

'I just don't know if I can sleep in here,' Carla says softly. Then she shoots me a smile. 'Of course I can. I'm being silly. It's perfectly fine.' She drops her shopping bags on the bed.

'Are you sure?' Marjorie asks.

Carla scrunches up her face and brushes her nose with the back of her hand. 'Yes.' She nods quickly. 'Of course. I'm sure it will be fine. If we could open the windows maybe? Oh, they're already open.' She puts a hand on her chest, as if breathing itself is an effort.

An Oscar-worthy performance that could teach even Meryl Streep a thing or two. Had we been alone, I'd be slow clapping right now.

'No, no, Carla,' Marjorie says sternly. 'This won't do at all. Let me think… Unfortunately, Nick's old bedroom is his office now. And we transformed the spare bedroom into Karlie's room, so there's no other bed…'

Nick appears behind her. 'Wow. Talk about a blast from the past.'

'We have a bit of a problem,' Marjorie says. She explains

the situation. Carla, meanwhile, has made a remarkably swift recovery. She's checking herself out in the mirror while brushing her hair with the hairbrush. I am dying to slap that brush out of her hand and scream at her to keep her hands off Carla's things.

'It does smell a little like a mausoleum…' Carla says softly. She stands and turns to Nick. 'My allergies, Nicky. You know…'

'Maybe, Nicky…' Marjorie says to Nick.

Oh, no. Please don't.

'What?' Nick says, oblivious.

'Maybe if you and Ellie could move in here for a couple of days? Would that be all right with you, Ellie? Then, Carla could have the master bedroom.'

Nick rubs his chin. I will him to say no. *Say no, go on, say no. Say we have allergies too.*

'If it's just for a couple of days…' He looks at me. 'What do you think, babe?'

I force a smile. 'If it's just for a couple of days…'

'Oh,' Fake Carla coos, frowning. 'I can see Ellie doesn't want to. Please. Forget I said anything. This will be perfectly fine, I'm sure.' She puts a hand on her chest and makes a little wheezing sound.

At this rate, I suspect I might kill her before sunset.

'No, darling. I insist,' Marjorie says. 'Ellie doesn't mind. Do you, darling?'

'Of course not,' I say. 'Nick and I are very happy to camp out in here for a couple of days.'

Fake Carla reaches out to take my hand. I stare at it, check it's not holding a grenade, then take it.

'Thank you, Jelly-Ellie,' she says. 'You're the best. You really are.'

'Well,' Marjorie says with a sigh of relief. 'I'm so glad that's all sorted. Let's go downstairs.'

'Yes. Let's,' Carla says. 'I could use a drink.'

A drink? Now? I check my watch. 'Oh, god.' A stab of panic punches my gut. I look around for my phone.

'What's wrong?' Marjorie asks from the doorway.

'I forgot Karlie.'

FOURTEEN

'Mummy!' The sight of my little girl always fills me with joy, and this time is no different. For a split second, as I bend down to hug her, I forget about everything and all is right with the world again.

Unfortunately, it doesn't last.

'So how was it?' Lauren asks, eyes wide. 'What is she like?'

We're standing at her front door. Karlie has her arms full of party bags – masks, lollies, feathers, tiaras… She lifts them to show me.

Lauren hands me Karlie's overnight bag. 'She was an angel. She can stay anytime. Those two had the whole house in stitches with their shenanigans.'

I tame down Karlie's hair, which seems to have been electrified. 'I'm glad. That's really great.'

Lauren tilts her head at me. 'Is everything okay?'

'Yes! Why wouldn't it be?'

She crosses her arms over her chest, unconvinced. 'So? How was it?'

'It was great! It still is, in fact. She's there right now.'

'Really? Oh, that's so amazing. I've been thinking about it all day. Marjorie must be beside herself to have her back. Where has she been? Did she say?'

'Here and there. Paris mostly.'

A gaggle of childish laughter erupts behind Lauren. She looks behind her. 'Want to come in? It's just the cousins and my sister and Alex. Maybe have a drink?'

I wondered all the way over whether I should confide in Lauren. Lauren is my closest friend here and I adore her. Also, she hasn't been in Lindleton all that long, so she never met Carla. Her husband, Alex, grew up here, but he went to a different school, so I don't think he'd pick her out of a line-up either.

But Alex trains at Nick's gym, and if I confide in Lauren, it's going to make its way back to Nick. I can't have that. I need proof first.

'Thank you, but I should take her home.' I take the bags off Karlie. She's jumping up and down, talking at a million miles an hour about what they ate and what they did and what games they played and all the clowns and Bethany has a dog called Bobo and she got so many *awesome* presents for her birthday and…and…and…

'Okay, well, if you're sure.' Lauren tilts her head again. 'You're all right, yes?'

'Yes! Perfectly fine. Just tired. I'll see you on Monday.'

'Call me if you want to gossip about anything. I'm dying to know how it all went and I don't know if I can wait that long.'

As I buckle Karlie into the car, I explain that Nick's sister is visiting. 'Her name is Carla.'

'Uncle Nick has a sister?' she asks, bug-eyed. 'But he didn't have one yesterday!'

82

I start the car and explain that Carla has been away, and now she's back, and she's visiting for a few days. Karlie loves the fact that Nick's sister is called Carla. 'Just like Karlie!' she squeals.

I grit my teeth, my hands gripping the steering wheel. 'No, not like Karlie,' I say. But she's moved on anyway. She's busy rummaging through her bags of treasures and describing each item one by one.

The afternoon light is beautiful, there's a nice breeze, and I find Carla and Marjorie sitting on the terrace. They are deep in conversation but stop abruptly at the sight of me. I immediately wonder if Fake Carla was talking about me.

Karlie hurls herself at Marjorie, lifting her bags of goodies in the air. 'Grannie Margie! Look what I've got!'

I have to say, I was initially torn about the nicknames Karlie adopted for Nick and Marjorie. I loved that they encouraged her to call them Uncle Nick and Grannie Margie, but wasn't it too early? Nick and I had only been together for six or seven weeks when we moved in with Marjorie.

But they soon cast my doubts aside. Marjorie dotes on Karlie and so does Nick. God knows my daughter hasn't had a lot of family until now. I've lost count of all the times Karlie asked me why she didn't have a dad like the other kids at school, and why she didn't have grandparents like the other kids at school, and why it was just me and her at Christmas? And at Easter? And...and...and... I didn't have any answers for her, but I hated myself for not giving her a proper family.

Now, Karlie is the happiest I've ever seen her. She just *loves* it here. She adores her Uncle Nick and her Grannie

Margie. She loves school and she loves her teachers and her friends, and they all adore her back.

Karlie leans against Marjorie and stares at Carla.

'Karlie, sweetheart, this is Carla,' Marjorie says softly.

'Hello,' Karlie says.

Carla slowly takes off the sunglasses that seem to be glued to her face and narrows her eyes at my daughter.

'How nice,' she says dully. 'I just love children.'

Karlie, sensing this is not someone to be easily seduced, moves on with a half shrug. She unpacks her treasures onto the table and shows them off to Marjorie, one by one. A peacock feather. A plastic tiara that she puts on Marjorie's head. Strands of colourful glass beads that she loops around Marjorie's neck.

'Do you want to come upstairs and put these away?' I ask Karlie.

'She's all right here,' Marjorie says, clearly enjoying herself. I glance at Fake Carla. She has put her glasses back on and is leaning back in her chair, catching the last of the sun.

'All right,' I say. 'I'll be upstairs, then. I'll be right back.'

I walk into Carla's bedroom – her old bedroom, our bedroom now – and I stop. Nick's and my things have been dumped everywhere. Clothes are draped over the back of chairs, our toothbrushes lean in a glass on the dressing table, my skirts and tops are strewn over the bed.

Nick has his back to me. He's putting clothes into the wardrobe, and even though he hasn't turned around yet, I can tell how tense he is, just from the ripple of his back muscles.

I pick up a silk skirt from the bed. 'Did she do this?'

I don't know why I ask. Of course she did. Nick turns, but the sight of him makes me take a step back.

His face is rigid with anger. He snatches some papers

from under a pair of boxer shorts on the bed and holds them up in his fist. 'What the hell is this, Ellie? What the hell are you doing to me?'

I stare at the papers in his hand. 'What are you talking about?'

He takes a step closer, his fist curled tightly around two crumpled envelopes. He shakes them so close to my face that for a moment, I think he's going to punch me. Which is ridiculous. We have our arguments, but not very often, and I've never felt physically threatened by Nick.

'What is it?'

'Why were you hiding them from me? I found them in the pocket of your jeans.'

He drops the envelopes to the floor. It's the two bills from last night, the ones I picked up from the mat when I came in.

'I saw the bills on the mat, and it was our date night, and I didn't want you to think about money for one night. I was going to give them back to you.'

He stares at me for a few seconds, then sits heavily on the bed, gripping his head in both hands. 'Sorry.'

'I don't know why you're so upset…' I say.

He pushes his fingers through his hair. 'I know. Sorry. I'm just really stressed right now.'

I sit down next to him and gently put my hand on his knee.

'I only meant to keep your mind off things for one night, that's all. I promise.'

He nods. 'I know.'

'Talk to me,' I say. 'What's going on?'

'I'm up to my neck in debt, Ellie. What do you think? I'm really struggling here.'

'Oh, honey.' I put my chin on his shoulder.

'Mum won't lend me any more money. The bank won't either. The gym could do really, really well. Everyone who goes there loves it. They tell me it's the best gym in town, but I don't have enough equipment. You know what happened when I went to that seminar? I was surrounded by successful franchisees, Ellie. Everyone in that room was making a success of it. Except me. Do you have any idea how that made me feel?'

I nod.

'I'm stuck in a loop. Because if I don't have enough equipment, people won't sign up for a membership. And I need members so I can make enough money to repay the loan. It's not rocket science.'

'I know that.'

I put my hand on his shoulder. My heart is beating hard. I've never offered it before, but now I feel I must.

'I have my dad's money, the inheritance. Twenty thousand pounds.'

He turns abruptly. I sit up.

'What are you saying?' he asks.

'I was going to keep it for a deposit on our house, when we moved, eventually…'

He drops to his knees in front of me. 'If you do this for me, I will buy you a house made of marble.'

I smile. 'I don't want a house made of marble.'

'Gold then. Solid gold. With diamonds.'

'I don't want a house of solid gold. I just want…' I hesitate. 'I just want a house for you and me and Karlie and for our other children, when we have them. Just an ordinary house. But once the gym gets up and running the way you want…'

He grabs my hands. 'It's for us. I'm doing it for us. For you and me and Karlie, and for our babies when we have them. That's what I'm doing it for. For all of us.'

'I know that.'

He presses his lips hard against my hands. 'You will do this for me?'

I swallow. It's the entirety of my money, but it feels right. 'Yes,' I say. 'I will do this, for us.'

He grabs my face with both hands and kisses me hard on the lips. 'Thank you. I love you so much, future Mrs Goodwin.'

It's only then that I become aware of a shadow to the side of the door. I turn around just in time to see Carla's face, staring right at us.

FIFTEEN

Karlie was exhausted from the party. I gave her an early dinner and a bath. Now, Nick is reading her a story in the living room, and then he'll take her up to bed. I can hear them from here: Nick doing funny voices and Karlie letting out joyful giggles that make my heart soar like a kite on a windy day. It's not conducive to falling asleep, but I don't care. I love hearing the two of them like that.

'What are you making?'

I turn around. Carla is here.

'Spaghetti bolognese.' And then I add, 'Nick's favourite.' I study her face. *Do you know what Nick's favourite dishes are?* I want to ask. But what would be the point? I know she doesn't. Who cares if I catch her out in a lie if there's no one to witness it? I already know she's fake. It's everybody else who needs to know it too.

'Do you need something?' I ask.

She stares at me, her eyes narrowed. She opens her mouth to say something just as Nick walks in. 'Hey, sis, do you want a glass of wine?' He opens the cupboard.

'Oh, yes, please,' she says cheerily. 'That would be nice. Would you like one, Ellie?'

I smile at her. 'No thanks, maybe later.'

Nick turns to me. 'The princess is tucked up in bed reading her book about the universe. Is that all right?'

'Of course. I'll go up in a minute.' I turn to Fake Carla again. 'Did you want something?'

'No,' she says lightly. She takes the wine Nick offers her and walks back out to the terrace, and I wonder why she came in in the first place.

'She's so…weird,' I say softly after she's gone.

'Don't say that,' Nick says.

I turn to him. 'You don't think she's weird?'

'Of course not.' He takes a sip of wine. 'What's the matter, Ellie?'

I go back to chopping onions. 'She didn't have to take over our bedroom and shove us into her old one. And I'm surprised you let her.'

He frowns at me. 'It's because of her allergies. And it's only for a couple of nights.'

I bite my tongue. 'She didn't have to transfer half our clothes over. And she didn't even take care of them. I'll be ironing your shirts for days.'

'Come on. It wasn't half our clothes.' He leans back against the counter next to me, takes another sip of wine.

'Why were you arguing with her before?' I ask.

'Arguing?'

'I saw you when you came back from town, while I was getting her room ready. You looked annoyed with her.'

'You're dreaming.'

'No, I'm not. I was watching you, and you didn't look happy.'

'I'm telling you, we were not arguing. What is it with you

and Carla, anyway? I thought you were desperate to see her again.'

'I was.'

'So why are you so unfriendly towards her? Even Mum noticed.'

Because it's not Carla. He puts his glass down on the counter next to me. I take a sip from it.

'Is it because you're jealous?' he asks. His eyes are twinkling. He's clearly teasing me but for some reason it makes my blood boil.

'Why would I be jealous?'

There's a bowl of cherries on the counter. He takes one, puts it in his mouth and pulls the stem off, watching me the entire time.

I put the knife down and put my fist on my hip. 'No, please, tell me. Why would I be jealous? I'm fascinated to hear!'

'Because Mum loves her more than you.'

My jaw drops. What a ridiculous thing to say. Of course Marjorie loves Carla more than me. What's wrong with that? Other than the fact she's not actually Carla, that is. I open my mouth to argue. I am about to point out I've never been jealous of the fact Marjorie loves Nick more than me, that he's the apple of her eye and I'm not jealous about that, but I don't know what to say without blurting out that *she's not Carla.*

'Love is infinite. Don't you know that? Just because Marjorie loves her children doesn't mean she has less love for others. Including me.'

He chuckles. I stand on my toes, my face upturned. 'And I love *you* to infinity.'

He takes my chin between his thumb and forefinger. 'And I love *you* to infinity and back.'

I close my eyes and laugh. 'You're so competitive.'

'You bet I am,' he whispers. I can feel his breath close to my mouth. I can taste the slight tang of red wine on his lips when they brush against mine. When he kisses me, it feels like I'm falling.

'Aww, you two are so sweet!'

I snap my eyes open. Fake Carla is leaning against the door jamb, her arms loosely crossed over her chest, her glass dangling from her fingers.

'Can I help you?' I say.

She lifts her empty glass.

Nick pulls away. 'Looks like sis needs a refill.' He grabs his own glass from the counter and puts his arm around her shoulders. 'Come on, let's go and find something nice in the cellar.'

'Oh! I forgot about the cellar,' Carla says. Then she looks over her shoulder and winks at me.

SIXTEEN

I walk into the dining room to set the table and find Carla focused on the antique clock set on the mantelpiece.

Of course she is. It's a stunning piece. The clock itself is adorned with little angels blowing trumpets, and there are two matching candelabras on either side. I also happen to know it's a late nineteenth-century French antique and probably very valuable, although I've never asked. It would easily fit in her enormous handbag. Well. Maybe not *easily*, but I'm sure she'll find a way. I make a mental note to check at regular intervals that the set hasn't gone missing.

'It must be strange being back after all this time,' I say.

She runs a fingertip along the candelabra. 'Yes, it is.'

'Ah. There you are, darling,' Marjorie exclaims warmly. She has changed into a pretty silk blouse with a green and gold pattern and linen slacks. I beam at her.

'How are you feeling?' I say, moving towards her, anticipating the kiss, the press of her hand on my arm, the warm smile.

Except it wasn't me she was addressing. She was talking to Fake Carla.

'Hello, Mother. How was your nap?'

'Very nice, thank you. I feel invigorated. Shall we have a sherry before dinner? Ellie?'

'Of course,' I say. 'I'll get it.' I'm about to walk to the cabinet where we keep the sherry when something occurs to me.

I turn around. 'Carla? Would you mind getting the glasses? And the crystal ones for the dining table, if that's all right.'

She looks at me like I've asked her to recite Pi to a hundred digits. My pulse quickens. 'The crystal glasses?' I repeat. 'They're in the same place they always were.'

Marjorie looks at Carla, frowning. Then she says, 'Above the sideboard, sweetheart.'

Carla does a quarter turn, then another, like a ballerina on a music box. Finally, having correctly identified the sideboard, she walks over to it. But even then she seems hesitant, as if waiting for someone to correct her.

I catch Marjorie watching her with a small, confused frown on her face.

'I'll bring out the sherry,' I say. She had no idea where Marjorie kept the glasses. None. In fact, she wasn't even sure which sideboard Marjorie was talking about. Or maybe she doesn't know what a sideboard is. Maybe they don't have those where she comes from.

Hell.

I just hope that Marjorie has noticed it, too. I think she did. And if I can trip Carla up a couple more times, then Marjorie will have to face the fact that something isn't right.

'This smells wonderful,' Carla says, twirling spaghetti on her fork. 'Thank you so much, Ellie, for preparing this meal. You're very sweet.'

'You're very welcome,' I say. And because Nick accused me of being unfriendly earlier, I add, 'And you're very sweet too.' Which makes no sense since she hasn't done anything, but nobody seems to notice.

'Mum says you found a job as soon as you moved back to town,' Carla says. 'How very lucky for you.'

'Yes. I was very fortunate.'

'Jobs around here must be hard to come by. But Mum said the woman who worked at the local hairdresser got hit by a car.'

'Yes,' I say.

'A hit and run,' she says.

'Yes, that's what I understand. Terrible,' I say.

'And just as you arrived in town, too. It's like it was meant to be. That's so lucky. For you, that is. Not for her.'

'I was fortunate to find work right away, yes,' I say.

'Incredible coincidence and such good luck. What was her name?'

I have to think for a second. 'Erm… Tracy,' I say. 'Why do you ask?'

'No reason. I thought I might have known her from school.'

'I don't think she grew up here,' I say.

'I see. And is Karlie settling well into her new school?'

'Yes, she is. Thank you. She loves it here.'

'What does her dad say about her moving here? It must be hard, no? If he has to travel from London to visit. Does he come every weekend?' She clicks her tongue. 'Oh, I'm sorry. I've upset you again. You already said. He's not in Karlie's life.'

I look at her. 'It's all right. You haven't upset me.'

'Are you sure? Because I would hate to. I know how sensitive you are.'

I bite the inside of my cheek. 'It's perfectly fine.'

'He was not a nice man,' Marjorie says. 'We don't like him at all.'

I smile at her.

'Oh?' Carla looks at Marjorie. 'Why? What did he do?'

'It's not my story to tell,' Marjorie says.

Carla looks at me expectantly.

'There's not much to tell,' I say, concentrating on my food. 'I went to college in London to study early childhood education and he was my professor. He told me he was separated from his wife. I thought he wanted to marry me. I fell head over heels for him. Then I got pregnant with Karlie. It wasn't planned. I was on the pill, but I must have… Anyway, I was over the moon. But when I told him…' I take a breath. 'He told me he was married, not separated, and he wanted me to have an abortion. I said no. He said if I told anyone he was the father, he'd tell everyone I seduced him and got pregnant on purpose to blackmail him.'

'And did you?' Carla asks.

I look up, my jaw slack with shock. 'No! My god! Of course not!'

Carla laughs. 'It was just a joke, Ellie.'

I stare at her, mouth agape. 'What is wrong with you?'

Marjorie reaches out to me over the table. 'Carla was just teasing,' she says.

Carla tears off a piece of bread. 'It was a joke, Jellybean. Forgive me. As I said, I forget how sensitive you are.' Then, in a low voice, she adds, 'but it's all coming back to me.'

Well, at least she got my nickname right.

'Come on, babe. Don't look so put out.' Nick laughs. 'Carla was just joking.'

I feel my cheeks flush with embarrassment. I brush my hair away from my face. 'I'm not put out,' I say. 'I got the joke.' But I am wondering, was it a joke? I don't know. I'm going mad. I can't tell a joke from a straight-up insult any more.

'Anyway,' I say, keeping my tone light to show I'm totally over the joke, 'I left college and to cut a long story short, I became a hairdresser instead. So, no, he's not in Karlie's life. But let's talk about you. Is there anyone you want to see while you're here?'

'No, not really.'

'No? Surely you want to catch up with some of your old friends?' *Of which I am not one, clearly.* 'What about Robert?'

'Who?' Nick asks.

'Robert. You remember Robert. Carla's first boyfriend. What do you say, Carla? We could invite him for dinner.'

'Don't you mean Tom?' Marjorie says, frowning.

I swallow my disappointment. I was so hoping Carla would go along with it. *Robert? Of course! How is dear Robert?*

I turn to Marjorie. 'You're right. Tom. That's who I meant.'

Fake Carla shrugs. 'Water under the bridge, Ellie. I wouldn't know Tom from Bugs Bunny.'

'No, you wouldn't,' I say.

'Let's talk about something else,' Nick says. He shoots me a look of warning.

'If you like,' I say.

Nick opens his mouth to speak, but I beat him to it. 'Do you remember the tree house?'

I know how ridiculous my questions are. I know I sound petulant at best, and at worst… well, unhinged. But I don't know what else to do. I don't know how to make Nick and Marjorie question the identity of this woman. So, I ask stupid questions Carla should know the answer to, because that's all I can think of.

Carla smiles but doesn't reply.

'We had such fun there,' I say, pressing on.

'We did,' she says, with a touch of hesitation. Then, satisfied nobody has corrected her, she resumes eating.

'It's still there,' I say. 'Although worse for wear. Do you remember where it was?'

'Where is what?'

'The treehouse?'

Again, Nick frowns at me. Carla scrapes a little bread on her plate. After a beat, she asks. 'Near the old well, isn't it?'

Nice try. It's nowhere near the old well, but it's interesting to know she's already had a good look around outside. I glance at Nick and then at Marjorie. They're both frowning at me. Like there's something wrong, with *me*. For a moment I wonder if maybe they don't know where the old treehouse is either.

'It's over there, in the oak tree,' Nick says, looking at me like I've lost my mind.

'I know that,' I say, laughing. I shake my head. 'Never mind.' I turn back to Carla. 'Do you still follow football?' Again, in terms of segue, it's pretty clumsy. Also, I already know the answer to that. It's a no. I can't picture her in the stands pouring beer over her head.

She blinks and shakes her head. 'Football?'

'I was trying to remember which is your favourite football team,' I say. 'You remember those player cards you used to glue in your school books? Red and white?' I tap my chin with my finger. 'Now, who was it again? I just can't remember…'

Carla bursts out laughing. 'Oh, Ellie.' She reaches across the table to take my hand. I don't take it, but I don't bite it either. 'You're so funny. I haven't seen you in twelve years and you want to talk about a treehouse and some football team I liked when I was a child?' She laughs again, and to my dismay, Nick and Marjorie do too.

'I just want to know what you remember about your

childhood, that's all,' I mumble. 'Some of your favourite memories. I'm just making conversation.'

She shakes her head, chuckling. 'You really should move on. It's a big wide world out there. Spread your wings. Don't be so obsessed with the past. Or my past, I should say. Truly, it would be adorable if it wasn't so…'

I wait for her to say it. *Creepy?*

'…silly,' she says.

Then Nick adds, 'Ellie.'

And it takes me a moment to get it, even as they all laugh. *Silly-Ellie.* Ha ha.

SEVENTEEN

'Shall we have some cheese?' Marjorie asks.

'I'll get it,' Nick says.

'No, I'll get it,' I say, pushing my chair away. I have to get out of here. I have to collect myself before I scream.

In the kitchen I put the cheeseboard together, but I barely know what I'm doing. I really mustn't let her get to me. And I know Nick and Marjorie didn't mean to laugh *at* me, they're just indulging Carla. I know all that. But it still hurts. Also, I do look childish and petulant and silly, whereas she's lovely and kind and magnanimous.

I have to pull myself together.

'How long are you planning to stay, sis?' Nick says when I return with the cheeseboard.

Carla has her elbows on the table and is flicking through her phone with both thumbs.

'I don't know. A few days? Oh, Ellie, I do remember something from childhood. That girl who was murdered around here. Remember her?'

'Murdered?' Marjorie says, jerking her head back.

Carla taps her screen with a beautifully manicured fingernail. '*Girl missing in Lindleton*. Remember that, Ellie?'

'You mean Sophie?' Marjorie asks. She stares at Carla, looking confused. 'Poor little thing. Why are you bringing her up now?'

'No reason,' Carla says, still scrolling. 'I thought Ellie might be interested to know I remembered that.'

I help myself to some cheese. 'That's not what I meant. And I think you know that.'

Marjorie looks at me, her head tilted. 'Is everything all right, Ellie?'

'Yes, everything is fine. And, yes, of course I remember Sophie.'

'It was awful,' Marjorie says, shaking her head. 'Absolutely awful. Sophie Bonham. Poor little soul. And her poor, poor parents…'

'Did they ever find out who killed her?' Carla asks, tilting her head at me.

'She wasn't murdered. She went missing,' I say. 'But that's not the point—'

'She was a good friend of yours, wasn't she, Ellie?' Marjorie asks.

'Again, that's not the point. I wanted to ask about Carla's childhood—'

'I don't know about you, but that was a big deal in my childhood,' Carla says. 'Didn't you know her, Nicky?'

Nick's jaw twitches. 'We went out for a while.'

'That's right.' Fake Carla puts down her phone. 'I remember now.'

She's a good liar, I'll give her that. A consummate professional.

'I didn't mean for you to Google the news from thirteen years ago,' I say. 'I wanted to know what your favourite football team was, which has absolutely nothing to do with Sophie Bonham. But nice try, Carla.'

There's a beat where no one says anything. Then Marjorie says, 'You seem very upset, Ellie. Is everything all right?'

'Everything is fine,' I say, brushing a loose strand of hair out of my face.

Nick is frowning, the cheeseboard in his hand. 'Wasn't she in your class?'

'So? That's not the point!'

'That poor girl,' Marjorie says.

'Can we stop talking about Sophie Bonham? Please? I don't care about Sophie Bonham any more!'

A beat. 'What do you mean, any more?' Nick asks.

'Okay! Fine! I don't want to talk about Sophie Bonham at all. I want to talk about—'

'Why are you shouting, Mummy?'

I turn around so fast I give myself whiplash. Karlie is standing there in her pyjamas, her feet bare. She's rubbing one eye with her fist.

'What are you doing up, sweetie?' I scoop her up, my heart racing.

'I heard you shouting.'

'I'm sorry. I wasn't shouting. I was telling a story.' I hold her in my arms. When I turn around to face the others, they're all frowning at me.

'Why are you getting so upset, babe?' Nick asks. 'Is it because we're talking about Sophie Bonham?'

What is wrong with them all? Fake Carla wants to sell the place and throw Marjorie in some third-rate retirement home. She clearly won't answer a simple question about her own childhood, and yet all everyone wants to talk about is a girl who disappeared thirteen years ago.

'I'll be right back,' I say before carrying my daughter back to her room.

When I return downstairs twenty minutes later, having waited for Karlie to go back to sleep, I find Nick, Carla and Marjorie in the living room.

'How's my princess?' Nick asks. 'Is she all right? Do you want me to go up and read her a story?'

'No, she's gone back to sleep. She had a nightmare, that's all,' I lie.

'Come and join us,' Marjorie says.

'I will. I just want to… Never mind. I'll be right back.'

I slip into the kitchen and fish my phone out of my bag on the counter. I make sure no one is listening in and lean back against the sink. I check the Facebook post again, then punch the number for the detective into my phone. Maybe he can help me. Maybe he knows where this grifter, fraud, horrible person came from. Maybe he'll help me expose her. After all, it's his fault that she's here.

The call goes straight to voicemail.

'Mr Grayson, it's Ellie Hawke here, Nick Goodwin's fiancée. I need to talk to you about Carla Goodwin. You posted about looking for her and she left you a message? I just don't think it's her. I mean, I know it's not her. But she's pretending to be her. I'm not making sense, sorry. But I want to know how she found you and if you could help me expose her. I'm actually very worried about her being here, in this house.' I reel off my number. 'Please call me back. It's urgent.'

The moment I hang up I realise my mistake. I call the number again and leave a second message. 'It's me again, Ellie Hawke. If you could not mention to Nick or Marjorie about my message just now, I would really appreciate it. I haven't been able to speak to them about the issue yet. They believe she…that woman, really is Carla, but she's not. Please call me back urgently. Thank you.'

EIGHTEEN

I am sitting at the dressing table in this musty room, rubbing cream on my face and trying not to obsess over the fact that Mistress Manipulatrice next door is luxuriating in our large, airy, beautiful bedroom.

Nick is lying back on the bed, one arm folded behind his head, reading something on his iPad. I grab a tissue to wipe the excess cream off my face.

'Are you okay?' he asks.

I catch his eye in the mirror. 'Yes, why?'

'You look upset.'

Let's face it, I am so far from okay, I wouldn't know where to begin. 'I'm fine.'

'Okay.' He goes back to his iPad.

'You were very quiet at dinner,' I say after a moment.

'That's because I couldn't get a word in with you quizzing Carla all night.' He looks up. 'What was that about, anyway?'

I shrug. 'Nothing. Just making conversation.'

'You're not still thinking she isn't Carla, are you?'

'No, no. Of course not. I know she's Carla.'

He narrows his eyes at me. 'Don't be weird, Ellie. Please. These are happy times. I want you to be happy.'

'I know.' I nod at him in the mirror. 'And I am.'

'Really?'

'Really. I'm happy. Deliriously so.' I put my cream away. Nick puts his iPad down and pats the bed next to him.

'Come here.'

I smile and lie down next to him and rest my head on his shoulder. He kisses my hair, then picks up his iPad again.

'Your mum said something really odd earlier,' I say.

'What's that?'

'She said…' I frown at the memory. 'It was so strange. She said Carla hated me. When we were children, I mean.'

'Mum said that?'

'Yes. That's so odd, don't you think? Honestly, it worried me. She's all right, isn't she? You haven't noticed her forgetting things, have you? It made me wonder if we should talk to Dr Patel. It was such an odd thing to say…'

'I don't know. I think Carla used to say stuff like that.'

I prop myself on my elbow and look at him. 'Carla never said that.'

'Okay, whatever. I don't know. I think she told Mum you hated her or she hated you or something.'

'But that's ridiculous!'

'Probably.'

'She said that to your mum? When we were children?'

'Apparently.'

I lie back down and gaze at the photo on the pinboard. The one of Carla and me, aged thirteen. 'Carla wouldn't have said she *hated* me. We might have had an argument, and she might have said she didn't want to be my friend any more…' I try to remember specific arguments, but I can't. We rarely argued, but it might have happened once or twice. 'That must be it,' I say.

'Yeah, that's probably it. Don't worry about it.'

'Tell me the truth. How do you find her?'

He caresses my back. 'I think she's great.'

I nod slowly. 'Has she told you much about where she's been or what she's been up to?'

'Not really. Bits and pieces.'

I nod. I almost say it. *I don't remember Carla having allergies as a child, do you?* But I don't.

Later, I stare at the ceiling and count the stains. I'm hoping it's going to help me fall asleep. Nick, on the other hand, is already fast asleep.

I'm up to twenty-five when I hear it.

I hold my breath and wait. The noise stops. I breathe again. *There*. It happens again. Like a rat scurrying around. In *our* bedroom.

I shake Nick gently. 'Can you hear that?' I whisper.

'Mmm?'

It's not so much scratching as moving about now. And it's just on the other side of the wall.

'What is she doing?'

'Who?'

'Carla.'

'She's not doing anything. Go to sleep.'

She must be going through my wardrobe. That's where the noise is coming from. It keeps changing too. It's not so much scratching now as something being dragged along the top shelf.

She's going through my things.

Two minutes later, Nick is snoring softly against my shoulder. I gently dislodge my arm from under him and slowly push the covers away. I unhook my robe from behind the door, then tiptoe in my bare feet the few steps to the other bedroom. I turn the knob slowly, and then, ever so gently, I push the door ajar.

She has her back to me. She's wearing a powder blue nightgown, and she is elbow-deep inside the wardrobe.

I have nothing of value to steal. But then I remember the necklace that Marjorie gave me, and I am kicking myself for having left it in my jewellery box.

'What are you doing?'

I gasp and turn around. Nick is standing there, in his boxer shorts, rubbing his eyes with two fingers. Carla's bedroom door opens wide, illuminating the two of us.

'Can I help you?' Carla says, eyeing us up and down.

I straighten my shoulders. 'I just came to make sure you had everything you need. Do you have everything you need?'

'Erm…' She turns around and surveys the room. 'That's so sweet of you. A carafe of water with a slice of lemon would be good. And a glass.'

I blink at her. Is she seriously asking me to fetch her a carafe of water and a glass? From the kitchen? With lemon?

But then, I asked, so I can hardly baulk now.

I smile. 'Certainly. I'll be right back.'

But Nick holds my arm. 'Don't be stupid. Get your own water, sis. Come on, Ellie. Get back to bed.'

Back in our room, I slip back into bed. Nick stands with his hand against the door. 'Were you spying on her?'

I straighten the bedclothes around me. 'I heard her going through my things in the wardrobe.'

He looks at me like I've grown another head. 'She's sleeping in that room. Why wouldn't she move things around in the wardrobe?'

Of course, when he puts it like that…

He narrows his eyes at me. 'I have no idea what you're

doing. But I promise you, Ellie…' He points a finger at me. 'If you upset Mum, or you cause Carla to leave with your attitude…' He turns slightly sideways, but keeps his eyes trained on me. 'Don't test me, babe.'

'What does that mean?'

'I love you. I really do. But blood is thicker than water. Remember that.'

NINETEEN

I don't know what's wrong with me. There's even a moment, as the sun rises and I'm still lying in bed unable to sleep, when I start to think that she probably *is* Carla, and I've lost my mind. Then, I remind myself about the Wicked Sistas – impossible to forget – and that she clearly didn't know where Marjorie keeps the crystal and couldn't discuss a single topic about her childhood.

She's not Carla. I'm not going mad.

I don't think.

On Sunday morning, I walk into Marjorie's living room to take her to the farmers' market. This is one of my favourite things to do with Marjorie. We will stroll slowly while Karlie skips ahead. We'll be chatting away, buying groceries for the week as well as flowers for the house and maybe some hand-made soap. Sometimes I even indulge in scented candles for a touch of romance, although Nick says that's a waste of money.

I find Marjorie sitting with Carla on the sofa.

'I didn't realise you were up,' I say to Carla. 'I'm ready when you are, Margie.'

Marjorie looks up. 'Thank you, Ellie, dear. Carla wants to drive me today. We'll use my car.'

'Oh?' Then I realise that Fake Carla is in the process of changing Marjorie's bandage. 'Would you like me to do that?' I ask. They exchange a glance.

'That's all right. Carla is doing it.'

I feel a little stab of hurt. I watch Carla work and wince. I wish she were being gentler. Marjorie's wrist is still very tender, which is why I rub pain relief cream into it whenever I change the bandage. But I can't see the cream on the coffee table.

'There,' Carla says, balling up the bandage and dropping it on the table. 'You won't need that anymore.'

'Are you sure?' I ask. 'Marjorie, if you want the bandage, that's completely up to you.'

'Carla is right. I won't need it any more.'

'Is Carla a doctor?' I say.

Marjorie frowns at me.

'I was just joking.'

Carla smiles at me. 'That's funny,' she says, then stands up. 'Are you ready to go, Mother?'

'Yes. Let's.'

I swallow a sigh. 'All right, well, I'll go and get Karlie and we'll meet you outside.'

'We'll wait for you at the car,' Marjorie says.

'But there's not enough room,' Carla says. She hands Marjorie her cane. Marjorie looks confused.

'Of course there's room.'

Carla clicks her tongue. 'I know. You're right.' She hooks her arm into Marjorie's and turns to me. 'I was hoping to spend some time with my mother. It's been so long since we've seen each other.' She tilts her head at me. 'Would you mind terribly, Ellie?'

My hands instinctively ball into fists by my side. *She wants to be alone with Marjorie so she can say horrible things about me.*

'I'm sure Ellie understands,' Marjorie says kindly. 'You won't mind, just this once, will you, darling?'

Just this once. Hearing Marjorie say it makes me so sad. Like I'm someone to be handled with kid gloves, lest I start throwing things. *I'd forgotten how sensitive you are, Ellie.*

Karlie's footsteps come running down the stairs. She's squealing, 'Are you ready, Grannie Margie? We're going to the market!'

'Of course, I don't mind,' I say, sounding like I very much mind. And it doesn't help that my face is rigid with anger, but I can't help it. And yet I know I am playing right into Carla's hand. Marjorie will think me petty and jealous for resenting this outing with her daughter.

Because she doesn't know. *She's not your daughter.*

She's going to get in her ear, I can tell. She's already feeding her lies about me. She's doing her very best to drive a wedge between us.

And she's succeeding.

Behind me, Karlie lands on both feet. 'Are we ready?' she shouts, holding up two little wicker baskets in both hands.

I turn around. 'We're doing something different today,' I say, taking her hand and walking her out of the room. 'It's not a good market today, so you and me are going to make the house look nice and Grannie Margie and…Carla are going to do some very boring old shopping.'

Every cloud has a silver lining, and mine is that the grifter will be out of the house for at least a couple of hours.

Which gives me plenty of time to search through her things. And if there's something to find, I will find it.

Karlie pouts for a while. I make her help me clear the breakfast dishes, then I take her outside to play. She has her own little garden plot to tend to – Marjorie's idea, a brilliant one – and we went to the nursery last Thursday and picked up some seedlings.

But as we walk out, I'm surprised to find Nick dressed in his overalls, leaning a steel ladder against the open front door.

'What are you doing?' Karlie asks.

'I'm fixing the overhead light, princess. See up there?' He points to the light fitting. 'It's broken. And then I'll give the front door a lick of paint.'

'What paint?' I blurt.

He points to a tin of paint on the edge of the path.

'When did you get this?' I ask.

'This morning.'

'I thought you'd gone to the gym. Shouldn't you be at the gym?'

'I don't need to. I've installed digital keys, remember?'

'Oh, I'd forgotten.'

He climbs up the ladder. 'What's with the twenty questions, Ellie?'

Oh, I have a lot more than twenty questions, but Karlie is pulling at my hand. She wants to get started on her little garden plot, so I let it go.

I set Karlie up with her tools and gardening gloves. We place half a dozen forget-me-nots and bright gaillardias, and she is as happy as a lamb. I help her get started, showing her how to dig the little holes and how much water to put in, and then I stand up.

'I'll be right back,' I say, kissing the top of her head. I disappear around the back of the house, get in through the back door and walk up the stairs, rolling up my sleeves with every step, ready to perform a forensic search that would make a seasoned crime scene investigator proud.

'What are you doing?'

Honestly, these days I feel like a prisoner in a gilded cage. I can't take two steps without somebody asking me what I'm doing or where I'm going. I've only been in this room for two minutes, and I've managed to open the wardrobe, and that's it. Surely Nick should still be busy painting the front door, shouldn't he? So why is he here, narrowing his eyes at me, a streak of white paint in his dark hair?

'What do you mean, what am I doing?' I ask. 'I'm in our bedroom.'

'Come on, Ellie. You're going through her stuff. I was watching you.'

'I wasn't going through her stuff. I'm looking for my necklace if you must know. The one your mother gave me. What are *you* doing here?'

He doesn't answer. He crosses his arms and leans against the door, watching me with narrowed eyes. In case I decided to tear Carla's clothes to shreds, presumably. I desperately want him to leave, now, so I can get on with my search, but he doesn't budge.

'By the way,' I say lightly, 'why are you painting the front door?'

'Because it needs it.'

'But you never paid attention to that before.'

'Yeah, well, I've thought about it, and Carla is right. It's time to move on.'

'You want to sell?' I blurt.

He shrugs. 'Why not? You said yourself Mum can't stay here alone much longer… We could use the money…'

Oh my god. This woman is like a sorceress. She has enchanted them all.

'So Carla wants you to sell, and now you're selling? Does Marjorie agree?'

He pauses. 'Ellie, with due respect, it's not your house, so butt out.'

This is *her* doing. A week ago, Nick would never have spoken to me this way. *Butt out. It's none of your business. It's not your house.* A week ago, he would have discussed the situation with me. He would have sought my opinion. A week ago, we were a happy couple making decisions together.

Now, I am to *butt out*.

He pushes himself off the wall. 'Come on. Let's go. I've got stuff to do.'

I put my hand on his arm. 'Please don't rush into anything. Promise me.'

'Babe, thanks, but I know what I'm doing.'

No. You don't. She does, though, and she's even closer to getting what she came for than I'd realised.

'You really don't like her, do you?' he says.

'That's not true,' I scoff.

'Come on. All your posturing about how much you loved Carla, how much she was your best friend and all that crap. It's all an act, isn't it? It's upsetting Mum, you know. The way you are with her. She doesn't understand why you were so cold and rude to her at dinner last night.'

Because it's not her. 'I certainly didn't mean to be rude. And it's not fair to say I don't like her. I'm just getting used to her again, that's all.'

'Is that what you call it?'

I need to be careful. I don't want blood to be thicker than water quite yet. Not until I've found something out about the grifter. I bite my bottom lip. 'I'm sorry. You're right. I'll make an effort.' Then I click my fingers. 'I know! How about we throw a party for her?'

He frowns. 'A party?'

'That would be nice, don't you think?'

'You want to throw Carla a party?'

'Yes.' I put my hands on his chest. 'Look, I know I haven't been very friendly to her. You and Margie are right. I have to do better. I think a party would be nice. It doesn't have to be huge, just a few people for drinks, that's all. Lots of people in town have been wondering where Carla has been all these years. They'll be thrilled to see her again.'

'I don't know, Ellie. She's only here for a few more days. I can't imagine there will be time to organise a party for her.'

'Nonsense. And she hasn't said how long she's going to stay, has she? We could do it on Saturday.'

He shrugs. 'Run it past her and see what she says. Come on. Let's go.'

'Yes, let's,' I say brightly.

In the hallway, he turns to me. 'Haven't you forgotten something?'

I slap my forehead. 'The necklace. Silly me.' I laugh as I go back inside to fetch my jewellery box. I reach for it on the top shelf in the wardrobe, but my hand touches nothing but wood.

It's not there.

I feel around the spot where I keep it, but it's definitely not there.

'What is it?' Nick says.

'My jewellery box. It's gone.'

In two strides, he's by my side. 'You're going blind, babe.' He drags it across and pulls it down. He's right. It was there the whole time. Just in a different place. In fact, I see now that all my personal things have been moved around. My shoebox full of old photographs, my nice box where I keep my diaries, my jewellery box… It's like someone went through every little thing of mine, but didn't bother to put anything back the way it was.

I open the lid to check, my heart racing. Marjorie's necklace is still there, thank god. I bet Fake Carla was intending to swipe it on her way out.

Well, I got there first.

I clutch the box against my chest and follow Nick out.

TWENTY

'I think that's a wonderful idea,' Marjorie says. 'Thank you, Ellie, darling, for thinking of it.'

We're in the living room having some tea and I've brought up the idea of a party. I'm pleased at Marjorie's reaction. It's nice to be appreciated again – even if I'm doing it for the wrong reasons. Or I should say, for the right reasons, but she doesn't know that yet.

Karlie jumps out of her chair at the prospect of another party. 'I think it's a *wonderful* idea!' she squeals. We all laugh.

Except Fake Carla. She's busy scratching the armrest of the sofa with her fingernail as if removing a bit of dried egg. 'I don't think so,' she sighs. 'I hate parties.'

If ever I needed proof… Carla loved parties.

Karlie climbs on Carla's lap and takes her face in her hands. 'Auntie Carla, it's a party! Everybody loves parties!'

I swallow a sigh. Unfortunately, my daughter has also fallen under the spell. She's been clinging to Carla and Marjorie all afternoon like she'd been shipwrecked from the *Titanic* and they were the only two people left beside her. It was Marjorie who 'introduced' Carla as 'Auntie Carla', when she explained that Carla was her daughter but she hadn't seen her in a while.

'How long?' Karlie had asked.

'A long time,' Marjorie had replied.

'Like, a year?' Karlie had asked, her eyes big and round.

Every time I tried to lure her away, she turned me down. All she wanted was to play with *CarlaCarlaCarla* and ask a million questions. 'How many sisters do you have, Auntie Carla? How many brothers do you have, Auntie Carla? Where do you live, Auntie Carla? Where have you been, Auntie Carla?'

From the mouths of babes… I was interested to hear Carla's responses – monosyllabic, non-committal – and frankly she looked like she'd rather eat slugs than play with my child. But that's children for you. If they sense you don't like them, they'll stick to you like glue until you do.

'So, Saturday?' I say, smiling, as if Carla hadn't just shot down the idea. 'Just half a dozen people. I'm sure Tom would love to see you after all these years. You two separated on good terms, from memory.' Carla hated his guts after he dumped her for Maryanne in year nine. 'He's married, you know. To a French woman called Isabelle. She's lovely. You two could talk French, swap recipes for croissants. And I'll invite our old teacher Mrs Lopez. Remember Mrs Lopez? She lives not far away, just off High Street.'

'I *love* Mrs Lopez,' Karlie pipes up. That's because Karlie loves everybody, even evil Carla. Also because Mrs Lopez bakes chocolate biscuits for Karlie. Whenever we see her at the shops, she'll tell Karlie that she has something for her, wink wink, and to 'Pop over later, poppet'. Karlie will pick a bouquet of field flowers on the way, and the 'something' will always turn out to be four delicious, freshly baked, still warm triple chocolate biscuits. 'One for Mummy, one for Uncle

Nicky, one for Grannie Margie, and one for me!' Karlie will sing.

Carla shrugs. 'I might not even be here on Saturday.'

Well, that's one way to get rid of her: threaten to expose her to people who knew her back when.

'No!' Marjorie exclaims, her cup halfway to her lips. 'You're not leaving already?'

'No, Auntie Carla!' Karlie says, over the sound of my gritting teeth.

'All good things come to an end,' Carla says to Karlie. 'Better get used to it now, sweetie.'

On Monday, I am at work, blow-drying my client's hair while mulling over what Carla said. If she's leaving hallelujah then it will be much more difficult for her to execute her scam. Who knows? Maybe she's given up on the idea. Maybe I achieved what I set out to do, which was to protect Marjorie from this con artist.

Later, there's a moment when neither Lauren nor I have customers, and Lauren bombards me with questions.

'Tell me everything. Leave nothing out. Start at the beginning. What was it like seeing her again?'

The truth is, I am dying to tell Lauren. Lauren is a great friend. She's generous and funny and perceptive, and the perfect person to confide in.

But I can't. If I tell Lauren, she'll tell Alex, and Alex will tell Nick, and blood will be thicker than water.

I try to answer as truthfully as I know how. 'She's very different from what I remember.'

'In what way?'

I was sweeping hair off the floor and I stop. 'She looks like Carla, but it's this polished, photoshopped, perfect version of Carla that I don't recognise. When I think of

Carla, she's got wild hair from running and plasters on her knees from falling off skateboards, and she's wearing shorts and dirty sneakers and cheap purple sunglasses from Poundland. And she's laughing and—'

And she was wild and she was gorgeous and she never had a bad word to say about anyone – other than Tom – and she was loving and fun and talented and we had plans and…and…and…

'Oh, honey, are you okay?'

I turn to her, laugh and press the back of my hand against one eye. 'Totally! I caught an eyelash.'

'But where has she been all this time?' Lauren asks, returning to straightening magazines on her desk. 'Was she mad at her mother? Did she say why she never kept in touch with anyone?'

'Not really. She's been travelling. She lives in France now.'

The door chimes as Mrs Drinkwater walks in for her shampoo and style.

'Good morning!' we sing together. And I forget about Carla.

Until I go out for lunch.

I can't believe my eyes. I went out to pick up our sandwiches from the deli on High Street – ham and cheese for Lauren, mozzarella, and tomato for me – when I see them walk out of Barclays.

Nick walks out of the bank first, followed by Carla. Carla pulls her sunglasses from the top of her head and adjusts them over her eyes. Then Nick hands her a fat white envelope. She opens it and pulls out a bundle of banknotes.

My jaw drops. Is she counting money? In the middle of High Street? She pulls another wad of cash, and another, and another, until Nick finally notices, puts his hand on the envelope and moves close to her. She shoos him away and puts the envelope into her handbag.

Nick says something, then walks away with a backward wave. She doesn't seem to notice. She's still focused on the contents of her handbag.

Suddenly, she looks up, and for a second I think she sees me. I step back behind a tree until she walks away.

My heart is in my throat. Because that looked like an awful lot of money, even from this distance.

And I've just transferred twenty thousand pounds into Nick's bank account.

TWENTY-ONE

'I saw you in town earlier,' I say to Nick. I waited until after dinner because I didn't want to bring it up in front of Carla, but the whole time my mind was racing. Was that *my* money she was counting? Did Nick give it to her? Why were they together at the bank anyway?

Fake Carla and Marjorie have left the table and shut themselves in Marjorie's living room. I wonder what evil deed Carla is plotting now that can only happen behind closed doors. What lies is she spinning about me now?

I find Nick in the shed fiddling with his motorcycle. I lean against the wall, my hands behind me, fake nonchalant.

'I was walking across the road from Barclays. I tried to get your attention, but you didn't see me.'

He is crouched next to the bike, cleaning something with a rag. I can't see his face, but I'm sure his shoulders stiffen.

I take a breath. 'Why was Carla counting money in the middle of the street?'

A beat. 'You should ask her that.'

'I'm asking you. Did you give her money? It looked like

you'd given it to her. I saw you hand over the white envelope.'

He pinches the bridge of his nose between his thumb and forefinger. 'Frankly, I don't think that's any of your business.'

'Well, it kind of is because I've just given you my father's inheritance to spend on new equipment for the gym and the next thing I know you're handing over wads of cash to Carla.'

He stands up slowly, working his jaw back and forth. 'You are always so suspicious.' He wipes his hands on a towel. 'You're right. I did give her money. But it wasn't our money.' He turns to me. 'It was Mum's. She asked me to cash a cheque for Carla.'

'Why?'

'Apparently, Carla is in some financial trouble.' He tosses the towel on the bench. 'She asked Mum for help, and Mum asked me to go and cash that cheque.'

'How much?'

He shoots me a look. 'You should ask Mum that.'

'But it looked like a lot of money.'

'It was. But that's their business, don't you think?'

I bite my bottom lip. 'It doesn't worry you? That she's back and getting Marge to hand her money like that?'

He shrugs. 'It's up to them.'

I nod. 'Yes. I suppose you're right.'

The next morning, before I leave for work and while Carla is still in bed, I ask Marjorie.

'Nick says you gave Carla some money.'

'That's right.'

'I didn't realise she had money trouble.'

She wipes a crumb from the corner of her mouth, then

puts her napkin on the table. 'She confided in me about it. It's her husband's business in Paris. It's not doing so well.'

'Oh? What business is he in?'

'Property, I believe. I understand things are tight at the moment. She asked me for help, and since I could, I did.'

I wonder how Nick feels about that. I know he asked Marjorie for money not long before we moved in with her. We were visiting, and I overheard them discuss it in the living room while I was making some tea. 'Come on, Mother! It's not like you can't afford it!'

'Nicky, please don't raise your voice at me. I've already invested a great deal in your gym. You have to learn to manage your finances better. I'm sorry. This time, it's no. Don't argue with me.'

He stormed out and took off in his car in a cloud of dirt, leaving me behind without any means to return to our cottage. I knew he'd come back, and he did, about an hour later, after he'd cooled off. But while he was away blowing off steam, Marjorie told me about their conversation. 'I just want him to be happy, Ellie, dear. But I think for that, he needs to stand on his own two feet. With you. I think the two of you should make things happen, together.'

'On our own four feet,' I'd said.

She'd smiled. 'You're not disappointed, are you?'

'Of course not. I think you did the right thing.'

'I'm glad. Thank you, Ellie.' She patted my hand and sighed. 'To tell you the truth, I don't have much cash available anymore. I have shares, of course, and this house... I gave him what I could. Please don't tell him,' she'd added.

'Of course not.' But I was shocked. I had no idea Marjorie was struggling financially. If that's what she was saying. 'You could always sell the house,' I'd said. Then I added quickly, 'Not for Nick, I mean for you. You could enjoy living in a smaller house, somewhere more manageable, and then you'd have money in the bank.'

She looked at me like I'd just turned into a cabbage. 'I can't just walk away from this house! It's our family home! It's where my children were born, it's where my husband and I lived the best years of our lives. This house is a part of me, Ellie.' And then she'd added, aghast, 'Can you imagine if Carla came home and I wasn't here?'

I wanted to say, '*I'm sure she'll call first*,' but I didn't.

'How much did you give her?' I ask her now.

She smiles at me. 'Now. I think that's a rather personal question, Ellie darling.'

I feel like Marjorie is slipping through my fingers, just as Nick is. With every passing day, they are shutting me out a little more.

I don't have much time. This woman is too good. If I don't stop her now, Marjorie will lose everything.

The following day at work, I wait until I'm between clients to call Tom Baker, Carla's boyfriend when she was a teenager. Tom is a local plumber now, and we used him once when a tap was leaking. I call him on his mobile. We make small talk for a few minutes, then I say, 'You know Carla is back in town, don't you?'

'Yes, we saw her at the market last Sunday.'

'Oh?' That's odd. Neither she nor Marjorie mentioned it to me. Maybe that's not odd. Maybe it's the new normal.

'How did you find her?' I ask.

He chuckles. 'She looks amazing.'

'Yes, she does. Did you get a chance to chat?'

'Not really. Just to say hi. Why do you ask?'

'Because she's leaving soon, and I thought it would be nice for her to see some old friends before she goes. Are you and Isabelle free after work? Just a quick drink at the house…?'

'Um…' I hear the sound of pages being turned. 'That should be fine. What time?'

'Five thirty? Or is that too early?'

'Five thirty is good.'

'Great! I look forward to seeing you both. And be sure to bring Isabelle.'

'I will.'

Then I call Mrs Lopez, who says she would be delighted to see Carla again. I also invite Lauren and Alex, and their daughter Bethany. But Alex has squash tonight, so he won't come.

By four thirty, I don't have any more customers and I've cleaned up as much as I can. I leave work and swing by the bakery where I pick up some cream cakes. When I get home I can't see Marjorie's car, and for a panicked moment I think they've gone out. I haven't told Marjorie or Nick or Carla about this. What if they are out? What am I going to do with the guests if Carla isn't here? I'm going to look like an idiot, that's what, serving petits fours to five people I see every other day anyway.

'Marjorie?'

'In here, Ellie!' Marjorie says

'Where's Carla?' I ask.

'She's gone to the shops.' Then I hear the car on the gravel. 'There she is,' Marjorie says.

'That's good. Because I have a surprise for her.'

'Oh? What is it?'

I smile at her. 'It's a surprise.'

She narrows her eyes at me. 'What are you up to?'

I glance at the window. Carla is getting something out of the passenger seat. 'I invited Mrs Lopez, Tom and Isabelle for a drink. Then they'll get to see her before she leaves. And

Lauren and Bethany are coming too. The party starts at five thirty.'

'Oh!' Marjorie looks surprised, but then she grins. 'That's a lovely gesture. I'm sure Carla will be delighted.'

Hardly, I think. 'But don't say anything. I want it to be a surprise.'

She smiles and squeezes my hand. 'Your secret is safe with me.' I am so happy that Marjorie loves me again, that I kiss her on the cheek.

TWENTY-TWO

'What are you doing?' Carla asks.

'Just getting these glasses out,' I say.

I'm putting the crystal flutes out on a tray. My movements feel unnatural and forced. How hard can it be to put crystal flutes on a tray? It's like being in a play and suddenly you realise you have hands, but you've never noticed them before and you've got no idea what to do with them. And earlier, I cut the cakes I'd bought into bite-sized morsels and set them on a platter with napkins, along with some olives, cheese, and biscuits. It's a mess, really, but I can't think straight.

'Is someone coming over?' she asks, frowning.

I scratch the back of my head, pretending to check my handiwork. 'I ran into Tom and Isabelle,' I say. 'They said they saw you at the market last Sunday, but you didn't have a chance to chat properly, so I thought I'd ask them over for a drink.'

'Jesus Christ,' Carla mutters under her breath. 'Did you—'

She's interrupted by Marjorie walking into the room. 'How lovely, Ellie, darling. You really are an angel.'

Fake Carla rolls her eyes, but I ignore her.

'Thank you, Margie.'

'Where's my brother?' Carla asks, grabbing a piece of cake and shoving it in her mouth.

'Erm… I'm not sure,' I lie. I do know. Nick went to pick up Mrs Lopez, but I don't want to give Carla a heads-up. I want Marjorie to see for herself that *Carla* wouldn't know her old teacher, Mrs Lopez, from a garden gnome.

I hear the sound of voices behind me. 'Oh!' I turn around. 'Look who's here! Isabelle, Tom, so nice to see you. Welcome. Lauren! Bethany! Karlie?' I call out. Karlie comes running down the hall.

'Grannie Margie says we can play in her room!' she shouts. 'We can play with her dressing-up box, and we can watch *BLUEY*—' she bellows the word, '—on the telly!'

'Yes, I know. Say thank you to Grannie Margie.' There's a loud clatter of thankyous, then Karlie takes Bethany's hand and they run back down the hall.

I turn to Lauren. 'I'm so glad you're here,' I whisper. 'Come this way.' Lauren greets Marjorie. They know each other as Marjorie comes to the salon regularly. Then I bring her over to Carla.

'And this is Nick's sister, Carla.'

'Hello, it's so nice to finally meet you,' Lauren says.

'Lauren! Hello!' Carla says sweetly. She takes both her hands and kisses her on both cheeks.

'Oh!' Lauren giggles. 'Very French.'

'A friend of Ellie's is a friend of mine,' Carla says. And she looks so kind, so pretty as she holds Lauren's hands in hers that I think I'm going to throw up.

'Mum tells me Blossoms & Curls is the best salon in town

to get your hair done,' Carla says, and I'm impressed she even knows the name of the place.

'Does she?' Lauren smiles widely. 'That's nice to hear.'

Then, still holding her hands, Carla grows serious. 'I heard about Tracy. How is she?'

Lauren makes a face. 'She'll be okay. She's still in physical therapy. She will be for a few months yet. But she's okay.' Then she adds, 'Thank you for asking.'

Carla pats her hands. 'Of course.'

Well played, I think, *well played.*

I bring Isabelle over to greet Carla.

'Isabelle is French,' I say brightly. And to Isabelle, I add, 'Carla lives in Paris.'

'Oh, really? I didn't know that.'

'Didn't you?' I laugh. Of course she didn't know. Fake Carla wouldn't know a French stick if it fell on her head.

'Where do you live?' Isabelle asks in her lovely French accent. I glance at Marjorie. She is smiling benignly at her daughter.

I am buzzing with anticipation as Carla opens her mouth to speak, and we all find out she wouldn't know the Paris Metro from Paris Hilton.

'Nous habitons le huitième, avenue Montaigne, vous connaissez?'

'Oui, c'est très joli par là. Et vous?'

'Nous vivons dans le treizième!'

'Ah! Le treizième c'est très sympa, oui!'

My smile freezes on my face.

Marjorie laughs as she turns to me. 'I have no idea what they're saying, do you?'

'Not a word,' I say, gritting my teeth. What was I thinking? This woman is a consummate professional. Of course she speaks French like a native. She said she lives in Paris, and she's not going to get caught out in the lie.

I bite my bottom lip. It's fine. Totally fine. Just a small setback in my grand plan. And then I see Mrs Lopez arrive.

'Mrs Lopez! How are you?'

'So nice to see you again, dear. Carla!' Mrs Lopez exclaims. 'I heard you were back.'

'How are you, Maria?' Carla asks.

Maria? I chuckle. 'Why did you call her that?'

Carla tilts her head at me. 'Because that's her name.'

'No it's not,' I say, watching Mrs Lopez.

'Carla is right,' Mrs Lopez says. 'Maria Lopez. You didn't know?'

'Of course I did!' I lie, smiling broadly. 'I just wouldn't have called you that, that's all.'

Carla engages in conversation with Mrs Lopez, and I am astonished at the gall of her, the ease with which she plays the role. And yet, if you listen closely, and god knows I am, you can tell something isn't quite right. When Mrs Lopez asks her if she kept her cat, and what was its name again? Carla replies, 'Yes, I love cats. I don't have one right now because it's too difficult in the Paris flat.'

Deflection, deflection. And yet, when I glance at Marjorie, she doesn't seem to notice. She's just smiling at her daughter. I'm beginning to think Carla could forget Marjorie's name and she wouldn't think there was anything wrong.

Never mind. I have a whole arsenal of tricks up my sleeve, and I'm ready to bring out the heavy artillery.

I grab a fresh prosecco and walk over to the fireplace. I kick off my shoes, drag the white ottoman over and climb onto it.

'Everyone!' Lauren hands me a spoon, and I tap it against my glass. 'Everyone, if I may…'

Everyone stops talking.

'Thank you. I just want to say, on behalf of Marjorie,

Nick and myself, how thrilled we are to have you back, Carla. It's been far too long.'

'Hear hear,' Tom says, raising his glass.

'I'm still not sure where you've been all these years—' I laugh '—or why you never kept in touch, but I'm sure we'll find out one day!'

Everyone smiles and nods.

'Tom, it's very nice to see you here. I bet you're pleased to see Carla again. Carla, why don't you tell us some of your fondest memories of Tom?' I tilt my head at her. Tom chuckles nervously.

'Why?' Carla says, and judging from the look on everyone's faces, they're wondering the same thing.

'Just to take a trip down memory lane. So? No fond memories to share with us? What did you like best about Tom?' I wait. Nick is frowning at me. Marjorie, who so far was smiling sweetly, raises an eyebrow. Isabelle looks like she's swallowed a lemon. *It's all right,* I want to say. *It's all part of the plan. She won't have any fond memories whatsoever.*

'Oh, I know!' I click my fingers. 'What team did Tom play for? He was very good, weren't you, Tom? Carla used to go and watch you play all the time, remember that? And if the game was a late one, she'd sneak out of her bedroom window. Remember that, Carla?' I laugh heartily. 'What team was it again, Carla?'

Tom puts a protective arm around Isabelle's shoulders. 'Hey, it was a long time ago.'

I smile broadly and nod. Carla has her head tilted, and she is watching me. No one says anything. I wave a hand. 'Anyway, I just wanted to say, welcome home, Carla. I think I can safely say everyone here will know how much it means to me that you're back. Everyone here will remember how close Carla and I were.'

Polite, expectant smiles.

'We were inseparable. You remember, Tom? Carla and I were the best of friends, weren't we? Two peas in a pod.'

He coughs into his fist. 'I guess…'

'We spent all our time together, remember that?'

'Not really, to be honest. I was in the year above you both…'

'That's right. You're right. But Mrs Lopez – Maria – will remember. Won't you, Maria? You used to have to separate us all the time because we talked so much!' I guffaw at the memory. Maybe I shouldn't have had that second glass of prosecco. 'Remember that?'

Mrs Lopez gives a tentative smile. 'My memory, dear… these days…'

'Really? Well, never mind. You'll just have to take my word for it!' I laugh. 'Oh, wait. Here's another amusing titbit. Did you know Carla does not remember which football team she followed? And she *loved* that team, remember that, Tom? She had stickers of the players all over her schoolbooks. She got into trouble about that too!' I laugh again. Still no response. 'But I brought it up in passing, as one does, the other day over dinner, and poor Carla had no idea. None. In fact, I'm not sure she'd know a football game from a cricket game! Does anyone here think that's strange?'

Silence.

'Anyone?'

I scan the room, desperately trying to come up with something else, something decisive, something that would show irrefutably that there's something very fishy about Carla.

My mind is a blank.

'Of course, it's been a long time since anyone has seen Carla. Twelve years, three months and one week, to be exact. People change. Of course. Recollections vary. Of course.' From the corner of my eye I see Marjorie move to stand next to Carla. She takes her hand. My heart sinks a little further, if that was even possible. It seems all I'm doing is driving Marjorie to take her side. Then Carla whispers something I can't hear, which might have been, 'It's all right, Mother.'

'But to forget so much? One might wonder if that person even is—'

'I was always asking to be separated from you because I couldn't bear to sit with you,' Carla says.

The room gasps.

I smile tightly. 'You know that's not true.'

Nick shakes his head at me. 'Jesus, Ellie,' he mumbles.

'She was my best friend,' I tell him. 'But I can't recognise her any more.'

He takes a step back, raking his fingers through his hair. 'My god, Ellie, what are you doing?'

I can feel my chin wobbling. 'We were like sisters. I know something is wrong.'

He shakes his head in disbelief. 'Ellie, you were not like sisters. She couldn't stand you! She used to complain all the time that you were a leech. You wouldn't leave her alone. You followed her everywhere. She used to say you wanted to *be* her and it was creeping her out.' He turns to Fake Carla. 'Tell her!'

Fake Carla clicks her tongue. 'You're being very harsh, Nicky.'

'Tell her!'

She flaps her hand in his direction. 'Fine! Fine.' She turns to me. 'You were very clingy. You kept following me and I felt sorry for you because your mother died and you were like a sad puppy. We all felt sorry for you. That's why we let you come here all the time. But then you started copying everything about me. You wore my clothes—'

'We *exchanged* clothes!'

'Then I wanted to be in a band, so you wanted to be in a

band. I was learning the guitar, so you went and learnt the keyboards. When I couldn't stand it any more I'd tell you that you couldn't come over, but then you'd do something really nasty to me.'

I am beyond speechless. I turn to Marjorie. 'Don't you see? She's lying!'

Marjorie hesitates. She turns to Fake Carla, wringing her hands. 'Well… I mean… There was the incident with the burnt hair…'

'What burnt hair?' I ask.

'You two were upstairs, Carla came downstairs…' She shakes her head at the memory. 'Her beautiful hair, all burnt on one side.' She glances at Carla. 'I had to cut it short for you, sweetheart, didn't I?'

'But that was an accident! She wanted me to iron her hair, to make it straight. We used your iron, Marge, and Carla knelt next to the ironing board and put her hair on it and I ironed it, just like she asked. But the iron was too hot and we didn't know you were supposed to put water in it and as soon as I put the iron on her hair it melted. But I didn't do it on purpose!'

Marjorie looks at her hands.

'I even cut my own hair really short, so she wouldn't feel bad the next day at school.'

Fake Carla looks at me sadly. 'Ellie. You were copying me. Like you always did.'

'Oh my god. You are such a liar!'

'What about the time you broke her arm?' Marjorie asks.

'Excuse me?' My jaw drops. Honestly at this point it's spending so much time trawling on the floor, I'll be hoovering up dust bunnies soon. 'I never broke her arm.'

'Ellie, come on…' Carla says softly. 'In the woods. You pushed me out of the tree. I fell and broke my arm.'

Marjorie visibly shudders. 'It could have been so much worse. She could have broken her neck, Ellie.'

'But that's insane! I didn't push her out of the tree. She was climbing up and she was being stupid jumping from branch to branch and she fell! I'm telling you the truth, Margie. It was an accident. I told her not to do it.'

Carla looks at Marjorie, then back at me. 'I wish you'd stop calling her Margie. She hates the name Margie, you know. Honestly, Ellie…' She sighs.

'What?'

She clicks her tongue. 'The way you've wormed yourself into my family… It's so…creepy.'

The room is deadly silent, everyone waiting for what happens next. Mrs Lopez is refilling her glass from the bottle of prosecco. At this point I could sell popcorn and make a killing.

'I spent years looking for you,' I say, my bottom lip wobbling. 'I was prepared to move heaven and earth to find you. Just to make sure you were all right. But you wouldn't know that, would you? Because—'

'And did it ever occur to you that's why I didn't want to come home?' she asks. 'You looking for me, moving—' she raises two fingers to make air quotes '— heaven and earth to find me?'

I shake my head at her. 'I don't even know what you're saying.'

She looks at Marjorie who puts her hand on her wrist. 'Sweetheart.'

'It's fine, Mother.' She looks at me again. 'I ran away because of you, Ellie. To get away from you.'

I'm trying to smile as I stare at my glass, which is empty. 'You're lying.'

'Come on, honey.' I look up. Lauren has her hand extended towards me.

'She's lying,' I say.

'Ellie, darling…' Marjorie says softly.

'No, really, she's lying. You want to know why?'

'Cut it out, Ellie,' Nick says.

'Because it's not her.' I look at Marjorie. 'I'm sorry, Marjorie. It's not her. It's not Carla.'

TWENTY-THREE

I don't know what I was expecting. In my mind, Fake Carla would be exposed, everyone would be in shock, and Nick and Marjorie would have to believe what was right in front of their eyes: It's. Not. Her.

No one says anything. All you can hear is the noise from the TV coming from Marjorie's room, and the shrieks of laughter from the girls. *Thank god.*

Carla speaks again. 'You can imagine how frightening it was to find out you were back here, in my house, and about to marry my brother.' She turns to Nick. 'I'm sorry, Nicky. I know it must hurt to hear those things.' She turns back to me. 'And I'm sorry for you, too, Ellie. Truly. But you need to let go, sweetie. Grow up. Get out. Get a life.' She stares at me for a few seconds, her chin wobbling. 'Stop stealing mine. Please. It's very frightening.'

'Oh, come on!' I say.

She turns to Marjorie. 'How could you let her back in here after all these years, Mum? How could you? Can't you make her *leave*?' Then, with a sob she runs out of the room.

Marjorie rushes after her. 'Carla, sweetheart. Wait.'

Everyone else frowns at me. The villain. The evil twin. The arm breaker. The hair burner. And I'm still standing on my ottoman like a bride on a cake topper. A bride who's been left at the altar, obviously.

People shuffle their feet and begin making their excuses. *It's been lovely but…work tomorrow…you know how it is…* Not to me. They say it to Nick while casting furtive glances my way.

I get off the ottoman.

Lauren comes to me. 'What the hell, Ellie? What on earth were you thinking?'

'Jeez, I don't know. I thought I'd made it clear.'

She glances over her shoulder. 'Of course it's her!'

'Please, don't you start.' I look at the other guests filing out. 'Tell me the truth. What did you think of her?'

'I thought she was really nice!'

'Are you serious?'

'Yes, why?'

'Because she's not really nice, Lauren!'

She blinks a few times. 'She actually is!'

I shake my head. 'I mean, fine. On the surface, maybe. But that's because she's playing a part.'

Lauren studies my face for a moment. Then she leans forward. 'Nick told Alex you've been having problems. Want to talk about it?'

I recoil. 'Problems? What problems?'

'With Carla being here. He says you're not handling it well. I mean, obviously…but he says you've been so close to Marjorie and now her attention is on Carla…'

'That's ridiculous!' I hiss. 'The point isn't that Marjorie spends time with her, the point is that it's not her!'

Why am I screaming into the void like this? Why is no one hearing me? I feel like the person in that painting with the distorted figure, their mouth open, their hands over their ears. That could absolutely be a portrait of me right now.

Lauren looks away. 'Look… maybe you should…'

'What?'

'Talk to someone?'

'What the hell does that mean?'

'Nothing. Really. Just a thought. Anyway…' She glances over her shoulder, as if looking for an escape. 'I should get Bethany. And I'll drive Mrs Lopez home.'

I take her hand. 'Please tell me you believe me.'

She avoids my eye. 'I'd like to, Ellie, but Alex says—'

'Oh, fuck Alex!'

She jerks her head up.

I put my hand on my chest. 'I didn't mean that. I'm sorry. It's just that Nick doesn't see what I see, and I wish he wouldn't tell everyone that I'm crazy or whatever it is he says.' I bite my thumbnail. 'What did Alex say?'

She gives me a hard stare. 'That you're nuts.'

I take her hand. 'I'm not. I promise. And I'm really sorry I snapped like that.'

She looks away and nods. 'Well…I guess I should get Bethany and take Mrs Lopez home, then.' We both glance towards her. She's at the table, finishing off the cheese. I suddenly become aware of Nick who, for some strange reason, is picking up the cushions off the couch.

'What are you doing?' I ask him.

'I'm sleeping in my office tonight.'

'In your office?' I glance at Lauren, then at Mrs Lopez. They're both staring at us. Mrs Lopez grabs a flute at random and knocks back the dregs at the bottom.

I lower my voice. 'There isn't even a bed in there.'

He holds up a couple of cushions.

'Come on, Nick. Don't let her get the better of us. If you'd give me a chance to explain…'

'I can't talk to you right now,' he says, his arms full of cushions. 'I don't want to see you, or talk to you. And speaking of lying—' His tone goes up a notch, both in pitch and volume. I silently urge him to wait until Lauren and Mrs Lopez have left, but he doesn't seem to notice they're still here. 'You told Mum you wanted to organise a small party for Carla. You told me the same thing. You lied to us, Ellie, to our faces. You were trying to set some kind of twisted trap for her, but it blew up in your face. So no, I don't want to talk to you right now. And now Mum is really upset because of you. You know what she said to me just now? *"I can't believe Ellie would lie to me like that. All that pretending…I feel so betrayed."* That's what she said. Her words.'

I swallow, brush a tear away with my fingers. 'If I could explain to Marg – Marjorie…'

He thrusts a hand at me, palm out. 'Don't. Just … don't.'

And then he walks out.

'Bethany?' Lauren calls out. 'Come on, sweetie! We're going home!'

I am dying inside.

Bethany skips over. 'We're going home?'

'We're taking Mrs Lopez home first, then we're going home.' She finds Bethany's coat and puts it on her. Karlie watches from the doorway.

'I'll see you tomorrow, I guess,' Lauren says, and for a moment I wonder who she's talking to, because she's not looking at me.

'Right, yes.' I nod. 'Of course. See you tomorrow.'

TWENTY-FOUR

The next morning when I get to the salon, I find Lauren lugging a delivery box inside.

'Hi!' I'm a little shaky from lack of sleep. I hoist my bag on my shoulder and pick up another box.

She gives me a quick smile. 'How are you feeling this morning?'

'Oh, you know… I've had better days.'

We put our boxes down on the long table inside.

'I'm sorry about yesterday,' I say, opening the first box. 'What I said about Alex.'

'It's fine,' she replies.

'I shouldn't have taken it out on you.'

'Really, Ellie. Don't worry about it.'

'You're mad at me.'

'I'm not, really. But I'm worried about you.'

'Why? I mean, I'm worried about me, too, but why are *you* worried about me?'

She turns to me and puts one hand on her waist. 'Did you really do all those horrible things to her when you were kids?'

'No! I swear to you! She's lying. That's all she's done since she got here. It never happened. I mean, not that way.'

She tilts her head at me. 'Alex said some things that Nick told him.'

'I know. You told me, he told me. I'm jealous.'

'No, not that.' She pulls out another few bottles of shampoo. 'Nick says it's not possible that it's not Carla. Not remotely. She's been there for days and her and Nick, and Marjorie, have been talking the whole time. There's no doubt in his mind.'

'That's because he doesn't know her like I do.'

She tilts her head at me. 'Do you hear yourself? They're brother and sister, Ellie. And what about Marjorie? Does she not know her like you do either?'

'Marjorie just wants her daughter back. Fake Carla could be a whole foot taller and Marjorie would still think it was her.'

Lauren remains silent as we finish putting the bottles of shampoo on the shelves. She jerks her chin at the bottles in my hands. 'You're squeezing them too hard.'

She's right. They're about to pop their caps off. I sigh and relax my grip. 'I just wish somebody would take my side.'

'I'm trying, Ellie. We all are.'

We all are. What the hell does that mean? Who's we? Is Fake Carla part of *we*? And all this business about Nick talking to Alex about me, and Alex gossiping to Lauren… I can feel heat rise in my cheeks as I straighten chairs and magazines. And then it dawns on me. There is one person who will believe me. One person who has the means to help me.

I glance at the clock on the wall. I only have a few minutes left before we open. I pull my mobile out of my bag.

'I need to make a call. I won't be long.' I say, before disappearing through the back door that leads to the lane.

I lean against the wall and load up the number from my contacts.

Ashley - Vanishing Acts.

'Ashley? It's Ellie. We spoke a few weeks ago on Zoom, about my friend Carla?'

A beat. 'Ellie! Hi! How are you?'

'I'm fine. No, I'm not. Something's come up.' I bite my bottom lip. Back in the salon, the bell over the front door jingles. A customer? Already?

'I'm actually on my way out…' she says.

'It's not Carla,' I blurt.

Silence.

'The woman in our house, the woman who claims to be Marjorie's daughter, Carla, it's not her.'

'Okay…' she says slowly.

'At first, I thought it was her. Of course I did. Why wouldn't I? I mean, she didn't exactly *look* like Carla. I mean, she did, but she's incredibly beautiful, not that Carla isn't beautiful… but this woman is like a supermodel. Anyway, she didn't know that my nickname for her was Caramello, so that was a red flag.'

'Are you all right?' Ashley asks.

'Yes, I mean no. I'm not all right because this isn't Carla.' I say this last bit through clenched teeth. 'And she didn't have a mole below her ear. I confronted her about that, and she had a good reason, of course, because she's very good.' I laugh bitterly. 'Oh yes, very good. One of the best. She knew about the mole because of the photo, you see? Cool as a cucumber. So she said she had it removed and she showed us the scar—'

'Slow down, Ellie. You're not making sense.'

'—meanwhile, Marjorie thinks she walks on water and

there's no doubt in her mind that she's Carla, but that's because she can't accept the truth, and I'm the one looking like the villain here, but she—'

'Ellie, I don't know what you're saying.'

'—didn't know *anything* about the Wicked Sistas. Can you believe it? When I brought it up, I could tell she had no idea what I was talking about. And it's been going on and on like that ever since she arrived.' I look behind me and drop my voice to a whisper. 'She's after money. The house. Everything. She's already got money from Marjorie, can you believe it? The gall of that woman. And you know the worst of it? You know what that means?' I hiss the last part, my heart thumping. 'It means Carla is still missing.'

Silence.

I pull the phone away to check we're still connected. 'Are you still there?'

'Yes, look, Ellie, I should go. I'm running late.'

I put my hand over my eyes. 'I need your help, Ashley. Nobody believes me. Nobody. Not Nick, not Marjorie… Not even my friend Lauren. But if you work with me, I know we can expose this woman. And we have to find Carla! And we have to expose that grifter…that fraud—'

'I spoke to Nick,' she says.

'You have got to be kidding me.' I rub two fingers over my eyes. 'He didn't say anything to me. When did you talk to him?'

'The day after I spoke to you on Zoom, three weeks ago. You suggested I call him at his gym, remember?'

'Really?'

A beat. 'Ellie…Nick said some things.'

'Oh, I'm sure he did. What did he say?'

'That you are obsessed with Carla…'

I snort a laugh. 'Of course I'm obsessed. She's missing!'

'I understand, but Nick said that when Carla left,

Marjorie got the police involved and they got in touch with her—'

'So? I told you that. But that was twelve years ago.'

'—Carla told them she didn't want to come home. She was sixteen, and they couldn't force her.'

'We discussed this, Ashley. I don't know why you're telling me what I already told you.'

'Nick says you've been obsessed with Carla for years and that it's unhealthy.'

I am silent for a moment. 'I don't know why Nick said that.' And especially why he never mentioned the conversation to me. 'I mean, yes, he always thought I was making mountains out of molehills and I should just accept the facts, but that's because he was worried about his mother. He didn't want to upset her.'

'He said the postcard was definitely from Carla.'

'And how would he know?' I snap. 'He wouldn't know Carla's handwriting from the Rosetta stone. We wrote dozens of songs together. I know her handwriting as well as my own. Why are you doing this? So Nick was reluctant about the podcast. We knew that. So was Marjorie. I told you that too. Or maybe I didn't. But that's not the point!' I hold the phone in my fist and almost bite it. 'It's not her.'

'She called me,' she says.

'Marjorie?'

'Carla.'

Oh my god. 'Fake Carla? When?'

'The day before yesterday.'

'I can't believe it. How did she know…?' I slap my forehead. 'Of course. I told her about your podcast the day she got here. I told her all about it, how I tried to get you to take it on as a project. My god, she's good.' I laugh. 'So what did she say?'

'She called to set the record straight.'

'Oh right!' I laugh again. 'I bet she did.' In the background, the bell over the front door jingles again.

'She checks out, Ellie.'

'What does that mean?'

'Date of birth, where she went to school, her first boyfriend, that sort of thing. I called Nick back to confirm her answers. She checks out.'

'Where she went to school? Are you serious? Of course she knows where she went to school. It's down the road from the house. There aren't that many secondary schools in the area. And her first boyfriend? I brought him up the first day she was here. Tom Baker. She ran into him on Sunday at the market. It proves nothing.'

The back door to the salon opens and Lauren pops her head around. 'Ellie?'

I hold up one finger. 'I'll be right there.' She shoots me a look and goes back inside.

'Don't you think it's strange that this woman called you out of the blue to tell you she really is Carla?'

'Well, that's not why she called—'

'And somehow she gave you information that would have been blindingly obvious to anyone in her position.'

She sighs. 'It wasn't like that. She rang to say that she was never missing. She said she ran away because she didn't want to be around…certain people. For personal reasons.'

I let out a bitter cackle. Behind me, the bell jingles again.

'Oh, she's good. She's really good.'

The back door opens wide. 'Ellie!' Lauren calls.

I lift a finger. 'One minute.' Then back to the phone.

'She checks out, Ellie. She talked to the police to say she wasn't missing a couple of times. We checked with them—'

I can hear voices inside the salon. Lots of voices. Lauren is still standing at the open door. 'Ellie, I'm not kidding. I need you in here.'

'I'll be right there,' I say for the third time. She closes the door. She does not look happy.

When Ashley speaks again, her voice is soft, gentle. 'Ellie, maybe you should talk to someone.'

'Are you kidding me?'

'I just feel…'

'What do you feel, Ashley?'

'This obsession you have with Carla—'

'It's not an obsession.' I lean back against the wall, my hand over my eyes. 'She's my friend, my best friend, and she's missing. Now there's this psycho in the house pretending to be Carla, and I can't get anyone to listen. She's got everyone fooled, including you, and I'm telling you—' my heart is thumping as I tightly grip the phone '—*she is not Carla.*'

'Ellie!'

I turn around. 'What?'

Lauren has the door open wide. Behind her, three customers are staring at me wide-eyed.

'You're shouting. What the hell is going on?'

I shake my head. 'Nothing.' I bring the phone back to my ear. 'I have to go,' I say, uselessly, as it turns out. Ashley has already hung up.

Lauren frowns at me. 'Are you all right? Do you need to go home?'

'No.' I square my shoulders. 'The last thing I need to do right now is go home.'

TWENTY-FIVE

Lauren and I barely exchange three words all day. Then, at three thirty I go to pick up Karlie from school. I park where I always do. The other mums and dads at the school gates engage in friendly chatter, like they always do. I have no idea what anyone is saying. Something about the school raffle. I say yes to everything, then I see Bethany's dad, Alex.

'Are you okay, Ellie?' he asks.

I force a smile. 'Yes, why?'

'You look tired.'

Of course I look tired, I think, chewing at my bottom lip. I've barely had any sleep, and I've been at work all day, where I almost gave Mrs Henry blue hair and only didn't because Lauren noticed I was mixing the wrong colour and stopped me just in time. There's a psychopath in my house, nobody will believe me, and everyone thinks I used to boil Carla's pet bunnies just for a laugh.

'Sounds like I missed quite the party,' he says with a lopsided grin.

I sigh. 'I don't know what Nick said to you about me…'

'That you're not coping with Carla being back,' he says. Then he leans forward a little. 'He says you're jealous.'

'I'm not jealous!' I shout. I want to shout other things too, like butt out of my business, you're not helping, but I don't because Karlie comes running out with Bethany. It's probably just as well.

She's full of chatter about her day, as always.

'Is Auntie Carla at home?' she asks.

I grit my teeth. 'I think so. Why?'

She starts skipping, tugging at my hand with each step. 'I love Auntie Carla.'

I stop abruptly and pull at her hand. 'You don't know her! You don't love her, because you don't know her. All right? And she's not staying long anyway.'

I start walking again. Karlie's mouth turns down. She bows her head and walks silently. I feel awful. I want to explain, but how can I?

'I'll push you on the swing if you want,' I say. She narrows her eyes at me, like this is some kind of trick.

'What's that?' she says, pointing. We've reached the car, and tucked under one of the windscreen wipers is an envelope.

'A flyer, I suspect,' I say, dislodging the envelope.

Nick is having an affair. I thought you should know.

I look around wildly, but all I see is a sea of mums and dads picking up children's backpacks, ruffling hair or loading children into car seats. I stare at the note again, my mouth dry, my heart thumping. I must have stood there a long time because Karlie tugs at my free hand. 'Muummmmm! Can we go home now?!'

'Yes.' I crumple the note and shove it in the bottom of my handbag. There was no signature, of course, but I don't need one. I already know who it's from.

Fake Carla.

Karlie's babbling away again, but I don't register a single word. All I can think is, what if it's true? What if Nick really is having an affair and someone is trying to warn me? It's not like we're in a great place right now. Fake Carla made sure of that. And women are always flirting with Nick. God knows he's around a lot of attractive women at the gym. Oh god. The gym. Could he have met someone there? He does spend an awful lot of time there. I always say he's obsessed with his gym business, but what if he was obsessed with *someone* at his gym business? I bet lots of beautiful women ask Nick to be their personal trainer. I bet they're falling over themselves to train with him.

Now all I can think about is Nick and some gorgeous long-legged model type in extra tight shorts bending down to touch her toes. I can't touch my toes. I haven't touched my toes since before I had Karlie. I bite my lip. Maybe I should start training. Get into shape. Touch my toes.

Don't be stupid, I admonish myself. *Nick isn't having an affair for goodness' sake. It's her. She wants you out of the way.*

She wants you to leave.

TWENTY-SIX

I'm in Carla's old bedroom, my forehead against the window. Outside, Marjorie and Fake Carla are on the terrace. Karlie is sitting on Carla's knees putting flowers in her hair. Marjorie barely spoke to me when I went in to see her in the living room. Just a perfunctory, 'Yes, thank you,' when I asked if she'd had a nice day.

I could tell she didn't even want to be in the same room with me. I was longing to speak to her properly, to explain why I believe Carla isn't who she says she is, although I've probably said it all already. Then, when I asked if she would like me to massage her hands, she said, 'No, thank you,' with a small smile that felt forced.

'Hey.'

I turn around. Nick is watching me from the doorway. Last night, he went straight to his office. I lay in bed and after a while I got up and knocked on his door. He told me to go away. Then I said his name, and he shouted, 'Get the hell out of my face!' So I went back to our room.

I look at him now. He looks like he hasn't slept any more than I have.

'I spoke to Ashley at the podcast today,' I say.

He lifts his chin. 'Oh.'

'Yes. Oh. Why didn't you tell me you'd spoken to her?'

He sighs. 'I didn't think it was necessary.'

'Not necessary? You said I was obsessed with her!'

'Because you are!' he shouts.

'And you told Alex I was wrong about Fake Carla, and that I'm jealous, and that I'm not coping.'

'Don't call her that.'

I shake my head in disbelief. 'I can't believe you did that. I can't believe you said those things behind my back. Why would you do that to me?'

'Because it's true!'

I close my eyes and grit my teeth. 'Did you know Fake Carla rang Ashley too? Apparently, she checks out, according to Ashley.'

'Because she does.'

'She doesn't. She's hypnotised you. All of you. I was never *obsessed* with her.'

'What about all the things you did to her? Burning her hair… Breaking her arm…'

'I never did those things to her. She's making stuff up.'

'Ellie…'

'Before she came, your mother never thought a bad thing about me. And you never said I was obsessed with Carla before. She's putting these ideas into your head – I know she is. She's like a snake charmer or something.'

He rolls his eyes. 'Thank you so much.'

'No, really. She's got you all fooled. It's gone too far. I'm going to the police—'

'The police? Are you out of your mind?'

'I should have done it days ago. She's going to take your mum's savings, and then she'll take the house. She's a con artist, and she knows I know. But she's got you all wrapped around her little finger and for some reason, there's nothing I can do to convince any of you.'

He grabs my wrist. 'Ellie, you have to stop! Stop this madness!'

'No, I don't.' I stand up and yank my arm away from his grip. 'I'm going to the police. You can come with me if you want, or not. Up to you.'

'Don't you dare.'

'Try and stop me.'

'For Christ's sake, Ellie!' He slaps his hands on his head. 'You can't keep doing this. Mum is really upset. After that stunt you pulled last night…'

'She's a liar. She's not Carla. You haven't seen her in twelve years and you swallow whatever story she feeds you, and you go around and discredit me, and I've had enough, Nick. I'm done. I'm going to the police.' I grab my phone from the bed and look around for my bag.

He puts his hands on my shoulders. 'Ellie, stop.'

'Trust me, you'll thank me later.'

'You'll upset Mum even more. She's already confused and frankly, she's quite angry with you.'

My heart gives a little twist. 'I know that.'

'If you go to the police behind her back she'll never forgive you.'

'She will once she knows the truth about Fake Carla.'

'Oh my god. This is insane. You're insane.' He takes my wrists again. 'Don't go to the police, Ellie. You'll make Mum so upset. Tell me what I can do to prove to you she is Carla.'

I stare at his blue eyes. 'You want to prove it to me?'

'Yes.'

'I want her to take a DNA test.'

He recoils. 'Are you serious?'

'Yes. And then I'll stop. I swear.'

He narrows his eyes. 'You'll stop?'

'Yes.'

'You will accept the results?'

'Yes.'

He releases me and strokes his chin. 'All right. I'll talk to Carla.'

I breathe out. This is such amazing news, and unexpected too. It makes me wonder if Nick doesn't have his own secret doubts. I put my hands flat on his chest. 'But don't just talk to her, make her.'

He fixes me with a hard stare. 'I'll talk to her and Mum. I'll do it now.'

'Okay, thank you. But maybe say it was your idea.'

He nods. 'Mum would have a fit if she thought you'd suggested it.'

I give him a small smile. I know he's right, but it hurts all the same. Once upon a time, Marjorie trusted me like a daughter. Back then, before Fake Carla showed up, if I'd suggested something like that, she would have thanked me for wanting to protect her.

Now, she'd have a fit.

'She's going to have a bigger fit when the test returns negative,' I say.

'Ellie, don't.'

'Sorry.' I drop my head and rest my forehead on his shoulder. He puts his arms around me.

'Promise me you'll be nice until we get the results.'

I mumble something vague and non-committal.

'Promise me.'

'I promise,' I say finally.

I mean, I can be nice. Once the results come in, it will be over. I can be nice until then.

'You're not having an affair, are you?' I mumble.

'What did you say?'

I bite my bottom lip. 'I said I'll be nice.'

TWENTY-SEVEN

He did it. He tells me later that night that Carla was fine about it. They'll do the test first thing in the morning, and it should only take two or three days to get the results back.

'Really?'

He nods. 'Really.'

I bite my bottom lip. 'I don't trust her.'

'I know that,' he says.

'Be there when she takes the test, okay?'

'I will. I promise.'

For the next three days, I do everything in my power to *be nice*, make everyone happy, and it's no small feat. Everyone is walking on eggshells around me, except for Fake Carla who I bet wouldn't walk on eggshells for anyone. Meanwhile, Karlie is more enamoured with her than ever, and I have to pretend that's absolutely fine with me. So sweet, even, while gritting my teeth down to bloody stumps just watching her sit on Fake Carla's lap or taking her hand, or showing her around her little patch of garden for the umpteenth time.

Anyone else would think I was crazy. I wonder about that myself. I mean, do I really believe Fake Carla would hurt my daughter? Absolutely. With all my heart. And whenever I waver, she will do something unequivocally menacing. Like last night.

I was making a chicken casserole for dinner, and I was chopping onions when she came into the kitchen.

Be nice.

'Do you need something?' I asked.

'No, thank you,' she said. She reached for the knife block and chose the sharpest one. She took an apple from the bowl, held it on the chopping board with one hand and cut it in half in one quick motion, like she was cutting the head off a live chicken.

I was frozen, staring at her. Then she left the room, taking both parts of the apple with her.

Which sounds fairly innocent. Except she took the knife, too.

On Sunday, I offered to take Marjorie to her committee luncheon at the Botanical Society, but she said Carla would drive her. She said it in a way that made me think she'd rather Karlie drove her, if it came to that. Like she couldn't bear to be near me.

Dinner was a stilted affair, although Carla seemed oblivious. She brought up the house again. 'Should we tear it all down and start again?' she asked Nick for the umpteenth time. 'What do you think, Nicky? Or sell it as it is?'

'It's not actually Nick's decision,' Marjorie said without looking at anyone. 'It is my house, after all. And I'm not selling, thank you very much.'

In that moment, I caught Nick looking at Marjorie with a look of pure hatred. I'd never seen him look at Marjorie like this before, and it made my heart race. Then he caught my eye, and his expression changed completely.

'Mum's right, sis,' he said gravely. 'It's her house. She can do as she pleases.'

'Sorry, Mother,' Carla said.

Honestly, it's her. I sound like a broken record, even to myself, but it's her. She's like an evil presence in this house. She's driving us all mad.

On Monday morning I take Karlie to school, as always. As the other parents gather at the gate, I make my way over, just to say hello, but for some reason everyone has to be somewhere today and they disperse quickly. I guess I'm not the only one having a hard day.

I stop by Dot's Cafe to get two lattes to take away. Again, it's the strangest thing. There are few locals in the cafe when I walk in, all having animated conversations, until they see me, at which point everyone falls silent. Even the waitress, normally friendly, looks like she just sucked on a lemon. She barely speaks to me when taking my order, all the while exchanging glances with the other patrons. And when I pick up the lattes, I can tell they're not that hot, but I let it pass.

'Good morning,' I say brightly when I walk into the salon. Lauren was arranging a pile of magazines on the counter. 'What are you doing here?'

I put down the lattes in front of her. 'What do you mean?'

'I left you a message.'

'Oh?' I pull out my phone. I have a missed call and a message from Lauren from an hour ago. 'Sorry about that. It was at the bottom of my bag and I didn't hear it. What did it say?'

Lauren goes back to arranging magazines. 'That you should take the day off.'

'The day off? Why?'

She looks at me, eyes narrowed.

I tilt my head. 'Is everything all right?'

'Everything is fine.'

'You don't sound fine.'

'Actually, Ellie, take the whole week off.'

'The *whole* week off? Why? I'm not due any leave.'

'We're not busy enough.'

'That's not true. Mrs Jackson has booked in for her foils this morning, she should be here any minute, and Melanie is coming in for a colour, and Caroline is bringing her son at four after school for a trim, and…' I pause. 'Is it because of the other day when I was on a call outside? Because like I said, it won't happen again. And I'm very sorry it happened.'

'Don't. You already apologised. It's fine.'

'So what is it?'

She tilts her head at me, looking like she's trying to decide whether to say it or not. 'Did you stalk Tracy before you applied for this job?'

'Tracy?' I try to think. 'Who's Tracy? You mean, Tracy who used to work here?'

'Yes.'

'Right. Well, no. I never stalked her, why would I? I never even met her. That's such a strange question, Lauren. What's going on?'

She stands taller and plants a fist on her waist. 'Do you know what they're saying about you?'

'Who?'

'Everyone. That you're crazy. That you are obsessed with the Goodwins. Always have been. That you came back to town and stalked Nick—'

'That's ridiculous!'

'—and seduced him until he agreed to go out with you.'

'Oh for Christ's sake!'

'That you would do anything to insert yourself into that family, and it's really disturbing.'

'Disturbing?'

'That it was you who drove the car that hit Tracy.'

I feel a wave of vertigo. 'Excuse me?'

'Did you do that, Ellie? Did you run her over because you needed a job?'

My legs are wobbling. I put my hand on the counter to steady myself. It comes back to me now. Fake Carla mentioning over dinner how lucky I was that Tracy was hit by a car. 'Oh my god,' I mutter. 'It's her.'

'Why are you in that house, anyway? Why are you so upset that Carla is back? That's what everybody wants to know. Is it true that she ran away because of you?' She leans forward a little. 'Is it true you came to take her place in that family? Is that why you're saying she's not Carla?'

'Oh my god, no! It's all lies! It's her, she's telling everyone horrible lies about me to discredit me!'

The bell above the door chimes and we both turn. I try to gather myself and push my hair out of my face. 'Hello, Mrs Jackson, I'll be with you in one minute,' I say. 'Please take a seat.'

But Mrs Jackson stands there, her hand still on the door handle. Her face turns pale. She turns to Lauren. 'I thought you said…'

'It's all right, Mrs Jackson. Ellie was about to leave.'

'No I wasn't,' I say, with way more bravado than I feel. 'If you would take a seat, I'll be with you in just a moment.'

But Mrs Jackson doesn't take a seat. She clutches her handbag against her chest like it's a shield, then takes a tentative step forward and a few more sideways, her eyes trained on me.

'You can't stay here, Ellie,' Lauren says, her arms crossed over her chest. 'I don't want you here.'

I turn to her. 'I can't believe you're doing this.'

'You need help.'

'I thought you were my friend,' I say, my chin quivering. I grab my handbag and loop it over my shoulder. My legs can barely carry me to the door. The bell above it chimes happily when I open it, and I jump up to try and rip it off. It's like I want to take out all my anger and frustration on that bell. I hate that bell. I hate it so much I want to kill it.

Mrs Jackson screams, and Lauren marches towards me.

I raise my hand in the air. 'Fine. I'm leaving.' Then I run to my car, unlock it and sob all over the steering wheel. I desperately want to go and pick up Karlie and leave, drive off as far away as possible. Or at least back to London.

Except, of course, I can't. I have no money since I gave it all to Nick. Not even for petrol. Certainly not enough to get to London, and my salary doesn't hit my account until next Thursday. That's if Lauren pays it, which, at this point, is debatable.

And what about Marjorie? What will happen to Marjorie if I leave her in the clutches of that crazy woman? She is in great danger, and Nick won't see what's right in front of his face.

I lift my head and brush my tears away. I can't do it. Marjorie has been like a mother to me – although not lately, but that's not her fault. What if I leave and crazy Fake Carla kills her before the DNA test comes back? What if that was her plan all along? To kill Marjorie and get her grubby hands on the inheritance?

I start the car. There's no way on earth I can leave Marjorie behind in the clutches of that psycho. I'll just have to wait it out until the test results come back, and then everything will be fine.

That's what I keep telling myself all the way home. *Every-thing will be fine.* Even when I get to the house and see Nick's car in the driveway. *Nick is back. It's not even midday and he's back already. Why? I don't know.*

Everything will be fine.

I get inside and hear voices in the living room.

'Hi,' I say. Marjorie is sitting in the armchair by the bookcase. She stares at me when I enter, her lips pursed together. She doesn't greet me. Carla is perched on the window seat, and Nick is standing by the fireplace, frowning at the sheets of paper in his hand.

'What's going on?' I ask Nick. Then I notice the envelope in his other hand with a blue logo and the words 'Bioscope Labs'.

My heart skips a beat. I study his face. He looks like he's about to explode.

This is it. It's happening. She's about to be found out.

I swallow.

'The DNA results,' Nick says through clenched teeth, lifting the pages to show me. 'It's official. Meet my sister.'

TWENTY-EIGHT

It's like the ground has fallen away from under me. I grip the back of an armchair to steady myself. Marjorie is staring out of the window. Carla looks triumphant, and Nick is glaring at me.

'Did you hear what I said?' Nick asks.

My heart is beating in my throat. For some reason the first thought that pops into my head is, *did the post come already?*

'But that can't be,' I say shakily.

He raises his hands to the sky and lets them drop. 'Well, it is. Are you going to keep going on like this? Do you have any idea what you've put us through? What you *are* putting us through?'

'But it's not possible! She didn't know about the Wicked Sistas!'

Nick turns around, clasping his hands over his head. 'I'm done. That's it. I can't take it any more.'

'You need help, darling,' Marjorie says sadly.

And suddenly, I know how she did it. I turn to Carla. 'You took a hair from her hairbrush.'

'Erm…what?'

'You used it on that first day, upstairs in Carla's bedroom and—'

'It was a swab.'

'—you took one of her hairs and you—'

'Ellie, it was a swab.'

'—used that to prove you're Carla, but—'

'Ellie!'

I turn to Nick. 'Can you let me finish, please?' I point my finger at her. 'She used one of Carla's hairs from Carla's hairbrush. Oh, you're good. You're very good.'

'Are you deaf?' Nick barks. 'I'm trying to tell you, the DNA test, it wasn't a hair sample, it was a saliva swab. We both did it. Carla and I are siblings. It's right here.' He stabs at the paper in his hand with his finger. 'Ninety-nine point nine nine percent.'

My head is swimming. I'm finding it hard to breathe. I turn to Marjorie. 'Were you there when she did the saliva swab?'

'Of course.'

My head is throbbing. I turn to Carla. 'I don't understand. You are so unlike her.' I raise a hand in my peripheral vision to stop Nick from arguing. 'You never say anything about her past. Your attitude, your behaviour, it's nothing like the Carla I know. It's like you don't even know her.'

She sighs theatrically. 'I am her! What do you want me to say? That we found worms in the rice in the canteen? What? What can I say to convince you? I mean, I just took a DNA test and you're still not happy. Just tell me what you want from me, and I'll oblige. And then, if you can leave this house, move out, take your child and get the hell out, that would be even better.'

'Carla, sweetheart,' Marjorie says softly.

I stare at her. How did she know about the worms in the canteen? Is the DNA test real? Could it be that I was wrong all this time? I sit down and turn to Marjorie. 'I'm sorry. I made such a mess of things. I only ever wanted to protect you.'

'Maybe it's you we all need protection from,' Carla mumbles. 'How did Mother fall down the stairs, by the way?'

I lean forward like I didn't hear her correctly. 'I'm sorry?'

'You were in the house at the time.'

I shake my head like I'm trying to dislodge water from my ear. I mean, the conversation was going pretty badly, but this is next level.

'It's rather convenient when you think about it. Mum falls, and here you are to save the day and next thing you know, you've moved in.'

I stare at her, my chest tight. 'I wasn't even in the room. I was in the kitchen when it happened.' I turn to Nick. 'Tell her, Nick.'

Nick raises his shoulders. 'I told her I don't remember what happened exactly.'

'How can you not remember? You were upstairs. I was in the kitchen making tea! I heard her shout and I called out to you!'

He makes a face, as if to say, *What do I know?*

I turn to Marjorie. 'Please, tell her. I was nowhere near you when you fell.'

She nods thoughtfully. 'That's right. Or I think that's right, I can't remember but that sounds right.'

'Well. How lucky for you, Ellie. Not only did you move in, but you got the best room in the house, too.' She claps slowly.

'How dare you. The reason we moved your mother downstairs was that she simply couldn't be upstairs any more – it was too dangerous. And those rooms were connected so she could have a sitting room of her own.' I turn to Nick. 'You said it was a good idea.'

He shakes his head, like he doesn't know what to say. My chest is heaving with outrage.

Marjorie's face softens. 'Ellie, darling—'

'Don't call her that, Mother,' Carla says through gritted teeth. 'You'll only encourage her.'

Marjorie raises her hand to shush her. 'Ellie, my point is, I don't understand where these suspicions of Carla come from. It's like you have some kind of vendetta against her.'

'Do you know Carla is leaving because of you?' Nick says. 'Tomorrow morning.'

Carla raises one shoulder. 'If Ellie were to leave, then I'd gladly stay a few more days.'

'You need help, Ellie,' Nick says. He looks exhausted, and very sad. 'You really do.'

I shake my head, press my fingers over my eyes. This can't be happening. My entire life is crumbling, and I don't know why.

'I'm sorry, Carla,' I say softly. 'I really am. I don't know what I was thinking.'

'Yes, well, it's a bit late for that,' Carla says.

I brush off tears with my arm so roughly that my watch scratches the side of my face.

'You're not well, Ellie,' Marjorie says softly. 'You need to see someone. I could make some calls, find you a suitable institution. Dr Patel will give you a referral…'

I swivel to look at her. 'An institution?'

Carla leans forward. 'Did you hear what she said? Nobody wants you here.'

TWENTY-NINE

Upstairs, I sit on the edge of the bed, pressing my fingers against my eyelids.

I can't believe it. It's her. It's Carla. The DNA says so. She knew about the worms in the canteen.

My stomach is like someone squeezed it in a vice and then twirled it around a couple of times. I just don't understand how I could have been so mistaken. I feel like I'm in the wrong movie. All this time, I thought I had a starring role in *The Brady Bunch*, only to discover that I was cast as the psycho roommate in S*ingle White Female*.

I walk out of Carla's old room and over to our old bedroom and open the wardrobe. When my father died, my flatmate Bee gave me an enormous gift box from L'Occitane full of self-care body lotions. I still have most of the products, but I took them out of the box because it's so pretty, with bright colours and flowers all over it. It's where I keep my old diaries and old photos and mementos.

I reach in to grab the top journal, but something makes me stop. That's odd. I have a dozen journals, and I tend to keep them in size order, with the largest at the bottom.

So this one shouldn't be on the top.

I shake my head. I mean, I'm insane, so who cares? I pick it up and flick through it. As it happens, it has the entry about ironing Carla's hair.

OMG I burnt Carla's hair today. She wanted it straight so we got the iron from the kitchen and we put a towel on her desk and she knelt in front of it and I arranged her hair on the towel. I had to pull it straight with one hand and iron it with the other. I put the iron down on it and there was a horrible smell, like someone had lit a hundred matches all at once. It was horrible. Carla pulled away and it took a second before I realised her hair was still on the towel. I took the iron off right away but there was this brown mess sticking to it. Carla looked at herself in the mirror and ran out screaming. Her mum had to cut it short all the way around.

If only I could show her. I know she hates me, but at the very least, I could make her understand that I never meant to hurt her. I was never *obsessed* with her. For the life of me I just can't understand why she says she ran away because of me, when she wanted me to go *with* her.

I flick through more pages until I find the entry about Carla climbing up the tree like she was Rapunzel, before she fell and broke her arm. It's so clear from my diary that it had nothing to do with me. I wasn't even up the tree.

I come across another entry, earlier on, about Nick.

Nick is sooooo hot! Oh my god, I was at Caramello's today, and he came out of his bedroom just as I walked past, and we almost bumped into each other. I could see his muscles under his T-shirt. He looks incredible, and those blue eyes!!!! OMG I love him. Except he looked at me like what are you doing here? I wished I'd worn my nice new top, the one with the frilly collar. I'm soooo in looooovvvveeeee!!!!! I—

'Why are you still here?'

I gasp and drop the journal. Carla is standing in front of me, her face all scrunched up with anger. 'I'm not kidding, Ellie.'

I pick up the journal. 'Oh, really? I had no idea. I never know with you.'

She frowns at me, as if to say, '*What are you even saying right now?*'

I shake my head. 'Sorry. Listen. It's not what you think. If you'd let me show you…' I get up, flicking pages like a mad woman. Oh, wait, I *am* a mad woman. 'I wrote it all down… I never meant you harm. I—'

She brings her face inches from mine. 'Just. Get. Out!'

'What's going on here?' Nick says behind her.

She turns around, then flicks a hand in the air. 'I give up. You do it.' Then she walks out.

I sit down again. 'I wanted to show her my diaries…' I hand the journal to Nick. 'Read it. Please. You'll see that I was never jealous or wanting to harm her or wanting to *be* her or whatever it is you believe.'

He sits down next to me, puts the diary in his lap.

'Read it,' I say.

'Ellie…'

'Really. Read it. You'll see.'

'I think maybe we should take a break.'

My heart skips a beat. 'What do you mean, a break?'

'Ellie, babe, I'm sorry…'

'We don't need a break. We're great! It's been wonderful between us. This is just a small hiccup, that's all. I'll get better, you'll see. I'll go and see someone. I'll get myself sorted. There's no need to take a break, Nick.'

He shakes his head sadly. 'I'm sorry, Ellie, but it's over.'

I stand up. 'Over?'

'I'm afraid so. You have to move out.'

'Move out?'

'Not right now, of course, but in a few days.'

'No, no, no. Nick, honey. We moved here, remember? Me and Karlie. You love Karlie. We packed up our lives –

which, granted, weren't fabulous but we moved here to be with you because it's what you wanted. It's what you wanted, isn't it?'

He looks down at his hands. 'I thought I did.'

'You *thought* you did? Don't do this to me, to us! What about Karlie?'

'What about Karlie?'

'Karlie needs a family! Otherwise she just has me, and that's not enough! She'll probably leave me, too, because I am someone people leave, but she's too young to leave me, so she needs other people! She needs a family, Nick! She adores you! Uncle Nicky! And you'll be like her father, eventually, and she loves Marjorie! Grannie Margie! I'll ask her to stop calling her that. I'll explain it's Grannie *Marjorie*. But I can't take her away from her family, Nick, you're all she's got.'

'Hey, I love Karlie. She's my little princess. But this situation, here, it's not good for her either.'

I stare at him. 'But it is. It's really good for her. And we're getting married, and she can't wait. And she's going to be the flower girl, and one day she'll have a little brother or a little sister and—'

He shakes his head. 'We're not getting married, Ellie.'

I bite on a thumbnail. 'Is it because you're having an affair? Is that why you don't want to marry me?'

He looks at me for a few seconds. 'It's because you're crazy,' he whispers.

THIRTY

It's hard to think how I could have made a bigger mess of everything, and yet…I feel so awful for Karlie. All I ever wanted was for her to have a family, a real one, instead of just a loser mother, and for a wonderful moment she had a family, but I managed to screw that up. She's going to be devastated when she finds out we have to leave. But I can't even think about that now. I have to find us a place to live.

I go downstairs and find my phone in the living room, then walk out around the house, making sure I'm out of sight from everyone.

I lean against the wall and call Bee. My best friend Bee, my one and only friend, actually, and the woman we used to live with in London before I came here. If there's one person who can help me now, it's Bee. Or I hope it's Bee, because if not, I have absolutely nobody left.

'Hey! I was just thinking about you!' she says cheerily. 'We haven't spoken in ages. How is everything going?'

I start to cry.

'Okay. What's up?' she asks, her tone suddenly all business-like.

'Where are you?' I ask between sobs. 'At work?'

'Yes… but that's fine. It's quiet today. What's happened? How's Karlie?'

'Oh, no. Karlie's fine. For now.'

'What does that mean?'

'It's me, Bee! I'm not fine. I'm terrible. I'm crazy. Did you know I was crazy? Could you tell?'

'Ellie, what are you talking about?'

I blurt out the whole story. Bee knew that Carla had returned but we haven't spoken since, only the odd text. I tell her how cold and distant Carla has been to me, and how I started to think it wasn't her. 'But it *was* her,' I say. 'I know that now. And it's not just the DNA test, it's that she knew about Mrs Lopez at school and the worms in the canteen and… Anyway, I know it's her, but now they're all saying these terrible things about me. That I was horrible to Carla when we were kids, and she hated me, and I just can't remember any of it. I thought we were really close.'

'Oh, honey, I'm so sorry. That doesn't sound good.'

'No, it doesn't, does it? Turns out I'm crazy and I have been for years, decades, my entire life, and I didn't even know it.'

'Ellie, I know you. You're not crazy.'

'I am, so clearly you don't know me as well you think. She says I was a leech, and that I engineered coming back to this house and being with this family because I'm obsessed with her, always have been. I want to be her, you see? And I pushed Marjorie down the stairs just so I could have her bedroom. That's how crazy I am. Oh, and I am the reason Carla ran away. Also Nick dumped me.' I sigh. 'Anyway, how are you?'

'No, Ellie, I'm sorry. I don't understand why they'd say all those things, if that helps. They sound like a horrible bunch.'

'But they're not. It's me. I'm the horrible bunch. Can we come and stay with you for a bit?'

'Of course you can.'

I let out a breath. 'Thank you, Bee. You don't know what this means to me.'

'I missed you guys. It will be nice to be with you again. Especially my Karlie. How is she?'

I sigh. 'She doesn't know we're leaving yet, so that's going to be hard. But she misses you, too. She asks after you all the time.'

'I just can't believe what you're telling me,' she says. 'It doesn't make any sense. All these years, you've looked for your friend…'

'That's because I'm obsessed.'

'And you always talked about her in such a beautiful way. I used to think I would've loved to have a close childhood friend like you.'

'Oh no, you don't. Trust me. Also, it was all in my head, so…'

She clicks her tongue. 'Ellie, hon… I don't understand. It really doesn't sound like you at all. All this talk of being horrible to Carla… Running away because of you… Did she say where she's been all this time?'

'Not really. She's very evasive, but then she would be. She probably thinks I'll stalk her or move in with her or something. That first day, I asked about her husband and I could tell she didn't want me to know anything about him. Which makes perfect sense now. I'd be scared of telling me, too, in her shoes.'

'Hang on. She's married?'

'To some kind of property guru or something she met in London, where she was busy running away from me. John Smith. Does that sound made up to you? She probably didn't want to tell me his real name. They live in Paris now. Or maybe she made that up too. Throw me off the scent. I can see that she was shocked to see me here, living in her old house and shacking up with her brother. I guess it does sound a little stalkerish. What do you think? Does it sound stalkerish to you? Of course it does. Forget I asked.'

Silence. I've probably bored her to death. She's probably lying dead by the phone. 'Sorry. I'm rambling. Are you still there?'

'Yes. I was just thinking about something you said earlier.'

'What's that?'

'Didn't you say you checked Births, Deaths, and Marriage records?'

I shudder. 'Yes. I see your point. Very stalkerish.'

'No, what I mean is, if she was married, wouldn't that be on her record?'

THIRTY-ONE

I find a log to sit on well away from the house and stay there for hours with my fingers pressed against my temples. I can't take any more of this. Every time I have a handle on things, something else happens. Carla isn't married. If she had been, as Bee rightly pointed out, her marriage would have been recorded. Even Marjorie looked surprised when she said it at lunch. I remember the way she looked at her. 'You got married in London?' I assumed at the time she was upset she hadn't been invited, and I could hardly blame her. But maybe it had rung a bell for her, too. Something she couldn't quite put her finger on.

And the bell was saying, *why was there no record of it?*

Eventually, it's time to pick up Karlie. Outside the school gates, the other parents stay well away from me. Some of them are whispering behind their hands. I wonder what they're saying. *She's insane, didn't you hear? She pushed Marjorie down the stairs just so she could have her bedroom!*

Karlie comes out, looking sullen. We get in the car. She

won't tell me what's wrong, but that's okay. I mean, it's not okay, but my mind is reeling from the conversation I had with Bee earlier and I can't think about anything else. *Wouldn't it be on her record?* Of course people can have a ceremony that isn't a legal marriage, but somehow, I don't think that's the case here.

I think she was lying.

I think she's been lying through her sparkling white teeth the whole time.

Except, if she isn't Carla, then how did she know about the worms in the canteen? Or that Mrs Lopez's first name is Maria?

My head is spinning. I have to think. The DNA test was a saliva swab. Could she have faked it?

Well. I'm going to say yes to that. It's probably a walk in the park to her. She probably fakes DNA tests all day. She's that good.

Karlie is quiet. Unusually so. Back home, she spends time in her room reading which is very unlike her. I tell myself she's tired and run her a bath.

I place Karlie's pyjamas on her bed. I wish I could see the DNA report. I bet Carla intercepted the real one and made a fake one. I don't know *when* she got to do that, but I bet she did.

But if she isn't Carla, how did she know all these things about our school?

And then I remember.

My diaries. They were not in the right order.

OMG I saw Nick today… Carla fell out of the tree and broke her arm. Mrs Lopez sent us to detention – again – because we talk too much. I don't care. I hate geography. I'd rather be in detention than trying to remember the names of all the rivers… Carla found worms in the rice today at the canteen. We almost threw up…

That's how she did it. Of course it is! She's been reading them. That's why they were in the wrong order. That's how she knew that I always had a crush on Nick. That's how she bewitched them all with her stories.

I help Karlie into her pyjamas. We go back downstairs. She sits at the kitchen table while I reheat the last of the quiche and add some salad. Back upstairs, I read Karlie a couple of chapters and then she falls asleep.

I slip into Fake Carla's room, pushing the door so it's only slightly ajar, and then I begin to search methodically. I open the drawers. They're almost empty. Just a few items of underwear, a couple of T-shirts and that's it. I already know how useless this effort is going to be. Anything important is going to be in her incredibly expensive and incredibly large handbag, which isn't here as far as I can tell.

I search anyway. It's not like I have a choice. She's here for nefarious reasons, and regardless of what happens between me and Nick after this, I have to stop her, somehow.

I go through everything, which takes no time at all, and I am no further than when I started a full three minutes ago. I run my hands over the bedcovers, I check behind the side table, and I look under the carpet. Nothing.

I'm about to leave but on impulse, I check under the mattress. Carla and I always used to hide things under the mattress.

And then I feel something, near the head of the bed. I quickly glance over my shoulder to make sure no one is watching, then I slide it out.

It's a slim red leather wallet, and inside is a driver's licence.

THIRTY-TWO

I take my phone outside and sit on the step. I left the wallet where I found it, but I kept the driver's licence. I pull it out from my pocket and take a photo which I text to Nick.

And then I wait. A few minutes later, my phone lights up with a text. *Where are you?*

Outside the front door.

Wait for me.

He arrives ten minutes later.

'What took you so long?' I ask.

'I was chopping carrots. Carla was there. I had to make it believable.'

I blink. 'Why were you chopping carrots?'

'I was going to make a stew.'

This is truly the strangest day. 'So where does she think you've gone?

'I didn't tell her. But she looked at me funny. Where is it?'

I open my hand. 'Susan Williams,' I say, tapping at the licence.

'I just can't believe it.' He drops his head and laces his fingers together behind his neck.

'I hate to say I told you so, but – no, actually I don't hate it. I told you so.'

He nods. 'Where did you find it?'

'In her wallet, hidden under the mattress in her room.'

He looks up. 'Why did you go and look under her mattress?'

'It doesn't matter. The point is, as you can see, it's her picture. There's no doubt about it. This isn't some random person's driver's licence that happened to make its way into a wallet that was wedged under the mattress. It clearly belongs to the woman pretending to be your sister. And as you can see, the date of birth is wrong. That woman is thirty years old, unlike Carla, who would be twenty-eight. The fact that she was born in the UK is the only thing this lying, conniving, ruthless psychopath has in common with Carla.'

Meanwhile, what I really want to ask is, '*Are you still breaking up with me?*' After all, I was right all along. That must count for something, surely?

'I'm not crazy, Nick. I never was crazy. She bewitched you all. That's the problem. We—' here I am generously including myself among the bewitched, '—were so desperate for her to be Carla, we never saw the signs.'

Then I remember. 'The DNA test. You said you were related.'

'We were. That's what it said.'

'But that's not possible.'

He rubs his chin. 'You know, I did think there was something odd about that report.'

I gasp. 'What?'

'Her name, it was different, like it was typed in a different font or something.'

'Oh wow.' I click my fingers. 'I knew it. She faked the report. My God she's good. We have to go and get it. Do you know where it is?'

'Where we left it. In Mum's room, on the mantelpiece.'

I try to think. 'Okay. Let's go back inside, and you go and get it.'

He nods, staring at the driver's licence in his hand. You get the sense he wants the words to change, that maybe if he stared long enough, the name *Susan Williams* would magically disappear and be replaced with Carla Goodwin, or even Madame Carla Smith.

'It's not a French licence, either,' I say. 'I know nothing of such things but wouldn't she need a French licence to drive in France?'

He ignores my question. 'And you found this in her room under the mattress?'

'Yes.'

'But why would you look under her mattress?'

It occurs to me these are strange questions at this point. I tilt my head at him. 'If you must know, I spoke to Bee about Karlie and me going to stay with her for a few days, and…' I study his face, waiting for an indication that, of course, it's off the table now. Nobody is going anywhere. I am not crazy, I don't need help, and we are not breaking up.

But as much as I search that beautiful face, I find nothing. I take a breath. 'Bee pointed out that Marjorie had asked for Carla's up-to-date records from Births, Deaths, and Marriages, and there was no mention of Carla being married. And yet this woman said she was married.'

He chews at his bottom lip. His face is taut, his jaw working back and forth. 'The fucking little bitch.'

I nod. 'Yes. My thoughts exactly.'

He drags his hands down his face. 'Jesus, Ellie. I'm so sorry.'

Music to my ears. 'I know,' I say, putting my hand on his arm. 'I know you are, honey.'

He stands and leans against the wall and bends down in

half, his face in his hands. 'Fuck!' he bellows into his palms. 'Fuck, fuck, fuck her!'

'Sshh. Don't shout. She'll hear you.'

'I don't know what to say.'

'We have to do something, Nick. We have to tell Marjorie.'

'Yes! Damn right, we do. And we have to call the police.'

Hallelujah. I can't believe this is finally happening. They're going to arrest her and I'll be there watching. No, I'll be there *clapping.*

'We have to tell Mum. Right now,' he says.

I nod. 'Yes. We do.'

'It's going to kill her.'

My heart breaks. He's right, of course. I know this is going to break her heart. And that is the last thing I want.

We go back inside the house. This time it's Nick who holds my hand tightly. He's walking fast, in long strides, and I can barely keep up. We stop at the door of the kitchen. I can't wait to see her face when he tells her, but she's not there. There's no one there.

'Go and find the report,' I say to Nick. I start up the stairs. If she's up there, I'll tell her that Nick wants to talk to her. But as I reach her room, I gasp. The drawers are open, as is the wardrobe.

And the mattress has been pushed off the bed base.

'Nick?'

I run out of her room calling his name. I'm about to run down the stairs when I notice that Karlie's bedroom is open.

Wide open.

'Karlie?'

I turn the light on. Her bed is empty.

'KARLIE!'

THIRTY-THREE

'What's going on?' Marjorie calls out from the hall.

I'm running, flying down the stairs. 'Have you seen Karlie?'

'What do you mean? Isn't she up there?'

'No. She's not.' I run from room to room shouting her name. 'Karlie? Where are you? It's not funny, Karlie!'

'Oh, dear,' Marjorie says, her hand on her chest. 'Has she gone outside, perhaps?'

'She shouldn't be outside,' I say. 'She's supposed to be in bed.'

I run out the door, Nick right behind me. 'Karlie!' I shout, my hands cupping my mouth. 'Karlie!' Nick slips past me and calls out her name as well.

'Where could she be?' Marjorie says behind me.

A wave of panic engulfs me. 'Where's Carla?'

'I'm not sure... She was in the kitchen earlier...'

'She's not there,' I say. I turn to Nick. 'I went up to her room just now. It looks like she did a thorough search. She even pushed the mattress off the bed. I think she must have seen the photo on your phone.'

'What photo?' Marjorie asks.

Nick ignores her. 'Oh, shit. You don't think…'

'Yes!' I shriek. 'She took her! That's exactly what I think! She's taken her!'

'Ellie,' Marjorie says, her hand on my shoulder. 'Of course she didn't take her. Karlie just slipped out, that's all.'

'But it's not her!' I shout. 'I found her wallet! Her driver's licence! It's not Carla! She took her!' I'm screaming, running blind. 'Where is she? Where's my baby?'

I'm running towards the woods on the other side of the garden. I'm shouting her name, my head swimming. I don't understand why she's not answering me. Everyone is shouting now.

'Karlie! Karlie, where are you?'

'Mummy?'

I stop. Turn. I can't see her. 'Karlie? Where are you?'

'I'm here, Mummy!'

I see her through silhouetted trees, standing in the middle of the orchard.

Oh my god. I run to her. 'Karlie!'

'What's wrong, Mummy?'

She's standing there, alone, her arms by her side, like a creature from a dark fairy tale. I fall on my knees as I reach her. 'Are you all right?' I check her all over. She's in her pyjamas, but strangely, she's also wearing her cardigan and slippers.

I wrap her in my arms. 'Why are you out here? You're not supposed to be here!' I scoop her up.

'What's wrong, Mummy?'

'Hey, nothing is wrong, princess,' Nick says. 'We didn't know where you were. You know you're not supposed to play this far from the house.'

'You're supposed to be in bed,' I say. 'What were you doing out here?'

Her face falls.

Marjorie meets us halfway, hobbling on her cane. 'Oh, thank god!' she exclaims. 'Is she all right?'

'I think so,' I say, even though she's sobbing. 'Auntie… Carla…said…we were…playing hide and seek!' she wails.

'She's not your aunt!' I snap. I'm too rough with her, I know that, but I can't help it. I'm still rattled by the terror of losing her. And yet I know it's not her fault. Again, *she* did this. She's showing me what she's capable of. She's telling me that if I come after her, she will go after my child.

Nick takes Karlie from my arms.

'I'm sorry,' I tell her. 'It's not your fault. Tell me what happened.'

'Auntie Carla—'

I close my eyes briefly. 'Sorry sweetie. Keep going. What did…Carla say?'

She wipes her nose with her sleeve. 'She said I should wait for you here. She said you'd come.'

I look at Nick in disbelief. 'Carla said Mummy would come?' he asks her.

She nods. 'We were playing hide and seek, and she said she would hide, and I should wait there, and then Mummy would come.'

I bite my bottom lip. I don't even have the words to describe how angry I am.

'Come on, let's get you inside,' Nick says, putting Karlie down at the front door.

'Where the hell is she? We have to call the police,' I hiss.

Nick puts his hand on my shoulder. 'Look.'

I turn to look. There are headlights on the road. A car has stopped. It's a taxi.

'Who is it?' Marjorie says, as Karlie leans against her and takes her hand.

I already know who's sitting in it. Susan Williams.

I run towards the car, but I'm too far away and it takes off.

She's gone.

I turn around and walk back to the front door. Marjorie has taken Karlie inside.

'We have to call the police,' I tell Nick.

He squeezes my shoulder. 'I'm on it.'

THIRTY-FOUR

'They should be here soon,' Nick says.

I managed to pull myself together for Karlie's sake. She may only be six, but she's smart enough to know this wasn't really a game, but something much more complicated. Something between grown-ups that she got caught up in. I made her a cup of hot milk and marmalade on toast, and now she's with Marjorie in Marjorie's room, watching Frozen on TV. Which means she's in heaven. She has no idea what all the fuss is about, but by the looks of the grin on her face, she's absolutely fine with it.

When I finally managed to get Marjorie alone and explained that Carla was never Carla, but a woman named Susan Williams, she almost collapsed.

'It's going to kill her,' Nick whispered to me.

'No it won't. She's stronger than that,' I replied. But I promised myself that I would do everything I could to soften the blow. 'We'll find her,' I said to Marjorie. 'The real Carla, I mean. I promise you.'

Now I'm on the couch in the living room biting my thumbnail. 'Where are they?'

'They'll be here.'

'I wanted to call them,' I say. 'You should have let me do it.'

Nick is sitting on the chair next to me, his elbows on his knees, fingers in a steeple against his chin.

'What's taking them so long?' I ask. 'She abducted my child for Christ's sake. Did you tell them that?'

'She didn't abduct Karlie,' he corrects. 'Karlie is here, and she's fine. She's perfectly safe.'

I wish he wouldn't speak to me like I'm five years old. 'She tried to abduct her, Nick.'

'That's not quite true,' he replies, in the tone of a long-suffering psychiatrist explaining to his patient – me – that the little green leprechaun dancing in the room is a product of my imagination.

'She must have realised you'd found her driver's licence,' he continues, 'and that's why her room—'

'Please don't call it her room. It's not her room.'

'—is in such a state. She used Karlie to create a diversion so she could get away. Karlie was never in any danger.'

'I can't believe you're saying that. You don't know that.' I rub my hands over my face. 'They should be here by now. Are you sure you called them?'

His mouth twitches. 'Of course I called them.'

I stand up. 'I'm going to call them again.'

'No, Ellie—' but I raise my hand to stop him. A car is pulling up outside.

They're here. Thank god.

They introduce themselves as DI Jordan – very tall and very thin – and DI McIntyre, who is short and built like a rugby player.

They want to talk to Karlie first—Nick did tell them

what had happened on the phone, although nobody mentioned the word 'abduction' until I do now. Then Nick explains it wasn't technically an abduction. He says I'm just overreacting, and that I'm a little hysterical but it's understandable under the circumstances.

I just don't understand why he's being like this. 'She snatched her out of bed, Nick!'

'We'll get to that,' DI Jordan says. He asks if I want a family liaison officer. I don't. I want to get on with it. I want them to find Susan Williams and throw her in jail.

'Then let's talk to Karlie if that's all right with you,' McIntyre says.

Marjorie brings Karlie out to the living room, holding her hand. My heart goes out to Marjorie. She looks awful, her face drawn, her eyes red, her mouth turned down. And to think she kept it together just now for Karlie's sake when she's just lost her daughter, again, makes my heart weep for her. I stand up and hug her. She hugs me back with a sharp intake of breath that threatens to turn into a sob. She pulls away. 'I'm all right,' she whispers. 'Thank you.'

I settle Karlie on my lap while Marjorie offers tea to the detectives.

'Everything is fine,' I say to Karlie. 'It was just a silly game, but these two policemen want to ask you questions anyway.'

She looks at me with wide eyes. 'Policemen?' This is a very exciting moment and leads to a million questions, such as why they're not in uniform (they're special policemen) and how often do they get to catch thieves (very often, apparently) and do they have lady policemen (Policewomen? Yes. Many. They're the best officers).

'Sweetie, you need to get back to bed soon. No more questions from you, okay?'

She nods. Then she answers all their questions with a clear gaze.

'Auntie Carla woke me up. She said Mummy wanted to play a game.'

They look at me.

I raise a hand. 'I didn't want to play a game if that's what you're asking. I had no idea what that woman was doing.'

'We understand,' Detective Jordan says. They prompt Karlie to resume her story.

'She said Mummy wanted to play a game. I said where's Mummy? She said she's outside, near the woods. She's playing hide and seek. She wants you to go and find her. I got out of bed. She helped me put my slippers on and a cardigan even though it's not very cold out. She said I had to be very quiet. She took my hand, and we went downstairs and we had to be very, very quiet, because that was the game. She had her coat on, and downstairs she had a bag. She took me to the woods and told me to wait there because that's where Mummy wanted me to go.'

McIntyre turns to me. 'Ms Hawke…'

'It's Ellie, please.'

'Thank you. Ellie. Did you ask Susan Williams to wake up Karlie?'

Karlie turns to me. 'It was Auntie Carla.'

'Of course not.' I blurt.

'Did you want Karlie to go to the woods?'

'She was in the old orchard. And no. I didn't. She should have been in bed.'

He turns to Karlie. 'Where was Mummy when all this was happening?'

'I don't know.'

'Did you see Mummy on the way out?'

She shakes her head.

'Thank you, Karlie. You're a very brave girl,' Jordan says, putting his notepad away.

'That's it?' I say.

'Yes. We have everything we need. Karlie can go back to bed now. Thank you.'

They look at Nick and nod, and I get the feeling that they're going to talk without me while I put Karlie back to bed. As if somehow, it's more important to hear the events of the night from Nick, than from me.

THIRTY-FIVE

'Is Carla gone for good?' Karlie asks as I settle her back in bed.

'Yes,' I say, caressing her hair.

'Forever?'

'Yes, darling. Forever. There's nothing to be afraid of.'

'I'm not afraid, Mummy. I'm sad she's gone, that's all.'

I swallow a sigh. *Right.*

'I liked her. She used to play with me.'

'I'll play with you. Every day. I promise.'

'Okay,' she says, in the tone of someone who knows they got a raw deal.

I read her a few pages of *The Magic Faraway Tree* and when I look up again, she's fast asleep.

'Is Karlie all right?' Marjorie asks when I get back downstairs.

I go straight to her and bend down to wrap my arms around her. She cracks the sob she's been holding onto for hours.

'Oh, Ellie! I wish I'd listened to you! I don't know why I

191

believed this…monster!' She pulls away. 'Will you ever forgive me?'

I click my tongue and sit next to her. I take her hand. 'There's nothing to forgive. She was a professional. You never stood a chance.'

'What was her motive, do you think?' Jordan asks.

'Money, obviously,' I say. 'I think she wanted the house.' I don't say the rest – that I think she wanted Marjorie dead, eventually, so she could inherit with Nick.

McIntyre leans forward in his chair. 'Tell me about your daughter,' he says to Marjorie.

She tearfully explains the background of Carla running away, the police contact they'd had with her, which the detectives seem to know about. She tells them about the postcard, the Facebook post, and finally her return. I interject here and there, explain that we were close friends and add some background.

From the corner of my eye I see Nick twitching.

'And you had no doubt this woman, Susan Williams, was your daughter Carla?' Jordan asks Marjorie.

Marjorie sighs. 'I'm such a stupid old woman.'

'Not at all,' Jordan says. He explains kindly that it's perfectly natural.

'We all thought it was Carla,' Nick says. 'All of us except Ellie, I mean.'

'Why was that?' Jordan asks me.

'I found her behaviour strange,' I say. 'And not at all like Carla.'

He makes a note. 'That wouldn't necessarily mean it wasn't Carla,' Jordan says. 'Was there anything else?'

'I just had a feeling,' I say.

'Ellie had difficulty adjusting,' Nick says.

'Excuse me?'

'What do you mean by that?' Jordan asks Nick.

'Well…' He frowns, crosses his legs. 'I don't mean anything in particular, just that… Well, we were all thrilled, as you can imagine. It was wonderful to have my sister back and we were over the moon, you could say, except Ellie who seemed to have a bee in her bonnet because Carla hadn't been very friendly to her when she arrived.'

I scoff. 'There's a bit more to it than that, Nick.'

'You immediately decided it wasn't her. The moment she walked in.'

'I didn't *decide* it wasn't her, Nick. It wasn't her.'

'I'm just saying, babe,' he says softly. 'You have to admit, you were always antagonistic towards her.'

'Ellie always knew it couldn't possibly be Carla,' Marjorie says, squeezing my hand.

'Thank you,' I say, glaring at Nick.

He shrugs. 'I'm just saying,' he mumbles.

'We should have listened to Ellie,' Marjorie says, pressing her handkerchief against her eyes.

'But how did you know it wasn't her?' Jordan asks, studying the driver's licence in a ziplock bag.

I tell them about the missing mole, which confuses them since people have moles removed all the time. 'But she seemed to know nothing about her own childhood—'

'That's not true,' Nick says.

'—which is why I asked Nick to make her take a DNA test.'

We all look at each other.

Nick stands up. 'The DNA test.'

He strides out of the room while Marjorie explains to the detectives that a DNA test was carried out which came back positive.

'So it was Carla.'

'That's what the test said,' Marjorie says.

'But Nick thought there was something wrong with the paperwork,' I say.

'Did he?' She frowns. 'He didn't tell me that.'

'I think he realised it after I showed him her licence.'

Nick returns. He frowns at Marjorie. 'I thought it was on your mantelpiece.'

'It is,' she says.

He shakes his head. 'It's gone.'

'Are you sure?'

'I looked everywhere. Carla must have taken it with her.'

'That's not her name,' I say.

He turns to the detectives. 'There was something amiss about it. Carla's name was typed in a different font, like someone had tampered with it.'

'I didn't notice that,' Marjorie says.

Again, I'm sure I catch that fleeting look on Nick's face, a flash of hate directed at Marjorie.

I shake my head. I must be dreaming.

Jordan is back to studying the driver's licence. He holds it up and looks at me. 'How did you know to look for this?'

'I was on the phone with my friend Bee. At that point, there was no question that this was Carla since I believed the DNA test results. I told Bee that Carla was married and she brought up the register check.'

'What do you mean?'

I turn to Marjorie. A dawning of understanding passes over her. 'Oh my goodness.'

'Marjorie checked the Births, Deaths, and Marriages records to see if Carla had gotten married.' *Or died*, I don't add. 'I'd asked her to do so,' I hasten to add. 'But there was no mention of marriage.' I sit forward. 'You should be out there. You should be looking for her. She tried to abduct my child.'

'She didn't, Ellie,' Nick says, sounding tired. 'We went over this.'

'Why are you defending her?' I ask.

'It's all right. We have police on the lookout for her,' Jordan says.

'Good,' I say, nodding. 'That's good. And you have to look for Carla, too. The real Carla.'

Marjorie gives me a small, hopeful smile. 'Maybe she's fine?' she says tentatively, but you can see her heart isn't in it.

'Was there anything else that made you think she wasn't Carla?'

'Many things. When I asked her about her childhood memories, she had none. Then—'

'She remembered Sophie Bonham,' Nick interjects.

I blink at him. What is it with him? 'I wouldn't say she remembered. She was looking it up on her phone, reading from old news items.'

'That's the young woman who disappeared a few months before Carla ran away, is that right?' Jordan asks.

'About a year,' Nick says. 'Do you think there's a connection?'

Why is Nick banging on about Sophie Bonham? 'Shouldn't we be looking for Susan Williams?' I say. 'You were asking me what else made me think she wasn't Carla.'

They nod. 'Yes. Go on.'

'Well, she didn't know about the Wicked Sistas. That was the band we were going to start. When I brought it up, she had no idea what I was talking about. That's when I knew, without a doubt, DNA tests notwithstanding. She should have known about the Wicked Sistas. We were obsessed with starting that band. We were best friends. She should have known.'

Nick sighs, rolling his head back against the seat. 'I think you should tell the truth, Ellie.'

THIRTY-SIX

'Tell the truth about what?' McIntyre asks.

I stare at Nick. 'Why are you doing this?'

Nick sits up. 'You were not friends, Ellie. That woman—' he points to the door '—might not have been Carla, but that doesn't change the fact that Carla, *our* Carla, couldn't stand you. At this point, I can't tell whether you're completely delusional or if you're just straight-out lying.' And before I have time to stop him, he's blurting it all out. That Carla hated me, that she only made friends with me because Marjorie asked her to after she heard my mother had died, that I used to do terrible things to her, like burning her hair and breaking her arm, and that she didn't know how to get rid of me.

I'm on my feet, shaking. 'That's not true! That's what *she* said, Susan Williams, but none of it is true!' I turn to Marjorie. 'You know that, don't you? I was onto her. That's why she fed you lies about me. But I did everything I could to protect you, both of you, from that woman.'

'And we're very grateful for that,' Marjorie says, motioning for me to sit down.

'But you still believe her instead of me?' I say to Nick.

'Ellie, sweetheart,' Marjorie says. 'It's not a matter of believing that woman. The truth remains that Carla had issues with you.'

I'm going mad. I really am. 'With due respect, Marjorie, I am not the issue here. The issue is the psychopath who pretended to be your daughter and tried to abduct mine.'

'You're absolutely right,' she says.

Jordan and McIntyre exchange a look. 'It's been a long night,' Jordan says, putting his notebook in his jacket pocket. 'You should all get some rest. We'll keep you posted on Susan Williams and review anything we may have about Carla from the time she ran away.'

'Yes,' I say, trying to regain control of the conversation. 'Please do that.'

I am so angry with Nick that I sleep with Karlie in her room. As I lie there staring at the ceiling, I try to recall at which point the focus of the police shifted from Karlie and the whereabouts of Susan Williams to my relationship with Carla.

I think you should tell the truth, Ellie.

The next day, I make breakfast for Karlie and take her to school. At the gates, everyone still gives me a wide berth, but I don't care. I pop by the salon and tell Lauren that Fake Carla is in fact called Susan Williams and she abducted my child.

'What? Is Karlie all right?'

'She will be,' I say, and burst into tears. I don't even know why I'm here or what I expected. Vindication? Apologies? But it's too soon for that. Who knows? She probably still believes I ran down Tracy with my car just to get a job. We both stand there, unmoving, with me sobbing from exhaustion more than anything.

'I don't know what to say' Lauren says finally.

'No. Never mind,' I say, then I walk out.

When I get home, there's a car I don't recognise. I walk in and call out for Marjorie.

'Up here, Ellie,' she says after a beat. I rush up the stairs.

'What's happening?' I ask.

The detectives are back, and they're in our bedroom, the one Susan Williams was using. Marjorie is there too, as is Nick.

'I thought you went to work,' I say to him.

'They called me,' he says, jerking his chin towards the police.

'They called you? Why?'

He shrugs.

The three of us watch from the doorway as they search through the wardrobe.

'Where did you find Susan Williams' ID?' Jordan asks.

'Under the mattress.' I point at the bed. The mattress is still pushed off its frame.

They keep searching, opening drawers and scanning the top of the dressing table, picking up items and putting them back down.

'Are you looking for something in particular?' I ask.

'Just taking a look,' Jordan says.

'Is this hers?' McIntyre asks. He has pulled my box from the shelf in the wardrobe.

'Actually, that's mine,' I say, reaching for it. He hands it to me, but lets go too quickly and I drop the box.

Marjorie lets out a gasp. I turn to her.

'What's wrong?'

She has her hand over her mouth and is pointing at the floor. 'Is that…?'

I look down at the contents of my box at my feet.

'No.' I start to shake. 'No.' I'm on my knees, rushing to put everything back in the box, but DI Jordan stops me.

'Can you step back, please?'

I don't want to step back, but there's nothing I can do. Jordan crouches on his haunches and picks up a photograph. The same photograph of the two of us that was on the pinboard in Carla's old room. Except that now Carla's face has been obliterated, like someone took a knife and stabbed it repeatedly.

'What is this?' he asks me.

I don't reply. He looks up at Marjorie, but she isn't looking down at the photograph. She's looking at the other items that have tumbled out of the box. I follow her gaze, and my hand flies to my mouth. 'Oh my god.'

'Ellie,' Marjorie says. 'What have you done?'

THIRTY-SEVEN

I waited for hours at the police station. At least they let me drive my own car. For a moment there I was sure they'd put me in the back of theirs, a hand pushing down on my head like I was a criminal.

Finally, I am brought into a small, airless interview room. I sit beneath a buzzing fluorescent tube for a long time, my stomach twisting a little more with every passing minute, until finally DI Jordan and DI McIntyre enter. McIntyre is carrying a thick manila folder. Jordan is carrying my box. They pull out two chairs across from me, taking their time lining up the edges of their files, fiddling with pens and notepads.

My heart is racing. My hands are shaking, so I put them on my lap. Jordan sets a small recording device down on the table and turns it on.

'Okay, Ellie – okay if I call you Ellie?'

'Yes.'

'Thank you. This conversation is being recorded. Would you like a solicitor present?'

He asks this as if it's a mere formality while making a note on his notepad.

'Why would I need a solicitor?' I ask, my heart thumping. 'Am I in trouble?'

'No. But you can have one if you like. It's up to you.'

'It's fine. I don't want a solicitor.'

'Very well. Can you state your name, please?'

I do as I'm asked. Jordan takes out an item from my box and holds it up. It's Carla's old mobile phone in a plastic sleeve. The same phone that tumbled out of my box earlier.

'Is this yours?' Detective Jordan asks.

It's a Nokia phone with a red and white Manchester United sticker on it. *MUFC Red Devils.*

'I already told you. It's not. It belonged to Carla.'

'Belonged?'

McIntyre speaks next. 'Can you explain to us, Ellie, why you have Carla's phone in your possession?'

'I can't. I don't know how it got there.'

'What about this photograph?' He tables the photo of Carla and me which is also in a clear envelope. He waits for me to pick it up. I don't want to. I can't bear to look at it, but I know I have no choice. I drag it across the table and study it. The sight of it makes my insides turn to water.

'Did you hate Carla?' he asks.

I shake my head which sets off a pounding headache. I press my fingers against my temples. 'No. And it wasn't me. I didn't do this.'

'So you don't know how the phone ended up in your property, and you don't know who disfigured Carla in this photograph or how it ended up in one of your journals. Is that correct?'

'Yes.'

'We'd like to ask you about the night Carla left,' Jordan says.

'All right.'

'Did you see her that night?'

'Yes.'

'Can you explain the circumstances?'

I tell them the story. I tell them about finding her in a complete panic, with her guitar and her bag all packed, how I tried to stop her, but she wouldn't listen. 'The last thing she told me was not to tell anyone, ever. Not where she went, or even that I'd seen her. Nothing.'

I fall silent. No one says anything for a moment, the only sound being the scratch of McIntyre's pen on paper.

'Now. We have a record in this file—' He lifts the manila folder '—that shows one of our colleagues contacted Carla Goodwin, on the sixteenth of October. That was four days after she ran away.' He flicks through a few pages until he finds what he's looking for. 'Officer Newman spoke to her on the phone. He asserted her identification by asking questions such as her date of birth, last address in Lindleton, mother's maiden name.' He looks up at me. 'Do you know Marjorie Goodwin's maiden name, Ellie?'

'No.'

He goes back to his notes. 'Carla Goodwin assured Officer Newman that she was perfectly fine and she didn't want to come home.'

I look up abruptly. 'That was over the phone?'

'Yes.'

'I thought it was a welfare check.'

'It was a phone conversation. On this phone.' He taps the plastic sleeve.

'So nobody actually saw her?' I ask, dumbfounded. All these years I'd assumed they had spoken to her in person.

'Did you talk to Officer Newman pretending to be Carla Goodwin?'

I press my fingers against my temples. 'No.'

'So how did this phone come to be in your possession?'

'I have no idea how it ended up in my box.'

'Would you be prepared to have your fingerprints taken?'

'Yes.'

'Thank you. We'll get it organised when we're done here.' McIntyre taps the photograph again. 'Did you scratch Carla's face out of the photograph?'

I rub my forehead. 'No.'

He leans back in his seat. 'Explain this to me, Ellie, because I'm confused. You keep saying you and Carla were best friends, so why is it that every single member of Carla's family believes she was running away from you that night?'

'Because Fake Carla, the other one, Susan Williams, has put all these ideas into their heads. Now they can't tell what's true and what isn't any more.'

'Nick says that you were obsessed with Carla and when she didn't want to hang out with you any more, you harmed her.'

I let out a laugh. 'Nick wouldn't have had the faintest idea what we were up to. He was two years older. He had different friends. He didn't pay attention to us.'

'But that's what Carla told him.'

'She couldn't have.'

'He says it got to the point where she became afraid of you.'

'That's rubbish.'

'So why would he say that?'

'I don't know.'

'Did you follow Carla after she left you at the lane that night?'

'No.'

'Did you kill Carla Goodwin because she wouldn't let you run away with her?'

'Oh my god! No!' I lean forward. 'She was my best

friend. I've been looking for her for years. Why would I do that if I'd killed her? Why would I spend all this energy looking for her?'

'That's an interesting question, Ellie,' he says, flicking his pen against the notepad. 'There are a few case studies about that. Criminals who are obsessed with the victim they killed and can't get enough. They still don't want to let go, so they make themselves the centre of the story by leading the search for a victim they know full well is dead. Is that what's going on here?'

'No!'

'Why did you tell Ashley Jennings from the Vanishing Acts podcast that Carla couldn't have sent a postcard because she was dead?'

'Oh, god. I didn't mean literally that she was dead. I meant it was the only explanation. She had to be dead since she never got in touch again and I couldn't find her. I tried so hard, and frankly that's what you should concentrate on. Finding Susan Williams and finding out what happened to Carla.'

'We are, Ellie. We're on it. You called the private detective who had been looking for Carla Goodwin. The one that Susan Williams contacted.' He flicks a page. 'Bill Grayson. You remember making that call?'

I look at him. 'Of course I remember. But he never got back to me.'

'He spoke to Nick who said he'd take care of it.'

'Did he?'

'You told Mr Grayson in your message that you didn't think it was Carla—'

'She wasn't.'

'—and asked him not to mention your call to Marjorie or Nick. Why is that? Why didn't you want Bill Grayson to tell Nick or Marjorie your concerns?'

'Because I knew they wouldn't believe me. Because they wanted her to be Carla.'

'But surely you'd want to share your concerns with them.'

'I'd tried that, but Susan Williams was too good. I don't understand the problem here.'

They exchange a look. 'The problem is that you can't give anyone any rational explanation as to how you knew she wasn't Carla Goodwin, other than some vague feeling you had.' He rubs his knuckle over his eyebrow. 'Nick thinks it's because you knew she was already dead.'

I push myself back against the table so hard that the chair bounces. 'That's a lie! I don't know why he would say something like that.'

'Let's talk some more about Nick Goodwin, if that's okay.'

McIntyre pulls out one of my journals from the box. The edges are spotted with protruding yellow tags.

'You wrote extensively about Nick in those journals. You were, what…fourteen? Fifteen?'

'About that, yes.'

'You write a lot about Nick. About how hot he is.'

I feel myself blushing.

He puts the diary on the table. 'There are lots of entries in that vein.'

I shrug. But inside it's fair to say I'm mortified. If I'd thought for a second that one day detectives would be reading my journals, I would have eaten them, page by page, before I'd let that happen.

'Why did you come back to Lindleton?'

'My father died. I came back to take care of personal affairs.'

'And you went to visit Marjorie Goodwin at the time, is that right?'

'Yes.'

'Did Marjorie Goodwin tell you that Nick had split up from his long-term relationship?'

'She said he was single, yes.'

'She said you perked right up when you heard that.'

'Really?'

'Nick says you were very keen to *get together* with him. He says you called him every day to make plans to see each other. He was surprised at that. He thought you had a life in London.'

'I have no idea why Nick is saying those things. I didn't stalk him, if that's what you mean.'

'Why did you settle back in Lindleton?' McIntyre asks.

My heart is like a drum. 'Nick and I fell in love. I was ready for a change.'

'I'd like to ask you about Blossoms and Curls. The hair-dressing salon where you work.'

'Yes?'

'Your predecessor, Tracy O'Ryan, was hit by a car and had to have multiple operations. She's still in recovery.'

I swallow. 'I know. I didn't run her over with my car,if that's what you're suggesting.'

'That's good to know. What kind of car do you drive, Ellie?'

'A Hyundai Amica.'

'What colour is it?'

'Silver. Why?'

They exchange a look.

'Did you break the top step at Marjorie Goodwin's house so she would trip and fall?'

'That's ridiculous!'

'Is it?'

I make moves to stand up. 'If we're done here…' But McIntyre leans forward, his bulky arms crossed on the desk.

'Hey, come on, Ellie. Let's cut the crap. We know you're

obsessed with the Goodwin family. We know you did something to Carla Goodwin because she wanted nothing to do with you. I think you've never stopped wanting to put yourself at the centre of this family. Searching for Carla was a way for you to indulge in your obsession with the Goodwins. You engineered your meeting with Nick, just like you engineered the job at the salon, just like you engineered moving into their house. We know you caused Marjorie's fall deliberately so that you would have an excuse to move in. We can't prove it yet, but we know.'

'That's not true,' I say, my throat constricting. 'And I fell down the stairs, too.'

Again, they exchange a look. This one says, *sure you did. The oldest trick in the book.*

'How did you know the postcard from Paris didn't come from Carla?'

'I told you. The handwriting wasn't right.'

'A person's handwriting changes between sixteen and twenty-eight. You don't seriously expect us to believe that was the reason.'

I rub my forehead. 'There was something else about it… I can't remember. I—'

'How well did you know Sophie Bonham?' Jordan asks, flicking a page in my diary.

'She was a friend from school. Why?'

He holds up the diary and reads: '"I saw Sophie with Nick today. She was all over him. So gross. They were hiding at the back of the gym. I don't know what he sees in her."'

God. I'd completely forgotten about that.

'Care to expand, Ellie?'

'Expand on what? I was fourteen years old. She was going out with my crush. It upset me.'

'Clearly,' McIntyre says, raising an eyebrow.

'What did you do to her?' Jordan asks.

'I didn't do anything to her!'

'You're sure about that? Because see the date here?' He taps on the page. 'Sophie Bonham went missing right about that time. And then a year later, your friend Carla ran away. You're connected to both of them. Care to expand on that, Ellie?'

McIntyre flicks to a page in his notebook. 'Why did you say, and I quote, "*I don't care about Sophie Bonham any more, I don't want to talk about Sophie Bonham at all…*"?'

I blink. 'Who told you that?'

'You said those things at dinner, in front of Nick and Mrs Goodwin. What did you mean by that, Ellie?'

'I was trying to keep the conversation on Carla – Fake Carla – but she kept bringing up Sophie.'

'You were very much in love with Nick back then, weren't you? But he was seeing Sophie Bonham. How did that make you feel?'

'What?'

'Did you follow Sophie to the Goodwins' house?' Jordan asks.

'No!'

'We know she left the Goodwins' house the night she disappeared around six. Did you follow her that night, Ellie?' Jordan asks.

'What did you do to her, Ellie?' McIntyre asks.

'Where is Sophie, Ellie?' Jordan asks.

My heart was already racing, but now it drops into my stomach.

Because I just remembered something.

I stand and grab my bag. 'I have to pick up my daughter from school.'

THIRTY-EIGHT

I park right outside the gates. We're not allowed to, but I don't care. I'm a few minutes early and I try to think but my mind is racing. Nothing makes sense right now. I think back to the day Marjorie fell. Nick was there. He came out to the landing like he hadn't heard anything and he was surprised about all the fuss. I think about the day I fell. Was he there? I remember waking up and seeing his face close to mine, looking at me with concern. Meghan, the cleaner, was there too, and Marjorie. Had he not expected them to be there? Would he have done something to me if they hadn't been? I think about that flash of hatred on his face when he looked at his mother. I thought I was mistaken, but now I don't think so. I think he hates her. Did he try to kill his mother and then me? Why? Because we were getting too close?

Because he was afraid we would find out what he'd done?

I pull out my phone. There's a Facebook page dedicated to finding Sophie Bonham. It's been dormant for years, but it still exists.

I load it up and zero in on the first photo. It's a group shot from when Sophie was on the rowing team. I zoom in on her face with two fingers, my heart pounding. When the detective brought up Sophie earlier, an image of her flashed in my mind. And that's when I remembered.

The necklace I found in the attic the other day. It wasn't Carla's, it was Sophie's. She wore that necklace all the time. And there it is, in that photo. I zoom in even closer. It's definitely the same necklace.

And it's in the attic, among Nick's old schoolbooks.

I get out of the car. By now the parents are huddled together, throwing furtive glances over their shoulders at me. I walk straight to Lauren which makes the other parents scuttle backwards, as if I had leprosy and was intent on shedding skin fragments all over them.

'Can you take Karlie home with you?' I blurt.

Lauren frowns at me, her mouth tight. 'Why?'

'Because—'

'No.' She shakes her head. 'No, actually, forget I asked why. I'm not taking Karlie home.'

The children are beginning to spill out of the front door. I grab her wrist. She recoils, wriggles her arm, but I hold on tight.

'Jesus, Ellie!'

'I need you to take Karlie with you. I wouldn't ask unless it was important.' Which is an amazing thing to say, considering we've always picked up each other's children. Now she looks at me like I've asked her to take an unexploded grenade home with her and stick it under her pillow.

'I'm not getting involved, Ellie.'

'Please, Lauren—' From the corner of my eye I spot Bethany running towards her mother. 'I'm begging you. I need someone to look after Karlie right now and I don't know what else to do.'

Lauren finally manages to snatch her hand away from

my grip. She grabs Bethany's hand. 'I'm sorry, truly. But that's not my problem.'

There are children everywhere now. I look around frantically, my heart racing. I look down at Bethany. 'Where's Karlie?'

She shrugs, and Lauren pulls her away. 'Leave us alone,' she says in a low voice.

I push the other parents aside, then the other children. 'Karlie?' I shout.

'I'm here, Mummy.'

I turn around. She's dragging her backpack and pushing a pebble with her toe.

I crouch down and hug her. 'Are you all right?'

She nods, still looking down. I pick up her backpack. 'Come on, let's get out of here.'

At the lights, I drum my fingers on the steering wheel. My mind is reeling. I can't have Karlie at the house right now. It's far too dangerous. I wish I'd made more friends, engaged more with the other mothers so I'd have options. Why didn't I make more friends?

'You okay, sweetie?' I ask in the rear-view mirror. She doesn't reply. She's tracing shapes on the window with her finger.

'Did something happen today?' *As opposed to yesterday when a stranger grabbed you from your bed and dragged you out to the woods?*

She meets my eye. 'Bethany says you're a liar.'

Ah. 'That's not nice. Why did she say that?'

'She heard her mum say to her dad that you lied to get your job.'

'I see.' Well, at least she didn't overhear her mother tell her father I tried to *kill* to get that job.

'I didn't. Bethany is mistaken, and I'll sort it out as soon as I can, okay?'

She doesn't reply. I stick my indicators on and pull over. I

turn around in my seat. 'Hey, Karlie. Look at me. I didn't lie
—' *or kill, or maim* '—to get a job at Bethany's mum's salon,
all right?'

She nods. 'All right.'

'We'll sort this out. I promise. I love you.'

'I love you, too, Mummy.'

'I love you more.' I put the car in gear.

'Where are we going?' she asks.

'To Mrs Lopez's house.'

THIRTY-NINE

I will forever be grateful to Mrs Lopez. Or, as Karlie likes to say, *Foreverandeverandeverforever*.

Karlie was ecstatic at the idea of spending a few hours with Mrs. Lopez, and Mrs Lopez was equally delightfully enthusiastic at the idea of spending time with Karlie. 'Let's bake chocolate biscuits,' she'd said, with a conspiratorial air. Karlie clapped and squealed with joy. They were so absorbed in their plans that neither of them noticed how upset I was. And if Mrs Lopez had heard any rumours about me, she hid it well.

Foreverandeverandeverforever grateful.

I thanked Mrs Lopez profusely and left.

I let myself into the house and drop my car keys in the bowl on the console table.

Silence.

I close the front door behind me. The sound of Marjorie's cane on the floor grows louder.

'Ellie.' She looks awful, her mouth tight, but there's

pleading in her eyes too. 'What happened? What did the police say? Did you tell them why you had Carla's phone?'

Her left hand is bandaged again. I reach for it but don't touch it. 'What happened to your wrist?'

'Nothing. It was bothering me again, that's all. Why did you have it, Ellie? You must tell me. I can't bear it. Why did you have Carla's phone?'

My chin wobbles. 'I don't know, I promise you. I don't know how it ended up in my box. I didn't put it there, Marjorie. I promise you.'

She looks at me for a moment. 'Where's Karlie?' She checks her watch. 'She'll be out of school by now. Is someone picking her up? Did you want Nick to do it?'

'No!'

She jerks her head up.

'She's with Mrs Lopez,' I say.

She nods. 'That's probably a good thing. You still haven't told me. What did the police say?'

'They asked a lot of questions.'

She holds my gaze, but her lips tremble. 'Did you hurt Carla, Ellie?'

I shake my head violently. 'No. I promise you, I swear to god I didn't. I loved her, Marjorie. Carla was my best friend. I would never, ever hurt her.'

Her eyes fill with tears. 'I'm just so confused.'

'I know.'

'I don't understand what's happening.'

'I know,' I say. 'I mean, I don't. I don't understand it either. But just…just give me some time. I'll figure it out. I promise you.'

She nods again, then quickly brushes a tear away. 'The police want to talk to me. I'm to go over there, soon.'

'Do they?' I'm surprised. Actually, I'm not. Of course they would. Carla was her daughter.

'Have they asked to speak to Nick?'

'At some point,' she says. 'They want to speak to me first.' She checks her watch again. 'Nick is going to drive me.'

'Where is he?'

'He's upstairs.'

I nod. But my heart does a little jig. *Good. I need him out of the house.*

I go upstairs to our bedroom. Nick has his back to me, pushing hangers in the wardrobe. On the bed are piles of clothes, carefully folded. His clothes. Not mine. They, presumably, are still in Carla's old bedroom. Unless he put them in the bin.

'What did the police say?' he asks without looking at me.

'They asked a lot of questions.'

He turns around. 'So they didn't arrest you.'

'Not yet.'

He goes to the chest of drawers and opens the top one. 'They want to talk to Mum. I'm taking her there now.'

'I know. She told me.'

'I don't know what to say to you, Ellie.'

Why don't you start by telling me how you came to have Sophie's necklace in your possession?

'Nicky?' Marjorie calls out. 'We should leave now.'

I swallow. 'We can talk later,' I say.

'Yeah, or not.' He moves past me and through the door, and without another word, he goes down the stairs.

I drop my bag on the bed, sit down and press my fingers on my temples. I wait for them to drive off. Then, as soon as the car is out of sight, I rush to the attic.

FORTY

Light is streaming through the little window, illuminating specks of dust in the air. I step over a roll of carpet and go straight to where I saw it last time: in the cardboard box full of Nick's old schoolbooks. I fish it out and hold it up to the light.

My heart sinks. It's the same necklace. I mean, I knew that already, but I would have given anything for that necklace in my hand to be different from the one I saw on Sophie's neck.

I slip it into my pocket. I've got to get out of here. I have to go to the police and show it to them and explain where I found it.

In my rush to get out, I trip on one of Nick's dumbbells that's fallen out of the bag. It sends me tumbling against the pile of suitcases full of Carla's old clothes.

I swear under my breath as I brush off my knees, and when I look up, wobbly from the fall, that's when I see it. A memory flashes in my brain, like an old Polaroid, as I stare at Carla's guitar case. I saw it before, right there, when I brought up the suitcases, but for some reason I didn't click.

I do now, as I stare at the dark denim padded guitar case, with the red logo on the front pocket and the brown shoulder strap. I am dizzy as I reach for it and slowly, shakily unzip a couple of inches. Specks of dust fly off as I push my fingers through the narrow opening and feel the edge of her guitar inside.

Carla had only one guitar, and only one guitar case. That one. I can still see her running towards the train station with it flung across her back.

But now it's here.

'You shouldn't be up here, Ellie.'

My heart explodes. I turn around. Nick is leaning against the wall, his arms crossed over his chest.

I hold his gaze for a second or two. 'What did you do to her?' I whisper.

'What are you talking about?'

I point to the case.

He shrugs with one shoulder.

'Oh, no, Nick. No.' I run to him and pummel his chest with my fists. 'What did you do with her? Where is she?'

'Hey!' He holds my wrists. 'Cut it out, Ellie!'

I yank my wrists away and take a step back. 'It was you. You had Carla's phone and you put it in my box. All this time I thought it was her, Fake Carla – Susan, whatever her name is – but it was you!'

Nick starts clapping slowly. 'Congratulations. You got me.'

'Did you…? Is…? Is Carla dead?'

'Yes. And before you try and punch me again, it wasn't my fault. She left me no choice.'

'Oh my god.' I can't breathe. I press the heel of my hands against my eyes. 'She never made it to the train station?'

'Correct.'

I feel lightheaded. Dark spots are dancing in front of my eyes. I bend down, my hands gripping my knees. 'You are evil,' I whisper.

'Maybe.'

I look up at him. 'You went to Paris and sent the postcard?'

'Yes.'

'Because you wanted Marjorie to think Carla was still alive?'

He stares at me, eyebrows knotted together. 'You kept looking for her. You kept asking questions. I wanted to shut you up.'

'Did you kill Sophie, too?'

He narrows his eyes slightly. 'What makes you say that?'

'You did,' I cry. 'I know you did, I found her necklace among your things.'

He frowns at my hands. 'You're not recording this conversation, are you?'

I can't breathe. I have to get out of here. I have to go to the police. I move to get out but he steps forward to bar my way and grabs my arm.

'Where are you going?'

'To the police.'

He lets out a laugh. 'Good idea. They already think it was you who killed Sophie, and then Carla. Oh, come on, don't look like that. That version is so much more interesting, don't you agree? Little Ellie who was so jealous, so enamoured of me, that when she saw I was interested in Sophie, she killed her. And when Carla discovered what an evil, manipulative little girl you were, you killed her too. That's what the police already think. That's what the evidence shows.'

'You pushed Marjorie down the stairs that day. It was you. Why? I thought it was about money, but did you try to kill her because she found something? Is that why we moved in? So you could keep an eye on her?'

He frowns at me, shaking his head.

I take a step back. 'You tried to kill me too. You were there, that day. You must have been. Why?'

'Honestly, Ellie, how did you get this far in life? Truly. Do you even have a brain?'

I take another step back. 'It was because of the podcast. You were worried about the podcast. That they'd find out what you did.' My vision blurs. 'Why did you do it? Why did you kill them?'

'You mean, why did *you* kill them.'

I'm going to be sick. 'Who is Susan Williams? How does she fit in?'

He shrugs. 'She looked like Carla, that's all. You're right. I wanted you to give up your stupid podcast idea. It didn't work. Honestly, Ellie. You just wouldn't give up. If you'd bought it that day at lunch, that she really was Carla, none of this would have happened.'

'The DNA test, all that, you faked it…'

He bursts out laughing. 'Of course, I faked it! We never got a DNA test done, Ellie! I just printed a page with a logo. Jesus, you're really slow sometimes.'

I can't breathe. 'You won't get away with this. I have Sophie's necklace.' I fumble for it in my pocket. 'I'm going to give it to the police. I'm going to tell them everything.'

He looks at me like I've grown another head. 'And what's that going to do? They'll just say you kept it after you killed her.' He extends his hand towards the hatch, as if inviting me to leave. 'Please. Be my guest. Go and tell the detectives you have Sophie's necklace. I promise not to try and stop you.'

'My god. You've been planning this for a long time, haven't you?' I shake my head. It makes no sense in light of everything, but I feel like my heart is breaking. 'You never loved me.'

He makes a face. 'Sorry baby. No. Nothing personal.'

'You brought me here to set me up for these murders. That's all it ever was between us. A setup.' My hand flies to my mouth. 'Oh god, did you hit Tracy? Was that you?'

He opens his hands and does a little bow. 'With your car. Yes.'

'You could have killed her!'

'You wouldn't have come back if you didn't have a job.'

'You almost killed her so I'd get a job? Why? Why was it so important to bring me here?'

'I thought it was obvious by now. To keep an eye on you. To stop you from looking for Carla.'

I'm going to faint. 'Why did you kill Carla?'

He lifts a shoulder. 'Collateral damage. She figured it out, about Sophie. She had to go.'

Rage erupts inside me like thunder, blinding me. I don't know what I'm thinking, or what I'm doing. All I know is he is screaming at me to stop, both hands in front of him, but I'm not listening.

Until I hear something crack.

He is staring at me, his eyes wide with surprise. He raises a hand to the side of his head and blood seeps through his fingers.

'You fucking bitch,' he says, more surprised than angry.

I look down at my right hand. I'm holding a barbell. I don't even remember picking it up.

'I'm sorry,' I say softly. Oh, god. I am sorry in so many ways. Because it has only now occurred to me that Nick has already killed two people, and we are alone in this house.

He stands there, looking bewildered, blood slowly running down his arm. Then his eyes turn glassy and he collapses to the floor.

I drop the barbell. I'm on my knees. 'Oh god.' He's hurt. He's really hurt. 'I'm going to get you some help, okay?' I look around for something to hold onto his head, something to stop the blood seeping out of him and at the same time I am fumbling for my phone. But I don't have my phone. It's in our bedroom.

'Nick?' I take his face in my hands. 'Oh, god. Nick? Can you hear me?' His eyes are open but vacant. I press my fingers against his throat and check for a pulse, but there's nothing.

Oh god. Oh my god. What have I done? 'Nick? Can you hear me?' I check for a pulse on his wrist. I bend to his chest and listen to his heart.

Nothing.

He's dead. Nick is dead. I killed him.

A shrill sound erupts and my heart explodes. Nick's phone. I dive into his pocket and dig it out, my hands trembling. The screen shows 'Mum'. I flick it to silent and wait, my heart pounding so hard it feels like it's bouncing off the walls.

Nick is dead. I killed him. I have to call 999. That's what I'll do. I'll explain everything. The necklace, what Nick did to Sophie and Carla... but I don't know what Nick did to Sophie and Carla. Only that he killed them.

I think of Karlie. No. Don't think of Karlie. It'll be all right. They'll believe me. They'll understand that it wasn't me. I'll tell them I found the necklace among Nick's old schoolbooks.

They'll believe me.

And I'll tell them what he said. I'll tell them he admitted to everything, even running Tracy down with my car. It'll be fine.

Oh god. Who am I kidding? They'll never believe me.

I hear the sound of a car pulling up to the house. I stand

up and crane my neck to see out the window. A man emerges from the driver seat of a sedan.

DI McIntyre.

I crouch down and hold my head in my hands. Why is he here? And what am I going to tell him? I stand up again, slowly, on legs that feel like they're made of ribbons, and peer out. McIntyre is opening the passenger door.

Marjorie gets out.

FORTY-ONE

I can't breathe. They'll never believe me. Marjorie certainly won't. She'll think I'm even more evil than she thought. I didn't just kill one of her children, I killed them both. That's what she'll think.

All I can think about is Karlie. Who will take care of her if I'm in jail? I have to think. I need to buy myself some time. I grab the edge of a carpet roll and yank it hard until I've got enough to pull over him. When I look out the window again, McIntyre is driving off.

I make my way down the stepladder with shaky legs, then push it up so it retracts. It clanks as it folds back and I close my eyes, my heart pounding in my throat.

'Nicky?'

It's Marjorie calling from downstairs.

'Yes, Marjorie?' I call out, pushing up the trap door ever so slowly.

'Ellie, is Nick up there?'

There's a pole that dangles from the centre of the trap door. I push it up, quietly, until the door is fully closed against the ceiling.

'No, Marjorie, he went out.'

I give it one last sharp push, and the latch engages with a click.

I hold my breath.

'But his car is here,' she says.

I am shaking so much I can barely walk. I brush my hair away from my face and lean over the balustrade.

'Maybe he took his motorbike,' I say.

She frowns at me. 'He was supposed to pick me up. He didn't tell you where he went?'

'I was asleep. I only just woke up,' I say.

She narrows her eyes at me. After a beat she says, 'Please come downstairs. We need to talk.'

'I'll be right down,' I say. I go into the ensuite bathroom and grip the basin. I stare at my reflection. There's a streak of blood on my forehead. My hair is wild. I look crazy.

I take off my soiled shirt and jeans and scrub my hands with the nailbrush as hard as I can. I don't want to take a shower because Marjorie might find that suspicious, but I rinse my forearms, and wash my face. I dry myself, make sure the basin is clean, then go to my bedroom and change into some fresh clothes.

And then I go downstairs.

Marjorie is standing by the window in her living room. She turns to face me fully, her head tilted. 'What's wrong? What happened?'

I swallow. 'I don't know what you mean.'

She narrows her eyes at me. 'You look very pale, Ellie.'

I nod. 'It's been a long day.'

'Yes. Yes, it has. Nick didn't tell you where he went?'

I feel the corners of my mouth pull down. My chin wobbles. 'Oh, Marjorie… I did something—'

Her mobile phone rings. Marjorie raises a finger at me. 'It might be Nicky.' She hobbles to retrieve her phone from the coffee table and checks the screen. She sighs. 'It's not him. It's McIntyre.'

'The detective?' I shriek. 'Didn't he just drop you off?'

She raises an eyebrow, and my stomach drops.

'I saw you drive up, when I woke up.'

To my relief, she puts the phone back down without taking the call. 'Yes. He drove me home because I couldn't reach Nick.'

'So why is he calling?'

'I don't know. I don't have time to deal with him right now.' She turns to me. 'What was it you wanted to tell me?'

Jesus. What on earth was I thinking? I can't tell Marjorie that I killed her son and his body is in the attic in a pool of blood.

'Nothing important,' I say.

'Well. Whatever it is, it can wait. Oh, I wish Nick was home.' She puts her fingers against her lips. 'I have to be somewhere.'

'Where?'

She looks at me. 'Some of my friends have come together. They want to talk about Carla, and…'

About me. They want to talk to you about me. About what to do with me.

'Nick was going to come with me,' she continues.

'Do you want me to drive you?' I ask. I wouldn't mind some time alone to think. I have to figure out what to do about Nick.

I'm going to be sick.

'Would you? I left him a message on his phone. Then he could join me later, if he wants. I'll leave a note, too. I don't want him to worry.'

I swallow. 'Of course.'

She hobbles to the console table where there's a notepad and a pen. She picks up the pen and rubs at her wrist.

'I'll write it,' I say.

'Would you?'

'Of course.' I take her place.

'Just tell him that I've joined the others,' she says. She thinks for a second while I write it down. 'He didn't want me to go, you know.'

Well, he won't care now.

'Please write, "I've thought about it, and I know it's the right thing to do. I'm sorry".'

I do as she asks, then she takes the pen from me and scribbles at the bottom. *Mum.*

I stare at the word. She's never going to hear it again. The only people who could call her that are dead. And at least one of them is my fault.

She stands up straight. 'All right. Let's go. We can talk more on the way.' Then she looks right into my eyes.

'Ellie, darling, I'm sorry. But there's something I have to show you.'

FORTY-TWO

For a moment there, I thought she was going to say, 'Nick's body is in the attic. I want to show you.'

That's because I'm going mad. Even more mad. But then she put on her coat and I grabbed my car keys. My legs can barely carry me.

'What do you want to show me?' I ask.

'You'll see.'

The sun is starting to be low in the sky. We start walking to the east side of the house, on the yellow grass, towards the wood. She has her arm locked into mine, and I can't help but think that it's very likely this is the last time we will walk together like this.

'Marjorie?'

'Yes, dear.'

I hesitate. We walk slowly in the direction of the old orchard. I swallow. 'There's something I need to tell you.'

'Mmm?'

How to explain what Nick did? I take a breath. 'The postcard you received from Carla, from Paris,' I begin.

'What about it?'

'You know how I always said something bothered me about it.'

'Yes, I know.'

'Nick sent it,' I whisper.

She doesn't reply. I don't even know if she heard me. I almost say it. *Nick killed her, and twelve years later he went to Paris to send a postcard so you'd think she was still alive.*

I can picture it in my mind so precisely, I can even make out the postmark.

I stop abruptly.

'We're not there, yet,' she says. 'But it's not much further.' She points with her cane to the well, about twenty feet away. I start walking again, but my heart is racing.

'My father died on March 9th,' I whisper. I feel lightheaded.

'Yes, I know.'

'I called you the next day to tell you. And that's when you told me about the postcard.'

'I remember,' she says.

I think I'm going to faint. 'But the postmark was dated the 12th of March.'

She doesn't reply.

'Which means that, when you told me about the postcard in that phone call… you hadn't received it yet.'

'There we are.' Marjorie says, as if I hadn't spoken. We've reached the well. The metal sheet that normally covers its opening is leaning against the side.

'Did you know it wasn't her?' I ask in a whisper. 'Have you always known?'

Marjorie taps her cane on the brickwork. 'Look in the well, Ellie.'

I lean over and look down.

And then I see stars.

FORTY-THREE
MARJORIE

Of course I knew it wasn't her. Carla would have had to crawl out of the hole she's been in for twelve years, and I'm quite certain we would have noticed.

Just thinking of it reminds me of a nightmare I once had, not long after we disposed of her body. I dreamed I was sitting up in my bed, reading, and she appeared in my room. Not like Carla, of course, but a ghostly figure, her hair dripping with mud, her face dirty and gaunt, and her eyes cloudy and white. She raised an accusing finger at me and I screamed. That's how I woke myself up: screaming. I never took that brand of sleeping pills again.

Poor Ellie. For days after Susan arrived – my daughter's 'stand-in' – Ellie would look at me and wring her hands together with that pained expression on her face. *I'm so sorry, Marjorie…*

That stupid girl thought she knew my daughter better than I did. She thought she could pick out the imposter and I couldn't. And not only that, but she thought she could throw a party and tell the whole world about how clever she was. *It's not her. I'm so sorry.*

Some days it was all I could do not to slap her across the face. Wipe that sweet butter-wouldn't-melt expression right off. Did she think I didn't know what she was up to with her stupid little party? Did she think she could outsmart me? She thought she was setting a trap for Susan when all this time she was playing right into my hands.

I briefed Susan about who would be there and how Carla would have remembered them. Of course, I'd been briefing her for days. Ever since that little con artist decided to stay and indulge in a little blackmail. Like I said to Nicky, '*You lie down with dogs…*' Still. Nobody would accuse me of not knowing how to make lemonade out of lemons.

'You hated her,' I explained to Susan. 'With a passion. I would ask you to be nice to her because her mother had died. You didn't mind so much at first, but then you couldn't get rid of her. She had taken to following you around like a sad puppy, copying your clothes, your hair, your games. She would insist you sit together in class. She would exclude the other children from your games. When you told her you didn't want to be friends any more, she'd hurt you. Once, she pushed you out of a tree and you almost broke your neck. She set your hair on fire. It got to the point you became afraid of her. You said she was dangerous, but I didn't believe you, and neither did your brother. And then you disappeared. And it's only now, upon your return, that you have finally told me the truth. You disappeared because of her.'

All lies, of course, but in the scheme of things, not a bad story at all. Perfect for my purposes, in fact. Ellie would get what's coming to her, and she would only have herself to blame. That stupid, stupid girl, calling me for years, asking about Carla.

'Have you heard from her? Don't you think that's strange? Will you check Births, Deaths, and Marriages, Marjorie? Just in case?'

The number of times I'd wanted to say, 'Yes, dear. I've had long phone conversations with my daughter. She's marvellous, thank you. I'll let her know you called.' But I couldn't do it. There was always the remote possibility someone would find her body, no matter how unlikely. What would I do then? The police would want to see phone records and there would be none. No. I couldn't risk that, but I was so weary of Ellie ringing me and asking about Carla that I took a risk anyway. I made up some story about receiving a postcard from Paris. It was a spur of the moment thing. I thought she would leave well enough alone after that. How was I to know Ellie's father had died and she was coming to Lindleton for the funeral? She'd started the conversation by asking about Carla, as usual. She had sounded rather shocked, and only then did she tell me her father had passed, and she would be coming back to Lindleton.

'No need to stay overnight,' I told Nicky. He was sprawled in the armchair, one leg hooked over the armrest, his cheek resting in the palm of his hand. I'd had to summon him from the gym and only when I told him that 'We have a problem – it's Ellie,' did he agree to come and see me.

'In fact, it's better if you don't stay overnight,' I said. 'Just take the train, buy a postcard, any postcard, and mail it to me. I've written down what it should say on this piece of paper.' I handed it to him.

He frowned at it. 'Don't you think you're overreacting? Just tell her you lost it. Tell her your cleaner put it in the bin or something.'

That would be just the kind of thing Meghan would do. I shook my head. 'Please, darling. I receive a postcard from my daughter after twelve years of silence and I throw it in the bin? Ellie would never believe it.'

He stared at me from below his long dark eyelashes. I

always thought he had the most beautiful eyelashes, for a boy. I didn't point out that it was his fault we were in this wretched mess in the first place, but let's say the words hung between us regardless.

I really thought that was going to be the end of it. Ellie would see the evidence with her own eyes, she would finally let sleeping dogs lie and I'd never have to hear another word about it. For the first time in a long time, I thought that I would finally get Ellie out of my life.

How wrong I was.

FORTY-FOUR

MARJORIE

'It's not her handwriting,' she'd said.

I'd given Nicky a sample of Carla's handwriting. A school essay I'd found in one of the boxes in the attic. He probably hadn't looked at it closely, if at all.

'We need to tell the police,' Ellie had insisted. We were having tea in the front room. I was trying to contain the rage that was building inside me. I'd gone through so much trouble, sending Nicky to Paris, having her over for tea, showing her the postcard... I could feel my face trembling with it. She thought I was upset at the idea that the card wasn't from Carla, but I said to her, 'Ellie, you're not making any sense! Of course it's from Carla. Who else would it be from?'

She stared at it in her hand for a long time. I wanted to snatch it and throw it in the fire. 'Do you have samples of her handwriting?' she'd asked. Well, yes, of course, she was my daughter. I had school notebooks and mother's day cards and god knows what, but I was hardly going to pull them out since it wasn't Carla's handwriting.

I dabbed at my eyes. 'They're in the attic, in boxes. I don't feel like looking at them, if you don't mind.'

'That's okay. I have notebooks from when we wrote songs together. I'll dig them out when I get back to London.'

I nodded but inside I was gritting my teeth so hard I could have pushed them inside my skull. She started to talk about taking the postcard and a sample of Carla's handwriting to the police. Through the pounding in my head I could hear words like: *Opening an investigation… It's been going on too long… Missing… Search for her…* I could barely restrain myself from strangling her right there and then. I changed the conversation to her daughter, Karlie, who was staying with her flatmate in some hovel in Croydon. 'I didn't want to bring her for the funeral. She's so young.'

'Of course,' I'd said. 'How long are you staying in Lindleton?'

'Until Friday.'

'Then you must come back before you leave. I know Nicky would love to see you.'

Needless to say, Nick never gave Ellie a second thought until she started calling about Carla. At the mention of his name, Ellie's face lit up and a blush came over her cheeks. And that's when I got the idea. Nick was single since Edwina had ended the relationship, something I'd been sad about. I was very fond of Edwina. But since Ellie was also single, it presented a unique opportunity to keep her close, and I knew without a doubt that we had to keep Ellie as close as possible. In London, I'd have no idea what she might be getting up to. I would lose sleep wondering if she'd gone to the police and reported Carla missing.

That's what I told Nicky after she left. 'You have to keep her here. She's single, so are you, she always had a crush on you, we all knew it, so for goodness' sake, don't let her go back to London where she's going to do god knows what. Just do what you have to to keep her here.'

It worked like a charm. Nick called her and asked her for

a coffee, to catch up for old times' sake. Then, he swept her off her feet, which was hardly a *tour de force*. Women fall in love with Nick at the drop of a hat, and Ellie always had a crush on him. Nick declared he'd never been in love before and he would do anything to be with her. He pursued her in London, until finally, Ellie agreed to move back to Lindleton with Karlie.

Again, I thought we were more or less home and dry. Nick would spend time with Ellie, he'd convince her that Carla was perfectly fine, just selfish and self-centred, just like she'd always been, and she'd return when she felt like it. He'd assure her that he recognised her handwriting. 'The way she did her B's, see? That's exactly the same. And who keeps the same handwriting anyway?' Then once she finally accepted the truth right in front of her face, Nick would end the relationship and send her and Karlie back to their old life.

Unfortunately, things didn't turn out that way. Ellie simply wouldn't accept the facts. Instead, she dug even deeper, no pun intended, and started to talk about involving a true crime podcast.

This was no longer a case of keeping her close. I had to get rid of her.

First, I faked the fall. When I say 'faked', I did fall on purpose, but not as hard as I made it look. There's nothing wrong with my wrist or my ankle. But I wanted Ellie and Nick to live here, with me, so I could take care of the things that needed to be done. In retrospect, I didn't even need to fake an injury. If I'd just asked, explained I needed help, she would have happily moved in. Ellie is a nurturer through and through. She is happiest when she's taking care of other people.

I tried to talk her out of the stupid podcast. How would it make me look? A mother who isn't in the least concerned about her daughter's disappearance *after twelve years*? What would people say? I felt I'd done all that I could. I had gone to the police when she first ran away. I got them to talk to Carla. Of course it was me they spoke to, on Carla's mobile phone, but I imitated my daughter's voice and answered all the right questions. Then I told them I was fine but didn't want to come home. I replied to Ellie's barrage of texts and told her more or less the same thing. And I sent myself a postcard from Paris. Was that not enough?

A podcast was out of the question. That's why I asked Nick to break the step that day. Two falls in the space of a couple of weeks might raise the alarm, but a broken piece of wood would make sense. Ellie wouldn't expect me to be up there, since I could barely walk unassisted. Supposedly. I went up silently, I waited for her to finish her video call with the podcast people, and when she came out, I pushed her. I knew it was unlikely she'd die immediately, and I was all set to finish her off by slamming her head against the floor.

But I hadn't expected Meghan, my cleaner, to show up unexpectedly. What was she even doing here? She had no reason to be here, and for a moment I actually considered killing her, too, just for being in the wrong place at the wrong time. She told me later that she couldn't come the next day for some reason, so she wanted to get her cleaning done early.

I started to despair. How could I get rid of Ellie without raising suspicions? A car accident? A hit and run? But we'd already done that with Tracy. Would another hit and run seem suspicious? Maybe Ellie could just disappear. As far as I knew, Ellie had very few friends and no relatives. Certainly nobody that would start a podcast about what really happened to Ellie.

But then Nicky called. 'You'll never believe this woman I just saw.'

FORTY-FIVE

MARJORIE

Nick had gone to London to attend the FitTonePlus franchisees seminar. The way he tells it, he was drinking with others in the hotel bar that first evening when he saw her. She was seated at a table, chatting to a man in a grey suit. He did a double-take. Not quite a 'I thought I'd seen a ghost' double-take, but if he hadn't known better, he would have wondered if that was Carla.

He didn't want to come across as ogling, so he watched her in the mirror behind the bar, all the while chatting to the others. And that's when he saw what she was *really* doing. She'd leant forward, as if to make a point, and her hand had gone from the man's arm, to his shoulder, and in one swift motion, she'd swiped his wallet from his jacket pocket. Nicky couldn't believe what he'd just seen, but he was sure he wasn't mistaken. The woman who looked so much like Carla was a pickpocket.

Nick finished his drink and waited until she was ready to leave to corner her. He offered her a deal: two hours of her time, a nice lunch in the country, and a little role play. 'Nothing kinky, just say your name is Carla and you're my long-lost sister,' he'd said. He'd even throw in five thousand pounds. Not of his own money, of course. Nick doesn't have five thousand pounds lying around, but he knew I'd pay. If she said no, then he'd have no choice but to march her to hotel security and tell them what he'd seen. She still had the wallet in her possession. She would have certainly been arrested.

She chose the lunch.

When Nick called to tell me, I didn't believe for one moment it would work. A complete stranger was to play the role of Carla in front of Ellie? And be convincing enough that Ellie would believe it? It would never work.

'Just meet her,' he'd said. So, I told Ellie I was going to see a specialist for my non-existent nerve pain in London, and I asked her to drive me. I would stay overnight and return with Nick. I thought it was best not to meet overtly, so we agreed to be in Harrods at the same time, on the second floor, in the jewellery section.

Did I think she looked exactly like Carla? Did I get the shock of my life upon seeing her that first time? No. But I agreed with Nick that she could pass as Carla. I still needed to speak to her, however, so I called her later that day.

I asked questions about her background, where she grew up, that sort of thing. I wanted to gauge her voice, her intonation, and her speech mannerisms to see if it could work. She didn't sound like Carla but only in the way nobody aged twenty-eight sounds like they did at sixteen. I believed she would pass. In the end I agreed. Frankly, the thought of *finally* being rid of Ellie and her suspicions was far too tempting not to. Also, I was running out of options.

I was very firm in my instructions. I told her the arrangement would be for two hours only and not one minute more. She would be thoroughly briefed and told *exactly* what to say.

She would not veer from the script. She would never speak of it, and in exchange we would not report her to the police.

Nick would hire a private detective and ask that he put up a Facebook post searching for Carla. Susan would call the number and claim to be Carla. That way, if Susan ever tried to blackmail us later, we could always say we believed she was Carla in good faith, since she called the detective and said so. Just a little insurance.

It was all agreed until the last minute before she was due to come when she changed her mind. Not about the task, but about the money. She asked for ten thousand pounds instead of five. I should have heard the alarm bells ringing, because they certainly were loud and clear. That girl was a grifter through and through. But instead of listening to my doubts, I settled on eight thousand pounds.

And let's face it, she was excellent. Not gushing enough for Ellie's taste, but that was my fault. I told Susan she should be pleased to see Ellie again, surprised to learn that Ellie lived here with Nick, as would be expected of Carla, and overall friendly. But don't be *too* friendly, I'd instructed. You're not going to keep in touch, so don't encourage her. Make it clear that you have moved on with your life and you two are now very different people. Ellie picked up on the missing birthmark, but I'd briefed Susan in case that came up. 'Should anyone ask, just say you had it surgically removed,' I instructed.

It was almost perfect. Or it would have been, if we hadn't forgotten one important detail:

grifters will grift.

I don't know what Susan was expecting when she came to the house, but clearly she was impressed by the size of the property and everything inside. And when stupid Ellie suggested she should stay longer, Susan saw an opportunity to make even more money. Serious money. Never hire a con artist to do a job for you if you don't want to be conned yourself. I've learnt this lesson the hard way. She announced that she would stay a few more days, and she would take the best room, thank you very much. And for her troubles, she'd like another payment – this time twenty-five thousand pounds on top of the eight thousand I'd already agreed to.

I was livid. Nick wanted to throw her out immediately and call off the whole thing. We'd go to the police and accuse Susan of impersonating Carla for money, just like Ellie had said, but I stopped him. 'Think about it. If Ellie doesn't buy it, then she'll never stop looking until she digs up Carla with her bare hands. We don't have much choice.'

I wasn't completely honest with Nick in that moment, because I knew that we had been handed a golden opportunity – one that would solve all our problems once and for all. If Susan wanted to stay, she'd have to earn her keep. And that girl was fulfilling her role to perfection. Frankly, if I'm being honest, I had more in common with Susan than I ever did with my own daughter. All I had to do was remind her at regular intervals by whispering the words in her ear.

You hated her. You were afraid of her. You would do anything to get away from her.

Ellie had no idea what was coming her way.

FORTY-SIX

MARJORIE

It was going swimmingly. In fact, it was almost over, until Ellie found Susan's identification.

I had to think fast. I was in my room lying down on the couch when Nick arrived with a picture of Susan's driver's licence on his phone. He thrust it at me. 'Ellie found this.'

I sat up. 'What? How?'

Behind him, Susan came in. 'I'm sorry. I hid my wallet under the mattress. I didn't think she would—'

'Why did you have it in the first place?' I asked. 'It's not like you needed to drive!'

'I—'

I shushed her with one hand. I needed to think. 'Where's Ellie now?'

'I told her to wait for me outside,' Nick said. 'She's sitting on the steps. I told her not to do anything until I got there.'

I got up and paced the room. 'Why did she go looking under your mattress?' I asked Susan.

She shrugged. 'No idea.'

'I thought the DNA report had settled the issue,' I said.

'So did I,' Nick said. 'I saw her upstairs, I broke it off with her, like you said—'

'How did she take it?' Susan asked.

'Badly, as expected. She got angry, then she cried.'

'So…was she supposed to move out?' Susan asked, frowning. I glanced at Nick. We held each other's gaze for a second or two.

'Something must have happened since,' I murmured, ignoring Susan's question. What we did with Ellie was none of her business. 'I really thought you were smarter than this.' I glared at her.

'Whatever,' she replied. 'So, what do we do now?'

'You have to leave,' I said. 'Immediately.'

'What about the rest of my money? I'm not leaving without my money.'

'You'll get your money.'

She crossed her arms over her chest and looked at me with narrowed eyes. 'Too right I will.'

For a moment I thought Susan would refuse to leave unless I gave her the money right there and then. How was I supposed to do that? I'd already paid her twenty. I didn't have the other thirteen thousand pounds lying around. 'We'll make other arrangements,' I said. 'You'll get your money. You have my word.'

'And your word is worth how much, exactly?'

'Cut it out!' Nick barked.

'We're wasting time,' I said. 'Ellie isn't going to wait forever. She could be calling the police while we're arguing.'

That seemed to put the fear of God into Susan. 'How am I supposed to leave without her noticing? She's outside, you said so yourself. And even if I get out the back way, I don't have a car.'

I nodded to Nick. 'You go and talk to Ellie. Keep her out there.' I turned to Susan. 'I'll get you out of here.'

It wasn't how I'd envisaged the final part of my plan, but I could see how it might work.

The police would come because of what had happened to Karlie. All I needed to do was to make sure the police found Carla's phone among Ellie's things.

The final piece of the puzzle.

And then, we would tell them everything.

Especially about Sophie Bonham.

FORTY-SEVEN
MARJORIE

It was because of Sophie Bonham that Carla died. I know that if anyone ever found out what I did, they would be shocked. *Her own daughter!* But I never could get close to Carla. Whereas Nick had been the perfect baby, angelic and sweet and loving, Carla had felt like she belonged to somebody else. Even in my womb she'd kick and wriggle like she couldn't wait to get out of there. As a baby, if you tried to pick her up she would fight you, her little face scrunched up like a raisin, her arms and legs pushing against you. It was the same as a toddler and all through her childhood. By the time she turned thirteen, we were like strangers passing each other on the stairs.

She loved Joe, I think. She certainly never loved me. Joe said that it was because Nicky and I were too bonded. We were our own little unit that left no room for Carla. But Nicky always wanted to be with me. He wanted to be held and cuddled and sung to. He wanted me to brush his hair, rub his back and kiss his little cheeks. He belonged to me in a way that he never belonged to his father. Then, when Joe died, Carla didn't love anyone any more, until Ellie came along.

I spoilt Nicky. I know that. But what was I supposed to do? It's hard on children when their father dies, and as a mother, you do everything you can to make them a little bit happier. When Nick was seventeen he asked for a car. He was obsessed with cars and couldn't wait to learn to drive. I bought him a Volkswagen midsize SUV in slate grey. My friends all said it was too much – that I should have bought him a cheap second-hand car, or even better, make him work for it. But I just wanted him to be safe. I wanted him to be encased in something that wouldn't collapse like a paper accordion if it hit a tree.

It happened in May. It was raining. Carla was at football practice that night. Nick was dating Sophie Bonham at the time. I didn't like it one bit but Nicky was madly in love. Puppy love, you might say. Sophie was only fifteen so of course that was a concern to me. She would come over to the house sometimes after school and they'd study in his room or listen to music. I always made sure they kept the door open.

'She's too young for you, darling,' I said once, and not for the first time.

'She's only two years younger than me,' he replied, blushing furiously. 'And we're not doing anything, Mum!'

'Fifteen and seventeen isn't the same, Nick. It really isn't.'

He closed the door in my face.

Sophie had been visiting Nick again that afternoon after school. They were together for quite a while, and then I heard raised voices. From him, mostly. I went up a few steps to listen when she came out.

'You're leaving already?' I said.

'Yes,' she replied primly. She'd left her boots in the hall and was about to put them back on.

'It's raining cats and dogs,' I said. 'Let me get my keys and I'll take you home.'

'I'll drive her home, Mum,' Nick said behind me. He'd only had his licence for a few weeks, but I wasn't worried. He was a good driver and they weren't going far.

I was in the living room watching TV when I thought I heard the front door. I looked away from the screen to see Nick standing there, soaked from the rain and dripping water onto the carpet. His trainers and the bottom of his jeans were covered in mud. He was shaking.

My heart sank. 'What happened?'

'It was an accident, Mum, I swear.'

He collapsed next to me on the couch, folding himself against me. He was wailing, his whole body shaking with sobs.

'Shhh…' I whispered. I caressed his hair, his back, just like when he was a little boy. He was crying so hard he couldn't speak. 'Shhh. Just breathe, baby. Everything is fine.' Between shuddering breaths, he told me they'd been fighting. I gathered that she had wanted to take a break.

Good, I thought. Maybe that's all it was. She broke it off and he's upset. Everything is fine.

I was praying that was the case, but deep down I knew whatever had happened between them was much worse than that. I'd never seen Nick in such a state.

'She was screaming for me to stop the car,' he sobbed on my collarbone. 'She kept saying, "*Let me out, let me out!*" Which was stupid because it was raining so much, but I lost it. I hit the brakes, and she got out and started walking in the middle of the road. I kept driving slowly behind her and I told her to get back in the car, that she was being stupid, that she'd get soaked, but she…she kept shouting for me to leave her alone… She didn't even turn around to look at me… And I don't know what happened! I didn't mean to… I don't know how…'

I took his face in my hands. 'Talk to me, Nick. Tell me what happened.'

'I didn't see her, Mum, I swear!'

'Is Sophie hurt?'

'She's… She's dead!'

'Oh god.' I stood up. 'What happened?'

'I don't know! I didn't see her!'

'What do you mean?'

'I turned my headlights off, okay? It was stupid, I know, but she kept shouting at me to leave her alone. I drove behind her anyway. I was really slow, I just wanted to make sure she was getting home safe.'

I shook my head, trying to make sense of what he was saying. 'You turned off the headlights?'

He nodded. 'I know. It was stupid, but she didn't want me to follow her but I did anyway and then…' He dropped his face into his hands. 'I didn't see her, Mum, I swear. She must have stopped walking but I didn't see her and I hit her but not hard, it was an accident!'

He wasn't making any sense. 'You *hit* her? With the SUV?'

'Can you please stop?' he cried, standing up. 'Stop asking me questions! I don't know! I told you! It was an accident!'

'Okay… It's okay, darling.' I wrapped him in my arms. 'It's going to be all right. Have you called the police? Are they on their way? What did they say?' I pulled away and held him by the shoulders. 'Are you sure she's dead? I didn't hear an ambulance. What did they say? I need to call our solicitor. Don't speak to anyone without a solicitor, you understand me? What did the paramedics say?'

'You're not listening to me, Mum! She's fucking dead,

okay? I didn't call anybody! Why should I? She's fucking dead!'

I felt like I'd been slapped. I stood there, in shock, unable to move or speak, my hand over my mouth.

Nick grabbed a fistful of hair. 'What's going to happen to me now?' he wailed. 'I won't go to prison, will I?'

'Where is she?' I said.

'It was an accident, Mum, I swear!'

'Take me to her.'

'Can we say we don't know who did it? We'll say she left and walked home, okay? Can we do that?'

I grabbed his face. 'I need to see her. Take me to her.'

I drove, in his car. I asked him how he knew she was dead. 'I just know, okay? I can tell.'

The weather was foul and there was no one on the road. Not that there would be as only three properties had direct access to this back road. There were no street lights. Nobody uses that road except as a shortcut to our houses.

She was lying on her front in the middle of the road. I stopped the car and ran, praying to god that she was alive, that Nick had been mistaken, but as soon as I reached her, I knew she was dead. Her head was turned to the side, although it was such a mess it took me a moment to see that it was her face turned towards me. Or what was left of it.

Suddenly, Nick was beside me. 'It was an accident.' He was calmer now. 'I should never have turned off the head-lights. I know that.'

'You can't turn off the headlights,' I said in a low voice. He hadn't just bumped into her, he'd *driven* over her. Repeat-edly. I felt sick. The rage with which he'd killed her, battered her down. Did she get out of the car because she was afraid of him? Did he chase her down the road? She must have been absolutely terrified.

'I'm sorry,' he whispered. He pressed the heel of his hand

on the side of his forehead. 'I don't know what…' Then he started hitting himself.

I grabbed his wrist and pulled it down and stared right into his eyes. 'You did this because she wanted to break off the relationship?' I whispered.

He jerked his hand away. 'It was an accident, okay? What am I going to do, Mum? Do I have to go to the police? Should I turn myself in? I'll explain – I'll say I don't know what happened, I got angry… Are they going to put me in prison, Mum?'

I shook my head. 'Nobody's going to prison.' And then, I did what any mother would do. I opened the boot of the car. I told him to pick her up by the shoulders and I lifted her legs. No one was around and we drove home in silence, except for the sound of Nick's sobs.

I knew what needed to be done. The well had been dry, or almost dry, for decades, even before we bought the house. It was so deep you couldn't see all the way down unless you shone a torch down. And even then, all you could see was a pool of water at the bottom. Nobody knew how deep it was.

And nobody would ever find her down there.

FORTY-EIGHT

MARJORIE

The next day, two uniformed officers came to talk to Nick. As it happened, I knew Bill – Inspector Aitken – from my involvement with the Police Benevolent Fund Charity Gala. I always tried to instil that kind of work ethic into my children. If you give your time or money to good causes, it will pay off in spades.

We sat in the living room as Nick told the story we'd rehearsed. He explained to the officers that he and Sophie had fought the previous night because he wanted to break off the relationship. She was very upset. He tried to console her, but she left his room abruptly without saying goodbye and ran down the stairs.

'What time was that?' Aitken asked.

Nick turned to me. 'About six p.m., wasn't it?'

I nodded. 'I came out to see what the commotion was all about,' I said. 'I found her crying in the hall. I offered to drive her home but she refused. She had her boots and her raincoat and insisted she'd be fine. I made her promise that she would take the main road. It's a longer route back to her house, but there are street lights, unlike the back road. She promised me.' I paused and looked towards the window. 'I didn't want her to walk home. I tried to convince her to let me take her. I really tried,' I said. 'But now I wish I'd tried harder.' I turned back to them. 'I've prayed she's all right ever since Gail called last night to ask where Sophie was. Nick and I even drove up and down looking for her in case she'd stumbled and fallen somewhere. We checked both the main road and the back road.'

'You didn't see anything or anyone?'

I shook my head. 'Girls that age can be very impulsive. Maybe she just wants to give us all a scare? She's just hiding somewhere, at a friend's house?'

'It's certainly a possibility we're looking into,' Aitken said gravely.

They asked what happened after Sophie left. This time I let Nick speak.

He told them I called up to him, and he came downstairs and we talked. He told me about the argument he'd just had with Sophie. We talked for maybe twenty minutes, then Nick and I cooked dinner together. Around then, Carla returned from football practice. The three of us ate at the dinner table, and about halfway through the meal the phone rang. It was Sophie's mother.

'That's when Mum and I went looking for her in my car,' he said. He looked so worried, which anyone would have interpreted to be about Sophie.

The two officers closed their notebooks, thanked us and left. Nick was never questioned again. He had an alibi: me. And we'd explained any car tracks on the back road. They had no reason to doubt us, and nobody in their right mind would ever suspect Nick of hurting a fly. He was charming to everyone, the kind of boy who helped elderly women carry their shopping. He was popular at school, he was on the school football team and the rowing team and excelled at both. Everybody loved Nick.

It was just over a year later that Carla came to me. She'd been behaving strangely all evening, refusing to have dinner with us and locking herself in her room. She was such an odd child. Nothing like Nick, who was always present, always charming. In comparison, Carla was dark and sullen. And she hated her brother, no doubt because she was jealous of him.

After dinner, Nick took off in the SUV to see his friends and I was cleaning up in the kitchen when Carla came in. She was white as a ghost. She was holding a silver necklace with a pendant in the shape of an angel.

'What is it?' I asked.

'Is Nick gone?'

'Yes, he went out. Why?'

Her bottom lip wobbled. 'I think she's down there, Mum.'

Honestly, after a whole year, I'd near enough forgotten about Sophie. The news headlines had moved on, neighbours had long stopped talking about her, the consensus was that she'd run away because she was upset about the breakup with Nick. So when Carla said that, I had no idea what she was talking about.

'What's down there?'

'I found this—' she held up the necklace '—by the well. It's Sophie's.'

'Don't be ridiculous,' I snapped, but my heart was racing. Carla started to cry. 'There's a smell down there, a horrible smell—'

'That's the sewage pipes. You know that. I had it fixed. There's no smell now.'

She was shaking. 'I had a look.'

'A look where?'

'In the well…'

It was all I could do to keep myself together. I picked up tins of chickpeas and put them on a shelf. 'For goodness' sake, Carla. The well is covered. How could you possibly look in there?'

'I pushed the lid…'

'And why would you do that?' I snapped. She looked startled. I made myself soften. 'I mean,' I said, more gently this time, 'it's dangerous. That's why Nick covered it.'

I should have bolted it. The problem was I didn't have the equipment and I was hardly going to hire a tradesman to do it for me. Nick and I found a piece of metal in the shed big enough to cover the opening, but there was only so much he could do to secure it. I kept telling myself that I should get the right tools and do it properly, but frankly I didn't know where to start.

'But why now, Mum?'

'What do you mean?'

'Why would Nick cover it *now*? It was more dangerous when we were kids. Don't you think that's strange?'

I was breathing too hard. I made myself calm down. 'Carla,' I said gently. I never called her darling, or sweetheart or any other endearment, the way I did with Nicky. I put my hand out. 'Let me have a look at that necklace.'

'It's Soph's, Mum. She wore it all the time. I'm telling you, I looked, and she's down there…'

'Give it to me, Carla.'

She handed it to me. I put it in my purse.

'We have to call the police!' she whined. 'I think Nick did it, Mum! He's not right in the head! I think Nick did something to her and I think she's down there and we have to call—'

I slapped her, hard. I just wanted to shut her up. Stop

253

talking. Be quiet. Stop this nonsense. I stood there, shaking, and the way she looked at me then, with her hand cupping her cheek, her eyes wide, I could tell that she understood that I already knew. She turned on her heels and ran upstairs to her room. I ran after her. She locked herself in with the bolt. I stood on the other side of the door. 'Listen to me, Carla. You don't know what you're saying. You're imagining things.'

I heard her voice, but it was too low to know what she was saying, and I realised she was on the phone. For a horrible, horrible moment, I thought she was calling the police so I slammed my hand hard against the door. 'Open the door!'

But then I heard her say, 'Ellie.' She was talking to Ellie. What was she saying to her? I banged and banged on the door and suddenly, it opened. Carla had her guitar, a travel bag and was wearing her jacket. She pushed me and ran past me to the front door. I ran after her but she was too fast.

I rang Nick on his mobile. 'It's your sister. She knows about Sophie and the well. She's ran off.'

'I'll get her,' he said.

I don't remember exactly what happened next. All I have now are snatches of memory I can't quite get hold of, the kind that linger after you've woken from a nightmare. Nick came home. He'd found her, like he said he would. He'd bundled her into the car.

'She's in the car?' I cried.

'She's not going anywhere.'

'What do you mean?'

He didn't even pretend to be upset. He said no one saw them. He had his hand over her mouth. And then he strangled her.

'What choice did I have?' he snapped. 'She knew about Sophie. You said so yourself.'

I screamed. I remember that. I screamed and screamed

and pounded his chest with my fists. 'What's wrong with you?' I said over and over. 'What the hell is wrong with you?'

He held my wrists so tightly I had bruises for days. 'No, Mum,' he said, his face an inch from mine. 'What's wrong with *you?*' And to this day, I don't know whether he meant because I couldn't see the trouble we were in now that Carla knew or because it was my idea to put Sophie down the well.

We stood there, staring at each other. 'How did you get her in the car?' I asked finally.

'I pulled her by the hair. She wasn't going to come willingly, if that's what you're asking.'

'Did anyone see you?'

'No. I saw Ellie coming out of the back road so I went down there and that's where I found Carla. I think she was on her way to the station. There was no one else around.'

'What about Ellie, could she have seen you?'

'No. She was going in the opposite direction. She was gone by the time I drove down there.'

And so, we put Carla down the well, too. I kept her phone. I read all of Ellie's texts and answered her, once. I gave the police Carla's mobile number and, when they called her, I pretended to be Carla. I answered all their questions. I said I was fine, I was living in Liverpool and I didn't want to come home.

For the next twelve years, I played the role of the concerned but resigned mother. And still, Ellie wouldn't let it go. Crazy jealous obsessed Ellie who desperately wanted to be Carla and hated Sophie enough to kill her.

Or that's how the story will go. Nobody will pick up Karlie and Mrs Lopez will call me. I'll be terribly worried and call the police. I'll say how awful Ellie looked the last time I saw her and the strange things she was saying. We'll find the note together – her suicide note. *I've joined the others...* We'll find the well open, and we'll look down there.

And then we'll understand the terrible, terrible things that Ellie has done to this family.

FORTY-NINE

ELLIE

My face hits water. My lungs are burning, my breath is trapped inside my mouth. Black water. Pain. Excruciating pain. Dots of light dancing in front of my eyes. Panic. Excruciating pain on the back of my head. Everything goes bright, like an explosion inside my brain. Then black.

I can't breathe.

I stand up like an arrow, coughing up a lungful of water and gasping for air. The water is only three feet deep, maybe four. Above me, the opening seems like a hundred feet away.

Marjorie is looking down at me.

'You wanted to know where Carla is? Take a good look around, sweetheart. That's right. There she is. Say hello to your friend.'

And that's when I see the skull bobbing next to me, and I scream. I scream as I stand among bones. I'm screaming so hard my ears are burning, my throat is on fire, my skin is scraping against the brickwork as I try to get away. 'Let me out! Let me out!!!!'

'I can't do that, sweetheart. You know that. How could I possibly get you out? And why should I? You left a suicide note. Or it will be once I tear off the other part. What was it you said? "*I've joined the others. I know it's the right thing to do. I'm sorry.*" You couldn't live with yourself any more, you poor thing. The police were about to arrest you. Everybody knows you're crazy, you're a stalker, you're insane and you killed little Sophie, and you dragged her here and threw her in the well. Yes. She's with you, too. The three of you together again. I'll tell the police I found the note and I went out and looked for you. I was so worried! But I couldn't find you. By the time someone does, it'll be a few days. I'm taking Nick on a little holiday tomorrow morning. To Brighton. We need a bit of sea air to recover from the horrors of the last few days. We won't be back for at least a fortnight. Enjoy whatever time you have left with your little friends, Ellie.'

'No, no! Don't leave me here! I'll say whatever you want me to. I'll tell the police I did it. Please! You can't leave me here! What about Karlie? What will happen to my baby?'

'Karlie will be fine. I'll call her father at the college. She has a father, after all. He can take care of her. Goodbye, Ellie. Please don't worry. It will be over before you know it.'

'No, no, no, no!!! Wait! Marjorie, I'm begging you! Don't leave me here!!'

But she's gone.

FIFTY

I'm still screaming even though I know there's no one to hear me. But still I scream until my lungs burn, because all I can think about is Karlie, my baby girl, my perfect child, and I have to do something, I have to get out of here, I have to get to her. My nails break as I try to climb the wall. I can't get a purchase. My fingers are bleeding. I can't even get a foot off the ground before falling back on top of Carla's and Sophie's bobbing bones and I'm flailing, twisting in the water to get away from them.

I sob, my face in my hands. What's the point of screaming anyway? Nobody can hear me. Even Marjorie will be back at the house by now. It will get dark soon, and I won't be able to see a thing. At least I won't be able to see Carla's and Sophie's bones.

I'm going to die here, with Carla and Sophie, or whatever is left of them. And everyone will think I killed them.

Even Karlie.

It's all my fault. It's my fault Carla died. I should have stopped her from running away. I touch the side of the skull.

'I'm sorry I wasn't there for you. I'm sorry I let you down. I should have gone with you and—'

'We'd both be dead.'

Where did that voice come from? I look up. There's a silhouette against the sky. Somebody's there, looking down.

'Marjorie? Oh god, Marjorie, you came back. Thank you! Help me out. I won't say anything I swear to god—'

'It's not Marjorie,' the voice hisses. 'It's me. Carla.'

I'm dead. I must be since I'm talking to ghosts now. I lean against the wall and drop my face into my hands. Is this what hell is? This well? Will I be here for eternity talking to Carla's ghost?

'Ellie! It's me. Susan Williams wasn't real. It's me. It's Carla. It's always been me.'

'No. No, no, no. You're trying to trick me. I know Susan Williams isn't Carla.'

'Ellie. We don't have much time so listen up. We broke your dad's lamp when we practised line dancing in your living room, and we hid the pieces in the shed. On your eleventh birthday, you kissed Jacob at the school dance and then worried you might be pregnant. You can ride a bike standing up, but I could never do it. Sometimes I faint at the sight of blood. We used to measure our height, and I was always exactly one inch taller. You've got a scar on your right knee from when we went rollerblading on the roof of the gym. I've got a scar on my left knee from when I fell out of the tree—'

'Caramello?'

'Yes.'

'But you can't be! You're a ghost! You're dead. You're… right here! Next to me.'

'I'm not, Ellie. That's Soph.'

'Oh god. But… but you're here, too! I know you are! She told me.'

'Trust me. I'm not. Also, there's only one body. One skull. Whatever's down there. Unless they killed someone else I don't know about…'

I'm going to be sick. I didn't exactly do a head count, but I'm pretty sure I only saw one skull. 'I don't understand what's happening.'

'I got out, and you will too. I'm going to tell you how.'

FIFTY-ONE

I am down on my hands and knees, completely submerged in dark, dirty water. I am in so much pain, I don't know how I'm going to do this.

I make my way around the perimeter, just like she said to do. And then I see it. Or rather, I feel it. It's a kind of tunnel opening, a hole full of water at the bottom of the well wall. I stand up and wipe the dirty, muddy water out of my eyes.

'I found it.'

'Good. You should only be in water for twenty feet or so. Go on. Big breath. I love you. See you on the other side.'

Big breath.

I am completely swallowed up in dark, muddy water and within seconds, I no longer know which way is up. The water is so thick I can't keep my eyes open. If I don't die here, and I very much expect to, then I'll absolutely die of cholera or typhoid or something shockingly horrible within five minutes of getting out.

It's all I can do not to panic. I'm crawling through a muddy hole that might have been wide enough for skinny sixteen-year-old Carla but is clearly not for me. At least there's only one way to go, so I can't get lost. I console myself with that thought as I crawl on my elbows, pushing water that has nowhere to go out of the way. Twenty feet, she said. *Come on, Ellie. Woman up. Twenty feet. You can do this.*

And then I get stuck.

I can't see, but I can feel tree roots that have pierced through the pipe. The opening is too narrow and somehow I've wedged myself. I fold my arms against my chest, my hands gripping my shoulders, but there's literally no wriggle room. My shoulders are stuck against roots and every time I try to push forward, my skin gets shredded.

Don't panic. I can do this. *Come on, Silly-Ellie. Think of Karlie. You have to get to Karlie.*

I wriggle my body forward by an inch. The pain in my head from being hit – what the hell did Marjorie hit me with anyway? A rock? – is excruciating. I scraped the skin down my leg on the way down and it stings like hell. The more I twist, the more I get stuck. I try to move backwards, but I can't. I have nothing to grip. My chest is starting to convulse from a lack of air. Swirls of sparks move against my eyes, black dots dancing among them. My lungs are on fire, my throat is closing and I want to scream for Karlie because I really am going to die and *God, Karlie, I love you so much, I'm so sorry I messed up, I love you so much—*

Something is happening. Against my closed eyelids, a light. I open them just a sliver. A narrow beam, a little way ahead. Is it real? Am I dreaming? Am I dead?

A hand. Two hands. They're grabbing my shoulders and they're pulling me through and I'm kicking and twisting and my lungs are on fire and suddenly…

Air.

I cough up water and mud, swallow gulps of stale, dusty, mouldy air which tastes like heaven. I drag myself the rest of the way in the dark. There's dim light now, and the last part is a vertical shaft. Carla has to wriggle around to push herself out of it, then she helps me out, too, and I fall out of the hole onto a tiled floor.

I'm on my hands and knees, panting and coughing. Carla does the same. At some point, I don't know how, we fall into each other's arms, laughing and crying. 'Is it really you?' I croak.

'Yes. It's me. I'm so sorry about everything. I missed you so much…'

I wipe tears off my cheek. 'I haven't at all. Never gave you a second thought.'

She smiles, makes a face and cracks a sob as she pulls me into a hug.

FIFTY-TWO

'Where are we?' I ask, trying to get my bearings.

'In the old scullery.'

'That squat little building behind the house?'

'Yes.'

'Jesus.'

'They used to pump the water into here. It's all gone now, only the old shaft is left.'

'I had no idea that led to the well.'

'Nobody did.'

No. They wouldn't.

I push a strand of hair off her face. 'What happened to you? Why did you stay away all these years?'

She tells me a story that I can barely follow. Nick killed Sophie, Marjorie knew and did nothing, and Carla ran away, but Nick caught her and strangled her. Or he thought he did. She came to when she hit the water in the well. They thought she was dead. She wasn't. She got out, just like she showed me. She ran away with nothing. No phone, no ID, no wallet, nothing. She started from scratch. She met lots of

265

shady people over the years. Her fake ID is good, but it's still fake. She could never get a passport or travel overseas.

'But why didn't you tell the police?'

'I tried that. I called anonymously and told them Sophie was in the well and that Nick had killed her and Mum had covered it up. The police laughed. They thought it was a prank. They hung up on me.' She shrugs. 'You've met Marjorie. She's a pillar of the community.'

I shudder. 'But how do you live? Do you work?'

She looks at me. 'I'm a thief, essentially. A con artist, a pickpocket. I'll do anything. Card tricks, hacking, whatever. I only steal from people who deserve it, by the way. I'm good at it.' She stares at me, as if waiting for me to disapprove. I take her hand.

'You did what you had to do.'

She nods. 'I was starting to relax. I figured they'd never look down the well now, and they'd never notice I wasn't there after all, or that there was a way out. Then one day Nick showed up at the hotel where I was doing a job on a guy who sold opioids for a living. He was part of a sales workshop on how to push their products on doctors who'd then push it on their patients, so he deserved to have his wallet stolen and his credit cards maxed out. And normally I'm good, but seeing Nick threw me off my game. He saw me and offered a deal in exchange for not telling security about what I was doing. As if I'd care. I wasn't going to do it, obviously, but I pretended to go along with it. Then Marjorie mentioned you, that you were living with them and engaged to Nick, and I knew. I just knew. They were up to something and you were not safe.' She raises one shoulder. 'So I came.'

I stare at her, tears burning the inside of my nose. 'You came for me?'

'They would have eaten you alive,' she says.

'But why didn't you tell me?'

'Oh, Ellie! I wanted to, so much, but I didn't trust you to keep it to yourself. They would have killed us. The both of us. They would have shot us and thrown us down that well. For good this time. I had to try and get you out first. I tried to warn you. I wanted to make you leave, to get you out of the house somehow because then I could explain. But in that house? I was terrified you'd tell Nick. Do you have any idea how insane Nick is? He's always been evil. I tried to tell my mother, but she never believed me. Nobody did. He was so good at looking like the perfect child in front of other people. I found knives under his mattress, once. I don't know what he did with them, but one time, the farmer up on the hill said two of his goats had been stabbed and someone had broken into his house and stolen cash. I was sure it was Nick. Trust me. He was nuts.

'But you never told me any of this, when we were kids, I mean.'

'I was terrified of him. He's a psychopath, Ellie.'

'Well, I know that now. He's been setting me up for Sophie's murder.'

'And mine. And make you look like you were crazy. They told everyone in town about you. That you were insanely jealous. That you hated me. That they were worried about your mental state.' Her face softens. 'I'm sorry, Jellybean. I really did try and make you leave.'

'The note on my windscreen, was that you?'

She nods. 'I didn't think you'd stay if you thought your wonderful Nick was shagging someone else.'

'Yes, well, clearly you don't know me very well,' I say drily.

She smiles. 'I did try. That's why I was so mean to you. I mean, other than the fact they wanted me to be.'

'Well, you nailed that part of the assignment,' I say. 'I

almost got arrested for your murder, you know. Just saying. Yours and Sophie's.'

'I would have bailed you out.'

'Oh, thank you so much. Quick question. When did you plan to do that? Because I had to sit through two hours of police interviews basically learning all the ways in which I'd killed Sophie and stalked Nick and killed you.'

'I would have told them everything eventually!'

'When? On my third appeal? After I'd languished in a horrible rat-infested prison for a hundred years?'

She clicks her tongue. 'You always exaggerate. I would have got you out after twenty.'

I laugh. And then I think of something. 'Is that why you kept saying they should bulldoze the property and start again? Sell it to a developer?'

She bursts out laughing. 'I wanted to see their faces! I mean, I had to come up with something to make it legit that I wanted to stay. They just thought I wanted more money, but I loved seeing them squirm whenever I mentioned selling the place! I actually made a tidy sum out of this.' She laughs.

I laugh too. 'You owe me!' I punch her arm lightly. 'I gave Nick twenty-thousand pounds for his gym. I bet that's the money he gave you.'

'Oh, I made more than twenty grand,' she says. 'So I'll totally pay you back.' And we're still laughing. I don't know why, but that's what we used to do. We'd start laughing, and then we couldn't stop.

But then she grows serious.

'I had to run away when you found my ID. I'm sorry I scared you with Karlie. I was really careful with her, I promise. It was Marjorie's idea to get Karlie out of the house to cause a diversion, but I would never, ever hurt Karlie in any way.'

'I know. You made sure she had a cardigan and slippers.'

'Where is she, by the way?'

'With Mrs Lopez. She's safe.' I tilt my head at her. 'But I thought you'd left? I saw the taxi at the end of the road.'

'I only went half a mile and came back through the woods.'

The inside of my nose stings. I don't know if it's impending tears or because I inhaled filthy, disease-ridden deadly water. I stare at her dirty, mud-caked face. 'You came back for me, again?'

'Of course not,' she says. 'I came back for Karlie.'

I laugh. And something in her eyes, in the glint of the moonlight, makes me twig.

I grab her hand. 'Oh my god! You have children!'

She holds up one finger. 'One. A girl. She's eight.'

'Oh wow, that's wonderful. What's her name?'

A beat. 'Ella.'

I blink about a million times, then tilt my head at her. 'You named your child after me? Of all the names you could pick?'

She mirrors my tilt of the head. 'It's with an "a", not an "i.e.", so no, not the same at all.'

'That's so creepy!' I say, but I have my hands over my mouth and I don't know whether to laugh or cry. For a moment we are twelve again, we are thirteen, fourteen, fifteen years old. All those times when we could finish each other's sentences, when we always knew what the other was thinking, when one look could send us into spasms of laughter. I stare at her, my eyes filling with tears, my heart expanding like a balloon. 'I'm so happy for you, that you have a daughter. And does Ella have a dad? One who's around, I mean?'

She smiles. 'Oh yes. He's around.'

'What's his name?'

'John. Smith.'

'Bullshit.'

'No, it's true.'

I laugh. 'Don't tell me he's a property mogul!' I half shriek.

'He's a painter and decorator,' she says. 'He paints houses.'

'Oh that's so great! I love painters and decorators!'

She laughs. 'He's great, he really is. He's wonderful.' She makes a face. 'He thinks my name is Susan Williams and that I sell insurance.' She shakes her head. 'Listen. We have to go to the police. Right now. We'll tell them about Soph and that we know Nick killed her and Marjorie covered it up.'

I scrape my teeth over my bottom lip. 'I can't.'

She grabs my hand. 'We can. You're not in that house any more. They can't do anything to you. They won't be able to pin Sophie's murder on you now because I can prove who I really am and tell them everything. As long as we stay away from the two of them, we will be safe. But we have to do it now.'

She crosses her legs and hoists herself upright.

I look up at her. 'I've got a problem.'

FIFTY-THREE

'You killed him?' she blurts.

'I didn't mean to. It was an accident. I was in the attic and I found your guitar and Sophie's necklace—'

'The necklace!' she cuts in. 'That's what I was looking for! Mum – God I hate calling her that – Marjorie took it from me that night. I thought she might have kept it in case it came in useful later because that's how she thinks.'

'Well, it looks like she gave it to Nick. I found it among his things. Wait. Is that why you were in my room that first day?'

'I was looking for it. I've been looking for that necklace everywhere. I thought if I could take it to the police it would help. Do you still have it?'

'I…' I get up and rummage through my pocket. I find it and pull it out.

'You're a genius,' she whispers. She looks back at me. 'What happened in the attic?'

'Oh, god, Carla! He was there! He admitted to killing Sophie, then he said you were collateral damage. I got so enraged, I don't know what happened but one minute he was

271

standing there and the next I'd picked up one of his stupid dumbbells and...he's dead.'

Her eyes are big and round like dinner plates. 'You left him there?'

'I pulled a bit of carpet over him.'

She slaps her hands over her mouth. 'And you're sure he's dead?'

I nod again. 'Positive.'

'What if Marjorie goes up there...' she muses.

'She can't get up there. She can barely make it up the normal stairs.'

She shoots me a look. 'She faked her fall. You know that, right?'

I blink at her. 'Really?'

'Everything they've done or said is a lie, Ellie. All of it.'

I nod. 'I knew that. It's been so sudden...'

My heart breaks. Again. Of course I heard what Marjorie said while I was crying at the bottom of the well, but I hadn't thought about anything else since. I didn't exactly have the opportunity. Now, the prospect of having to unpick months of closeness and affection... 'I thought she was like a mother to me.'

'Yeah, well, I told you. They're psychopaths. They don't care about anyone.' She takes in a sharp breath.

'What is it?' I ask.

A branch rattles against the window in the wind. I gasp.

'Come on,' she says. 'We have to get out of here.'

I nod, wiping my nose with the back of my hand. 'What are we going to do?'

'We need to come up with a plan.' She tries to think. 'If Nick is dead, then Marjorie will pin it all on him. She'll say she had no idea. It will be our word against hers.'

I wrap my arms around my knees. 'Do you think I'll go to prison? I think I should call Bee. Tell her to go and pick up

Karlie. I don't want Karlie to live with her dad. He never gave a shit about—'

'Listen to me. You won't go to prison. It was self-defence.'

'Well…not really.'

'Trust me. It was.'

'Okay.'

'But I don't want Marjorie to get away with it.' She nods to herself. 'I have an idea.'

We sit there, on the hard floor, while she tells me her idea.

'It's never, ever going to work,' I say.

'It will.'

'It's too crazy.'

'Trust me. I know her. It will work. And anyway, it's all we've got.'

I take a breath. 'Okay, then.' I push myself upright. 'Let's get started.'

Carla's hair and clothes are still dripping wet, as are mine. I pick up twigs and bits of leaves off the floor, off me, and weave them through Carla's hair. I rearrange it to make it even more limp, pulling strands over her face. There are blobs of mud at our feet and I pick some up and stick it up one of her nostrils. She laughs. I smear some on her face. She scrunches her eyes.

'You look absolutely terrifying,' I say.

'That's what we want.'

'Do that thing you used to do with your eyes.'

'What thing?'

'You know.' I roll my own eyes up to demonstrate, but I could never do it like Carla could. She lets out a bark of laughter.

'Okay, your turn,' I say.

She rolls her eyes all the way back so that only the white is showing.

'That is so freaky,' I whisper. And she laughs, like she used to. A big cackle that bursts out of her, followed by jerks of her shoulders, punctuated by a series of snorts. Honestly, if she'd laughed like that when she was pretending to be Susan, I would have known within a nanosecond that she was Carla.

'I'm going to get my phone. I left it in the treehouse with the rest of my stuff.'

We crawl through the window and into the night air. It's dark now, with only the moonlight shining through the trees. I've seen that window a dozen times and always wondered where it led to. Now I know. The old scullery.

Within minutes Carla is back with her phone. We bend down and scurry back to the house. The light is on in Marjorie's living room and the curtains are only half closed. We pause for a second, crouched below the window. Inside, Marjorie is leaning against the closed door, one ankle crossed over the other, one arm loosely wrapped around her waist. She's holding her phone up to her ear but she's not speaking. No cane in sight.

'She certainly doesn't look like a frail old lady,' I whisper.

'I told you,' Carla whispers back.

I think of how much love and affection I lavished on Marjorie, believing with all my heart it was reciprocated. I think of the many times I carefully unwrapped her bandages before gently massaging cream into her hands and feet. I think of how I became her personal chauffeur, cleaner, cook, bed maker and hair stylist, believing she couldn't do these things for herself.

Oh, and then she tried to kill me.

'Time to go,' Carla whispers. I nod. We scurry to the

back door of the house and carefully open it. Down the corridor, Marjorie's door is ajar.

'Please call me back when you can, Nicky, darling. I'm getting worried,' we hear her say.

Carla tilts her head towards Marjorie's door. I nod, then point to the ceiling.

'I'll wait for you upstairs,' I mouth. I have to get my handbag and phone, which I've left in my bedroom. The plan is that once Carla has finished, we're calling the police.

Carla pushes the door to Marjorie's rooms.

'Oh, Nicky, there you—'

I pause, one foot on the bottom step.

'Hello, Mother,' Carla says, in a voice that sounds like it's being beamed directly from the afterlife.

Marjorie screams.

FIFTY-FOUR

I didn't think it was going to work. I thought Marjorie would hit Carla with her cane. I thought we should fight her together. Two against one.

But as Carla pointed out, that would not achieve what we wanted. For one thing, it would have added the charge of assault on top of the murder I'd already committed. Considering all the clues out there that made me look like a deranged killer, I was getting quite the rap sheet.

'I know her,' Carla had replied. 'Trust me. It will work.'

And so, Carla appeared to her mother as a ghost. A ghost with an iPhone in her back pocket, set to record every word Marjorie said. Carla would ask her about Sophie, and then she'd ask about me. As far as Marjorie knew, I was still screaming down the well. Whatever Marjorie said to Carla would support my claim that I'd killed Nick in self-defence. I would tell the police that when I killed him, I feared for my life. It would have been true, eventually – I have no doubt about that.

I start up the stairs, slowly, quietly, stopping to listen occasionally.

I'm sorry, please forgive me! I had no choice! I had to protect him!

'Why did you kill Sophie, Mother?' Carla asks in her haunting voice. She is so convincing, there's a moment where I wonder maybe she is a ghost. Maybe it's me she fooled back there.

'I didn't! I swear to God, Carla. That was Nick. I only helped him—'

I leave them to it and go into my room. I wash my face in the bathroom. The rest of me is shockingly disgusting but I don't have time to shower. And anyway, I want the police to see me like this. I get my phone from my bag then return to the hallway where Carla's haunting voice is still bouncing against the walls. 'You will rot in hell for this, Mother!'

I have to say, Carla was always a good actress, but this performance is outstanding.

Marjorie gives a strangled scream, then nothing. A beat of silence, then a loud thud. I spring to lean over the balustrade. Carla's face is looking up at me.

'What happened?'

'She fainted.' She holds up her phone. 'Wait till you hear it. Trust me, I didn't think she could shock me, but she did.' She slips the phone back into her back pocket. 'Come on, let's go. Let's take this to the police.'

'I'm coming down,' I say. I get out my phone to call Mrs Lopez. I'm going to ask her to keep Karlie overnight. There's no way on earth I want Karlie here.

'Mrs Lopez, it's Ellie.'

'Oh, Ellie. How—?'

That's when I see it. A blood stain on the floor. I look down at myself to see where I'm bleeding from, but all I can see is dirt and mud.

'Hello? Ellie? Are you there?'

There's another one, one step below, even larger. I bend

down to touch it. It's wet. Again, I scan my body to see where it's coming from.

'Ellie, what's wrong?' Carla asks from below.

I look at the back of my legs, and that's when I see more blood trailing down the hallway.

'Hello?'

But I haven't been down there.

I drop the phone and run to the attic trapdoor. It's shut. I pull it down so hard the ladder almost decapitates me.

No. no, no, no. Surely not. No.

'What's happening?' Carla shouts behind me. I scramble up the ladder and flick the light switch. I push the carpet hard, even though it's already pretty obvious.

He's not there.

'What's going on?' Carla says from below.

I clamber back down. 'He's gone.'

'Gone?' Her hand flies to her mouth. 'I thought you said he was dead?'

'I was wrong.' My phone is still on the floor. I run for it and snatch it up. 'Mrs Lopez? Are you there?'

'Yes. Is everything all right?'

'Is Karlie there?'

'No. Nick just picked her up.' Then she adds, 'He didn't look too good. I was a bit concerned.'

How did he know? How could he have known that Karlie was there? But then I remember. I told Marjorie before Nick drove her to the police station.

I fly down the stairs on legs that feel like they're made of jelly. 'It's Nick!' I blurt at Carla. 'He's got Karlie!'

'What? How—?' She stops and turns around abruptly. 'Listen.' She pauses. 'A car.'

She's right. I heard it too. Tyres on gravel.

Behind her the front door opens.

It's Nick. He's holding Karlie's hand.

'Oh, god. Karlie.' I run to her but Nick points his finger at me. 'Stop right there!'

I stop in my tracks. The expression on his face is of pure hate. He's wearing a cap and there's dried blood on his temple. His face is white, his eyes are bloodshot, his mouth is set into a thin line.

Karlie's chin wobbles. 'Mummy?'

I feel a wave of dizziness come over me. I think of what Carla said earlier. *He's a psychopath, Ellie.* I'm still holding the phone which I bring back to my ear. 'Call—'

The front door slams shut.

'Hang up the phone, Ellie, or I swear to god—'

Karlie screams.

FIFTY-FIVE

Nick has slapped his hand over Karlie's mouth.

'Nick, let her go.' I put my hand out to him. 'Please, Nick. You're scaring her.'

'I will break her in half if you don't say something nice to Mrs Lopez and hang up the phone,' he says in a low voice.

I nod quickly. 'Yes. I'm doing it now.' I bring the phone to my ear but I'm shaking so much that I drop it. I scramble to pick it up. 'Everything is fine, Mrs Lopez, thank you.' I hang up and give him the phone. He shoves it in his back pocket, then he takes his cap off and throws it on the floor.

Carla looks paralysed at the sight of him. Or maybe because his hair on one side is matted with dark blood. Carla can't handle blood.

I extend my hand again. 'Let me have Karlie.'

'No.'

He takes his hand off Karlie's mouth and picks her up. She screams at the top of her lungs, limbs flailing. 'Mummy!'

'It's okay, sweetie. Mummy's here,' I say, as if that could possibly make any difference to the horror that's unfolding. 'Give her to me, please, Nick.'

'I said no. What do you take me for?' He hoists her over his shoulder and strides to the kitchen.

'What are you doing?' I shout, running after him.

'Nick, what are you doing?' Carla cries.

He opens the kitchen drawer and rummages through it.

I'm screaming, my hands reaching for Karlie. She's screaming, too, her eyes wide with fear. Carla is shouting. 'Let her go! What are you going to do?'

There are dots dancing in front of my eyes. I am so scared I think I'm going to pass out. I know now what this monster is capable of, and I don't know what he's going to pull out. Scissors? A knife?

Nick finds what he's looking for and slaps his hand over Karlie's mouth again. 'Shut up, Ellie!' he shouts. 'Just shut up!'

Carla grabs my arm. I stop screaming.

'It's okay,' she says. But it's not. Not by a long shot. But thank god it's not a weapon that Nick has found in the drawer. It's a bunch of keys. Still with one hand over Karlie's mouth, he strides back out of the room.

'What are you going to do?'

'I'm not going to hurt her,' he says. He opens the door to the utility room and flicks the switch. Then he puts Karlie down but still holds onto her, both hands on her shoulders. 'Just stay in there until I come and get you,' he tells her.

'Mummy!!!' she screams.

'It's okay, sweetie,' I say over his shoulder. 'Just wait in there, okay? Everything is going to be fine.'

Then he locks the door.

Karlie is still screaming, trying to kick the door down.

'Just wait, sweetie,' I say, trying to sound soothing, even though my throat is so tight with fear I can barely get the words out. But it doesn't matter. She's so loud, she couldn't possibly hear me anyway.

Nick lets out a breath, pushing the fingers of one hand through his hair. 'Let's go in there,' he says, jerking his chin towards Marjorie's rooms.

I glance at the utility room once more. I can't move. I can't bear to leave her in there, screaming, but Carla pulls at my sleeve.

'I'll be right back, sweetie!' I shout. She stops screaming. I stare at the door, frozen.

'Come on,' Carla says softly. There's a split second when Nick has his back to us as he pushes Marjorie's door open, and Carla does something with her hip, a little sideways jerk, then tilts her head down and sideways, her eyes trained on me. If there was a less discrete way to get my attention, I don't know what it is.

I look down at her hip. Protruding from the belt of her jeans is a small silver rectangle, like the top of a... I blink, then stare at her, eyes wide, mouth agape. *Knife handle?*

She pulls at my arm, and I follow her inside Marjorie's living room, and find Marjorie crouched in the corner, her arms wrapped tightly around her legs. She stands shakily at the sight of Nick.

'Nick!' she whines. 'I've been so frightened! What's going on, Nicky? Oh, god! What happened to your head? Are you hurt?' And I'm thinking, you're not just a horrible woman, you're also the biggest coward. You heard Karlie screaming at the top of her lungs, and you thought, *mmm...What should I do now? I know, I'll huddle in the corner*.

Marjorie turns to Carla and starts to shake, her mouth open in a silent wail.

'Oh, stop crying, Mother,' Nick snaps. 'She's not a ghost.'

Marjorie closes her mouth. 'What?'

He slams the door shut and turns to Carla. 'I heard everything you said back there. Everything.'

I think of that branch, the rattling in the wind. Except it wasn't the wind. It was Nick, next to the window, listening to us.

He tilts his head at Carla. 'So you got out. All these years I thought you were in there.'

Marjorie looks at Carla. 'Out?'

'She's not a ghost, Mum. She's Susan, except she's not. She's always been Carla. She's the one who tricked us all.' He puts out his hand towards Carla. 'Give me your phone.'

"I-I don't have it.'

'Cut it out, Carla! You recorded everything. I heard you. Give me the phone!'

'Give him the phone, Carla!' I shout.

Carla thrusts it at him. He takes it and fiddles with the screen.

I'm so sorry, Carla, I'm so sorry—

He holds up the phone to his mother. 'I can't believe you fell for this.' He taps the screen, then drops the phone on the floor and smashes it with his foot, over and over. Even when the phone has broken into pieces and you couldn't possibly use it to make a call, or for any reason whatsoever, he keeps going, letting out a little grunt with each whack.

'I want to get Karlie,' I say, my voice cracking. 'We'll leave, right now. You'll never hear from us again. I promise.'

'Don't be stupid, Ellie. Nobody's going anywhere.' He closes his eyes for a second. 'Everybody be quiet. I have to think.' Another second, and he opens his eyes again. He points his finger at me.

'You are going back into the well. Now, obviously, there's a way out, so you'll have to swallow some sleeping pills first. But the whole suicide note stands.'

'Nick, please…'

'And you'll have to take Karlie with you.'

I shake my head. 'No. Don't say that.'

'She's seen too much.'

'You said you weren't going to hurt her!'

'I lied.'

'Oh, god. Nick, listen to me. She's a child. She's not going to say anything. She has no idea what's going on here!'

'Honestly, Ellie, you have to be quiet. I mean it. You're getting on my nerves.' He looks at Carla. 'And you have to die.' He frowns and rubs the back of his neck. 'We can't get you in the well because Ellie here is going to commit suicide by jumping in, and when they find you both... Well, she's supposed to have killed you twelve years ago and you're obviously pretty fresh, so...'

Then he raises his arms and lets them fall. 'What am I saying? The solution of my problem is right in front of my eyes!' He turns to me. 'Carla escaped the well, just like she said, but she didn't escape me, she escaped you. Then she came back when she heard you were living here to warn us, me and Mum, but she pretended to be someone else so you wouldn't hack her into pieces, but you found out anyway, and you did kill her. And then you killed yourself. It's perfect.' He lets out a satisfied sigh. 'You both have to die. Right now.'

A sharp movement to my right. 'Oh god.' Carla has whipped out the knife – it was indeed a knife. In fact, it's the exact knife she took from the kitchen the other day when she sliced herself an apple.

She points it straight at Nick, her feet planted on the ground, her free hand raised slightly. 'Let Karlie out and let us go,' she says.

She's shaking all over. She doesn't sound in the least convincing. Even with the knife.

'What the hell are you going to do with that?' Nick says. 'Throw it at me?'

It happens fast. He takes two strides over to her and grabs her hair with one hand. Carla screams. She tries to stab him but he's too strong. In one movement, he has turned her around and put her in a choke hold, the knife in his free hand, pointing at her throat.

'Thank you,' he says. 'That's perfect.'

I'm screaming. Carla is screaming and he gives her throat a little squeeze. 'Shut up.' Then to me, 'If you don't be quiet, I will slice her throat.'

I slap both hands over my mouth. Carla's eyes are wide with terror.

'I'm sorry,' I whisper to her.

'Nick! No! You can't!' Marjorie cries.

'I can't?' he says, looking bewildered.

'Nick... It's too much!' Marjorie says. 'There has to be another way.'

'There isn't another way. Thanks to you!'

'To me?'

'This is all your fault!' he shouts.

'My fault?' she blurts.

'I told you to leave Sophie on the road,' Nick says, 'but no, you had to put her in the well. I knew it was a bad idea. I told you so, and I was right! And now look what you've done! Look what it's come to!'

'How can you say that? I did it all for you,' Marjorie says, her mouth trembling. 'For you, Nicky. To help you.'

He laughs bitterly. 'To help me? Are you serious? God, I hate you, Mother. You have no idea how much I hate you.'

'Nicky! Don't say that, baby.'

'My whole life you have treated me like I owe you. Like you did me a favour. All these years I have been beholden to this house, stuck to you, like a piece of gum under your shoe for the rest of our lives. It was bad enough being stuck with this stupid house, never being able to sell it, and then fucking

Ellie sticking her nose in where it doesn't belong. And now…' He pokes the knife at Carla's throat. He shakes his head. 'Help me? Is that what you call it? I could never be free of you, of this mess, of Sophie, until we both died. Do you have any idea what that's been like for me?'

Marjorie is crying. 'But I—'

'Spare me, Mother. Let me get this done. Goodbye, Carla. For good, this time.'

He puts pressure on her throat with the tip of the knife and she screams.

I am flying. I throw myself at him, head-first, shoulders square, and crash against his body as hard as I can. He slams against the wall, hitting his head, and cries out in pain. The knife has dropped from his grasp and is sliding on the floor.

I dive for it, expecting Nick to kick me or fight me for it, but he hasn't moved.

I'm scrambling for the knife, but I can't see it. Meanwhile behind me, Nick is yelling. 'Get her off! Get her off me!'

I turn around. 'Oh god.' Carla's body is slumped on top of one side of him. She's not moving, blood is seeping from her side.

'You…killed her?' I say.

'Get her off me!' he cries, but his words are slurring together. I don't know why he can't pull himself out from under her, but then I see that the side of his head is bleeding again. Hitting the wall must have reopened the wound. His eyes are strange, unfocussed and moving around in their sockets, like he's looking for something but he doesn't know what. When he speaks again, his mouth is distorted. 'Get… her off…me.'

'Get her off him!' Marjorie screams. I look back at her. She's on her knees, looking at me with so much hate I can feel it on me, like heat.

And she's holding the knife.

'It's all your fault…' she snarls, now with both hands holding the knife. 'I'll tell them you killed her,' she spits, glancing at Carla. 'That's what I'll say. You killed Sophie, and Carla, and now you're trying to kill us, too!'

She raises her arms, but before she has a chance to stab me, I've grabbed both her wrists.

She's screaming at me to let go, but I am strong. I am pure fury as I drag her along the floor by the hands, keeping them locked around the handle of the knife. She tries to fight me, to free herself from my grasp, her feet scrabbling against the wooden floor, trying to get a purchase.

But I'm too strong for her. Nick's slumped form is still slurring at me to get Carla off him, and I'm screaming, and Karlie is screaming in the utility room, and suddenly someone is slamming a fist against the front door. 'Police! Open up!' And Marjorie is screaming, trying to free herself from my grip and the police are banging on the door but I'm not letting go, and when I've dragged her, inch by inch, to where Nick is slumped, powerless, his eyes wide with fear, I raise Marjorie's hands in mine, Marjorie's hands which are still clasped around the knife handle, and together, we bring it down and plunge it into Nick's chest.

FIFTY-SIX

6 months later.

We held two funerals in the weeks following that terrible day. Nobody went to Nick's as far as I know. Not even Marjorie, because she's in jail. I wonder if she asked for a special dispensation. Prisoners can do that, can't they? In special circumstances? Anyway, if she did, the request was denied.

Nick's body was cremated, and I'm happy to say that I have no idea what happened to his ashes. I wonder if they sent them to Marjorie. I hope they did. She can look at them on her little metal shelf, if she has one in her cell. She can remember the last words he said to her: *God, I hate you, Mother.*

The other funeral was the saddest experience of my life. And unlike Nick, the occasion was packed. Everyone in Lindleton was there as we laid her to rest.

I was sad, but I was also glad that Sophie was finally out of that horrible, horrible well. All her friends and family came together and commissioned a marble angel for her grave, just like the one on her necklace.

I don't remember much about that day. I know that I

cried-hugged a lot of people, like Sophie's parents, and Tom and Isabelle, and Lauren, and Alex, and Mrs Lopez. It was Mrs Lopez who called the police. She feared something wasn't right and she was worried about 'You and Karlie,' she'd said. Not about Nick, not about Marjorie. About me and Karlie.

I know that Carla and I stood there, one arm around each other's waist. I know that I was so relieved she was all right, and that the knife wound was minor and she only fainted because of the blood.

And now, six months have passed. Some days it feels like yesterday. Some days, it feels like a lifetime ago. Some days, it feels like it never happened at all. Like it was all a nightmare, and then I woke up.

'Have fun at school!' I hug Karlie, then hold her sweet face and kiss her all over. It's been six months, but I still find myself hugging her about fifty times a day, which makes her squeal and wriggle and whine, 'Stop it! Mummy!!!!'

Children are so much more resilient than adults.

'And you have fun at school,' I say to Ella. I hug her tightly and hold her sweet face and kiss her all over. She's nine years old now and she looks so much like her mother it's scary.

Ella squeals and wriggles and wipes her face with the back of her hand, scrunching her eyes. 'Stop it, Auntie Ellie!'

Then they take each other's hands and run to the school, their little rucksacks bouncing on their backs.

'Bye, Mummy!'

'Bye, Auntie Ellie!'

'Bye, girls!'

I wave, then wipe tears from my eyes. I can't help it. I just love them so much. My therapist says the crying will pass, but I don't think I want it to.

Only when they've disappeared inside do I walk back to my car.

'She's grown so much.'

I stop and turn. Lauren is standing there, with a small, timid smile.

'Lauren!' I smile and hug her warmly. 'It's been so long! How are you? What are you doing here?'

She clicks her tongue. 'I just didn't have the courage to come sooner, but Alex finally made me. He says he's sick of watching me mope around the house.' There's a bench a few steps ahead. She points to it. 'Would you mind if we sat down?'

'No, of course not. Or we could go for coffee somewhere?'

She checks her watch. 'I don't have much time.'

'Of course.'

'So, how have you been?' she asks when we've sat down.

'Good, I'm good. We're good. And you?'

'Really well. And how is Carla?'

'She's great.'

'She was lucky you were there,' she says.

'I was lucky she was there when I was in the well,' I say.

Lauren nods, then presses her fingers against her eyelids.

'Hey,' I say gently, taking her hand. 'It's all right. Don't cry.'

She smiles. 'I know. I can't help it.' She sighs. 'And is Carla, Carla again?'

'Yes. And she's thrilled,' I say. 'She got married three months ago.'

'Oh, that's so nice.'

'It is,' I say. Although, for a little while, it was hard. She had to explain to John, her partner, that Susan Williams wasn't really her name, that she wasn't an insurance sales-person but a pickpocket and a thief, and that her brother was a killer.

John was wonderful about it all. John *is* wonderful, and I can vouch for that because I've come to know him a little over the past few weeks. He is tall, handsome in an under-stated way, with blond shaggy hair, and he absolutely worships the ground she walks on.

'She has a new job now,' I tell Lauren. 'She runs her own security company, advising clients on fraud risks.' I don't mention that one of her clients is the hotel where Nick caught her swiping someone's wallet. Basically, she's put her knowledge to use on the right side of the law. 'The money isn't as good,' she told me once, which made me laugh.

'How is Tracy?' I ask. I know she's on her feet again and back at the salon.

'She's good, really good. All better now.'

'That's wonderful.'

Lauren looks at me. 'I'm so, so sorry.'

I squeeze her hand. 'It wasn't your fault.'

She nods. 'I could have been a better friend.'

I click my tongue and put my arms around her. 'You were a great friend.'

She laughs. 'No I wasn't. I really thought you were mad. Or worse.'

'Stop it. None of it was your fault. Nick and Marjorie were very convincing. This was a plan they'd worked on for months.'

She lets out a sigh. 'I still can't believe it.'

'I know.'

'If I hadn't heard the recording on Carla's phone…'

Poor Nick, not sufficiently au fait with technology to know that the recording went straight to the cloud.

'Karlie looks so grown up,' she says. 'I was watching the three of you before. Was that Ella with her?'

'Yes.'

'And is Karlie happy to be back in London?'

'I think so. I mean, she's happy wherever she is. You know what she's like. We live with Bee again, so that's nice. And Bee and I have started our own salon.'

'I know. Mrs Lopez told me.' Then she says, 'Bethany really misses Karlie.'

'And Karlie talks about Bethany all the time.'

'Do you think we could set up a play date one day?'

I squeeze her hand. 'I think that would be brilliant.'

Later, when I go back home, I get out of my car, and for the second time today someone says my name behind me.

I turn around. This time it's DI Mike McIntyre leaning against his car, his arms crossed over his chest.

'Hello, Mike. You're a long way from home,' I say.

'I was in the neighbourhood, as they say. Do you have a minute?'

'Yes. Would you like to come inside?'

'That's okay. It won't take long. Marjorie's trial is coming up in a few weeks.'

'I know,' I say.

'Have you or Carla spoken to her recently?'

I think about Marjorie, languishing in prison. I don't know if anyone visits her. I know Carla doesn't. Occasionally, the phone will ring and a disembodied voice on the other end will ask if I'll accept a call from Marjorie Goodwin, and every time, I hang up. Carla tells me the same thing happens at her house. And she hangs up, too. Life's too short.

'No. Have you?'

He nods. 'We've interviewed her a few times.'

'In prison?'

'Yes.'

'I see.'

'She's not in a good way.'

'I'm so glad,' I say.

He chuckles.

'What's wrong with her?' I ask. 'I hope it's terminal.'

'It's more…psychological, shall we say. I'm told she cries all night, calling out for Nick. Mostly she's catatonic.'

'You've made my day,' I say.

'She's going to plead guilty to covering up Nick's crimes.'

I let out a snort. 'She doesn't have much choice. Carla got her full confession on her phone.'

'When Marjorie thought she was talking to a ghost.'

'That's right.'

He frowns and rubs the back of his neck.

'What is it?' I ask.

'Marjorie insists she didn't stab Nick. You did.'

I raise an eyebrow in surprise. 'Really?'

'She admits to helping dispose of Sophie's body in the well, and helping to dispose of Carla's body in the well, and of pushing you into the well.'

'That's a lot,' I say.

'Yes, but none of it is actual murder.'

'Not even mine?'

'You're not dead.'

I click my tongue. 'We really have the finest police force in the world, Detective.'

He chuckles, then grows serious. 'If Marjorie committed murder, then she should be tried for murder, not just accessory to murder. We know she didn't kill Sophie, or Carla. But she insists she didn't actually stab Nick.

'But she did stab him. I was there. It's not in question, is it? I mean, her fingerprints are all over the knife.'

'So are yours.'

'I told you. I scrambled to get the knife but then I dropped it. My fingerprints are just a smudge or two near the blade from when I tried – unsuccessfully – to wrestle it from her. Hers are all over the handle.'

He nods. 'She swears blind that yes, she picked it up, but then you dragged her across the floor and you made her stab Nick.'

I burst out laughing. 'Really? I dragged her across the floor? Is that what she said?' I laugh again. 'She's maybe thirty-odd years older than me, but she's fitter than me. She only pretended to be frail, remember? And even if I did drag her across the floor for whatever reason, what was I supposed to have done then?'

'She says you held her hands together around the knife and that you stabbed Nick.'

I laugh again. 'I don't know what to tell you. It never happened. She stabbed Nick because he was trying to kill Carla. I know that's strange, considering, but I'm not in her head. All I can say is what happened.'

'I get it,' he says. 'But I wanted you to know, because it's going to be part of her defence.'

'You mean it's her word against mine?'

'There's a bit more to it than that, unfortunately. There's evidence from scuff marks made by Marjorie's shoes that she was dragged, or dragged herself a few feet across the floor. There's your prints—' he holds up a hand to shut me up '— smudges of your prints on the knife. Her hands and wrists had bruises consistent with being clasped the way she described. The bruises on her wrists are shaped like finger-tips. The angle of the stab wound in Nick's chest isn't quite what you'd expect to be.' He puts his hands in his pockets. 'Look. You have nothing to worry about, you're not on trial here.'

'Oh, I'm not worried,' I say.

'Even if you did what she claims you did, Ellie, it's okay. You tried to get the knife off her, she didn't let go, and you managed to stab Nick anyway. You can absolutely argue it was self-defence or—'

'No,' I say firmly. 'I don't have to argue anything, because it didn't happen.'

'So how do you explain the bruises on her hands and wrists? The scuff marks on the floor?'

'We fought over the knife, yes. I told you that. She did drag herself to grab it. And yes I tried to wrestle it from her, which is why I guess she has bruises on her hands. But her story that I made her stab Nick or whatever? Please!' I laugh again and shake my head. I know nothing would happen to me if I explained what I did. And McIntyre is right. I could say that she wouldn't let go so I did what I had to do.

But that's never going to happen. I want Marjorie to go down for murder. I want her in jail for the rest of her life, unable to bear the idea that she killed her own flesh and blood, her precious, beloved son.

I rummage through my bag for my keys. 'She's a liar, Mike. She's been lying for almost fourteen years. So frankly, whatever fantasy story she's feeding you to get off the murder charge, she's lying. You want a solution to your problem?'

He tilts his head at me. 'If you have one…?'

'Oh, I have one,' I say, looking right into his eyes. 'Don't believe her.'

ALSO BY NICOLA SANDERS

Don't Let Her Stay

All The Lies

Made in the USA
Monee, IL
07 October 2024

67303496R00177